CANDLELIGHT

"HAVE DINNER WITH ME TONIGHT," RICK SAID GRUFFLY.

"I have some questions to ask you about the case, and something very important to discuss with you."

"I've got plans," Fran said with a smile. "Sorry."

"Cancel them," he ordered.

She stared at him, a look of disbelief in her eyes. "Every time I start thinking maybe there's something to you after all, you come on like some he-man. No thanks, Rick. As I said, I've got other plans."

She started to turn away, but Rick grabbed her upper arm. "This is a matter of national security," he said firmly. "As a representative of our government, I'm asking you for a favor."

"Oh, really?" she asked mockingly. "And all this time I thought you were interested in *me*."

His eyes blazed, and he pulled her even closer. "I *am* . . ."

CANDLELIGHT SUPREMES

THE PERFECT EXCHANGE

Andrea St. John

A CANDLELIGHT SUPREME

Published by
Dell Publishing Co., Inc.
1 Dag Hammarskjold Plaza
New York, New York 10017

ISBN: 0-440-16855-4

Printed in the United States of America

April 1987

10 9 8 7 6 5 4 3 2 1

WFH

For my aunt, Mrs. Glen Dyke, known to a generation of nieces and nephews as "Aunt Boo."

To Our Readers:

We are pleased and excited by your overwhelmingly positive response to our Candlelight Supremes. Unlike all the other series, the Supremes are filled with more passion, adventure, and intrigue, and are obviously the stories you like best.

In months to come we will continue to publish books by many of your favorite authors as well as the very finest work from new authors of romantic fiction. As always, we are striving to present unique, absorbing love stories —the very best love has to offer.

Breathtaking and unforgettable, Supremes follow in the great romantic tradition you've come to expect *only* from Candlelight Romances.

Your suggestions and comments are always welcome. Please let us hear from you.

Sincerely,

The Editors
Candlelight Romances
1 Dag Hammarskjold Plaza
New York, New York 10017

THE PERFECT EXCHANGE

CHAPTER ONE

Francine Barnette's large hazel eyes glowed with satisfaction as she studied the screen of her computer graphics terminal. She'd worked long and hard creating a diskette for entry in this year's computer graphics competition, scheduled to be held three months from now in Long Beach, which was just half an hour away from her office in Anaheim. As she stared at the results of her labors, she was filled with a sense of contentment.

"Oh, Fran, that's great stuff," a male voice exclaimed behind her. Glancing over her shoulder, she smiled in acknowledgment. "Really fantastic," Danny Romero said, a wide, impressed grin on his face.

"Thanks, Danny." She turned back to the computer keyboard, tapping in the command which scrolled all twelve of the final illustrations and designs slowly across the screen. One by one they flickered across the screen, a riot of blazing color and design that seized the attention and held it, an exotic feast for the eyes. "What do you think—can we count on at least an honorable mention this year?"

"Honorable mention! Fran, if you don't win at least first place, there just ain't no justice, lady. And just think what a feather in our caps a win would be for Barnette Graphics. Why, you'll be turning customers away, we'll be so busy."

Smiling, Fran typed instructions on the keyboard to the left of the electronic sketch pad, finalizing the art and closing out the diskette. When the tiny motors ceased their almost inaudible humming, she extracted the small diskette, marked its envelope with a felt-tipped pen, and slipped it into the pocket of her smock. Switching off the terminal, she took the diskette over to the processor, where the encoded visual information on the diskette would be converted into 35mm color transparencies. Blown-up copies of these slides would be displayed to prospective customers during the coming months, as examples of the quality of work they could expect if they brought their business to Barnette Graphics.

"Danny, would you mind processing these for me?" She glanced at her wristwatch. "I've got to make a couple of calls before everything closes."

"No problem." Danny stepped over to the machine and accepted the diskette, then began adjusting the controls. "Oh, by the way," he said, shooting her a quizzical glance, "Bill Munroe called—again. I didn't know what to tell him, so—"

"So you what?" Fran interrupted, an exasperated expression on her face. "Listen, Danny, after dating Bill for over a year, I finally realized he just wasn't my type, okay? So anytime he calls, you don't have to tell him a thing but the truth. I simply do not wish to speak to him. Is that clear enough?"

"Hey," he protested, his normally amiable face taut with concealed anger, "Don't take it out on me. How am I supposed to know these things? I'm paid to draw, not play Dear Abby!"

"You're right, Danny," she admitted. "Sorry."

With a nod she walked away. As she strolled through the broad, brightly illuminated work area, passing the drawing boards of employees who had already departed for the long Memorial Day weekend, she was unable to quell a feeling of a sense of pride. "For a twenty-eight-year-old college dropout, she muttered to herself contentedly, "you've done all right." Barnette Graphics had been in business for just over two years, but was rapidly becoming a name to be reckoned with in the booming southern California graphic arts business. The hundred-thousand-dollar outlay for her latest acquisition, the computer graphics system, was ample evidence of her growing success.

"Even if the bank still owns ninety percent of it," she wryly said, coming back down to earth. Entering the partitioned-off cubicle which served as her private office, she sat down at her desk and reached for the phone. She stopped as she caught sight of Jeanette Bowen, her office manager, in the doorway with a sheaf of papers in her hand.

"What is it, Jeanette?" she asked.

"About ready to take off?" Jeanette asked, a wistful expression on her face.

"You said it, kid. Reservations all made at the Ponderosa Lodge for tonight, bags all packed, and rarin' to go." She gestured at the telephone. "I was just getting ready to call the shop to see if they've finished servicing my car."

"Lucky devil," Jeanette murmured, entering the cubicle and sinking wearily into one of the chairs on the opposite side of the desk. "Tahoe's just beautiful this time of the year. Or so I hear, anyway," she added pointedly.

"Oh, ho-ho. Don't give me that 'poor little me' routine," Fran retorted with a chuckle. "I haven't had a vacation since I started this outfit, as you well know. And it's been three years since I saw Shelly. I've never met her husband, and we've been best friends since junior high."

13

"Well, I—"

"Hang on, Jeanette," she interrupted, holding up a hand as she reached for the phone. "Let me get this call out of the way, then we can talk. The garage closes in fifteen minutes."

She quickly learned that her car was indeed ready and that the mechanic would be delighted to deliver it to the office. She stretched luxuriously as she replaced the handset, feeling the workday tension beginning to ease out of her body. All that remained was to toss her two bags into the car, collect the diskette and the 35mm slides, and she would be ready for the richly deserved three-day weekend at Tahoe. She looked over at Jeanette and nodded.

"Okay, shoot."

"I just wanted to bring you up to date on all our current jobs before you took off." Jeanette glanced up from the papers in her lap, a wicked glint in her eye. "So you'll have plenty to worry about on your holiday."

"Thanks, kid. But if I didn't have faith in my people, I wouldn't be going." Fran sobered. "How does it look?"

"Not bad, actually. We've just about finished the Zimmerman Electronics presentation. All we have left is to process the masters into viewgraphs and we're done. It's due on Monday, as you know. Danny'll do the processing tomorrow. He volunteered to work, since his ex-wife has the kids this weekend."

"He's been pretty darned good about working weekends, Jeanette," Fran said. "We'll have to be careful not to take advantage of him. He's the only unattached male in the office."

"Right," Jeanette said thoughtfully. She made a note, then continued. "Anyway, the Maxwell brochure is coming along right on schedule, almost ready to go to the printer. I pick up the slides for Century Realty on

14

my way in in the morning." Stacking the papers on her lap, she smiled with an air of satisfaction.

"In other words, boss, relax and enjoy. We're in good shape."

"Fine. Just you and Danny working tomorrow?"

"Just us two old mules," Jeanette confirmed. "Kathy and Sam're off to Mexico for the weekend, and Chuck is planning to take his family to Dodger Stadium Saturday and Sunday."

"How about you and old Rodge?" Fran asked. "No plans?"

"Nope." Jeanette lowered her eyes. "I'm afraid that's all over, Fran."

"Jeanette! I thought Roger was special!"

"Me, too, for a while." Jeanette glanced out the window. "Hey, here's your car. And look at that hunk driving it!" Leaping up from her chair, she drew back the curtain and stared avidly.

Fran's blue Mazda RX-7 was nosing up to the curb in front of the office, gleaming from a fresh waxing and presumably filled with clean oil and a tank of gasoline. She stood up and walked out from behind her desk as Tony, the dark, curly-haired mechanic, swaggered through the front door, carrying her keys and a pink invoice slip.

"Here y'are, Fran," he said familiarly. "Service with a smile, just like always."

After examining the invoice, Fran took out her checkbook and wrote a check. When she handed it to Tony, he clutched at her hand for a moment, an insinuating smile on his face. "Y'know, there's still a little noise in that engine," he murmured suggestively. "If you'd just come out to dinner with me tomorrow night, I might be tempted to check it out for you—on my own time, of course."

"Are you telling me my car's not ready for a trip?"

Fran jerked her hand away, flushed with anger. "Because if you—"

"Hey, c'mon, Fran," Tony protested, back-pedaling swiftly. "When're you gonna lighten up, for Chrissake? The car's fine. I just want—"

"I know very well what you want, but you're not going to get it. Not now, not next week, not next year." As Fran paused to draw a breath, she caught sight of the appalled expression on Jeanette's face and stopped, ashamed of overreacting. Tony couldn't help being the swaggering, flirtatious playboy she knew him to be, but she was supposed to be a lady, not some shrill-voiced virago.

"Hey, listen," Tony began angrily, but Fran interrupted.

"I'm sorry, Tony," she said. "I really do appreciate your bringing the car to me at the office. I realize it's an extra service. But if there's going to be an extra charge —of any kind—I'll gladly come get it myself next time. Do you read me?"

"Loud and clear, lady." Stuffing the check into his shirt pocket, Tony hurriedly left the office, his face dark with anger and humiliation.

"Wow," Jeanette murmured. "You were pretty rough on him."

Fran glared. "Those macho studs are a big pain right in the you-know-where. Tony thinks he's God's gift to women. I've had my share of the Tonys of this world, thank you."

"And the Bills?" Jeanette suggested, raising an eyebrow. When Fran didn't reply, she added, "Don't let your problems with Bill turn you off on all men."

"You're hardly in a position to give me advice on men!"

Jeanette winced, her large blue eyes wide and hurt, and Fran was instantly ashamed of the cutting remark.

"I'm sorry, Jeanette. You didn't deserve that. Forgive me?"

"Of course." But Jeanette's eyes were cool as she turned away.

Inwardly cursing her thoughtlessness, Fran went back to check with Danny. He handed her the set of slides and diskette.

"They're great. Listen—have a good weekend. You deserve it."

Back in her office, Fran plucked her new tan raincoat from the rack and slung it across her arm, then hefted the two small overnight cases. Outside, her good mood of half an hour ago began to return. She was smiling with anticipation of the long delayed reunion with Shelly Hiller as she backed out of her parking slot and headed east toward the freeway.

A quarter of an hour later her RX-7 was merging with the heavy flow of traffic on the Orange Freeway, crawling along at a snail's pace with thousands of other southern Californians in flight from the crowded urban areas for the long weekend. In the distance ahead, the blue peaks of the San Gabriel mountains floated above the murky brown layer of smoglike peaceful islands, exerting their seductive pull on her. Glancing impatiently around at the sea of traffic, she tuned in an all-music station on the FM radio. She sighed and stretched, determined to force the pressures of business from her mind for the next three days. In the meantime, though, there was an eight-hour drive looking her in the face, and she was already aching with weariness.

Approximately four hundred miles to the north, another attractive young blond woman was preparing to depart her office for the weekend. She glanced furtively around the office, and when she was satisfied that nobody was paying any particular attention to her, Cindy

Linkwell switched off her desktop computer terminal. She extracted the program diskette and placed it on the surface of her desk. Then, with another surreptitious look around the office, she withdrew an almost identical, but blank, diskette from her purse. Quickly, she exchanged it for the one on her desk. Snapping her purse shut over the incriminating evidence, she stood and gathered her things.

"Hey, Cindy," a male voice called from across the room, startling her so badly she almost dropped her purse. "Gonna hit the tables in Reno again this weekend?"

"Not this weekend, George," she replied, with a shaky laugh. "I'm going to spend the next three days catching up on my rest."

"Lucky you," George said, a cynical expression on his bland, round face. Getting to his feet, he flicked his pudgy fingers disdainfully at the glowing screen of the computer terminal on his desk. "This damned STEALTH program has had us all putting in too damned many hours. What difference does it make if the Air Force develops invisible bombers? Quick as we perfect it, they'll steal it, and we'll be right back to square one. Right?" He snorted, not waiting for a reply. "I'll be glad when we're finished with this test program, I can tell you."

"Me, too." Cindy relaxed a bit, fluffing her hair with her free hand. George Carpenter was no threat, absorbed as he was in his own resentment of having to work too many hours. "At least this weekend will give us all a chance to catch up on our rest."

"Yeah, you, maybe," George muttered, staring with frank admiration at the movements of her breasts as she arranged her hair. "I'm working tomorrow and Sunday —again. Man, the Defense Department's gotta be really hot to get their hands on this stuff, to keep authorizing all this overtime."

"Well, I suppose it is—" Cindy began, eager to get away, but George cut her off, leaning forward and whispering theatrically.

"Whaddya suppose the Russkies would pay to get their hands on this stuff?" He gestured at the diskette in Cindy's hand. "If you could just smuggle that thing outa here and peddle it to the Reds, you could probably retire on what they'd pay you!"

"That's not funny, George," she replied, glancing around uneasily. "Listen, I've got to check this back in. See you Monday."

George sighed, the grin slowly fading. "You're right. I guess I need a day off worse than I thought, even if the money is good." He turned back toward his work area, waving at her. "You have fun this weekend, anyway," he said bitterly. "I'll be thinking of you as I tap, tap away at this damned test program all weekend."

Drawing a deep breath, Cindy turned toward the large open vault which occupied the far corner of the room, presided over by the classified documents and materials custodian who was methodically checking the top secret material back into storage until needed for the next day's work. Cindy's heart skipped a beat when she observed that one of the men from her group, Al Hedding, was on custodial duty today. Familiar with what she was working on, he could easily spot the bogus diskette for what it was when she tried to turn it in. However, he was obviously tired and bored, and simply glanced up and made a check mark against her name on a clipboard when she thrust the diskette into its slot and turned away.

"Hey, hold it a second, Linkwell!" he called sharply. Cindy spun around, her heart hammering with terror.

The room seemed to spin, and she clutched at a nearby desk for support.

"What—what's the matter?" she quavered.

"Hey, are you okay?" Hedding peered at her in concern.

"Y—yes, I'm okay. Just tired, I guess." She drew a couple of deep breaths, but her heart raced madly, frightening her. She'd suffered from angina since she was a child, and sensed an impending attack if she didn't calm down quickly. "What's the matter, Al?"

"Oh, you just forgot to initial this." He held out the clipboard, scowling. "Criminy, how long're you women going to have to work here before you learn the procedures?"

"I'm sorry, Al, really." She scrawled her initials on the sheet opposite her name. Hedding continued to watch her curiously as she handed the clipboard back, and she hurried away.

Outside in the corridor, she joined the flow of employees heading for the exits, chattering enthusiastically at the prospect of the long weekend. Cindy hurried along, head down, oblivious to the happy chatter.

Suddenly it was as if a giant vise had been slammed tightly around her chest. She staggered to a halt, leaning against the wall of the corridor. Her hands trembled visibly as she groped in her purse for the small prescription bottle, shaking one of the tiny white pills into her palm and placing it under her tongue. Almost instantly the crushing pain subsided, leaving her weak and trembling with relief. She breathed a prayer of gratitude for the effectiveness of the pills; the splitting headaches which were the almost inevitable side effect of their use were a small price to pay for the cessation of the terrible, death-dealing pain in her chest. After taking a couple of deep breaths, she continued on toward the exit.

Above the wide exit door hung a starkly lettered sign:

WHAT YOU SEE HERE, WHAT YOU DO HERE, WHAT YOU HEAR HERE—LEAVE HERE! HELP ELIMINATE TECHNOLOGY TRANSFER! Ignoring the sign, she stepped out into the open air, glancing up at the gray, lowering skies with an involuntary shudder. The air was cool and moist with the promise of rain, and she pulled the collar of her raincoat snugly about her throat as she walked toward the parking lot.

As she reached her familiar old battered Volkswagen bug and climbed in and switched on the ignition, she glanced back at the entrance of the building for possibly the last time, suddenly reluctant to leave it behind. Once she backed out of her parking slot and left with the top secret diskette in her possession, she was irrevocably committed to a course of action that would turn her into a fugitive, hunted by the authorities and subject to a long prison sentence if caught and convicted. At the forbidding thought her large gray eyes flooded with tears.

If only there was some way out, some way to right what she had already done and avoid what she was supposed to do during the next couple of days. She could go on with her life, figure out some way to repay her debts, and never, ever, permit herself to enter a casino again . . .

Then the sky rumbled with thunder and fat drops of rain began pelting the metal roof of the car, jolting her back to reality. And reality, she realized with a sinking sensation, was the stack of IOUs bearing her signature and the agreement she'd made to cancel them. No, she realized with a heavy sigh, there was no turning back. It was too late.

Shifting into reverse, she backed out of the parking slot. The windshield wipers swept the rain from the flat windshield, clicking with metronomic regularity as she guided the car toward the exit onto the highway. She took no notice of the plain white sedan which nosed out onto the highway a few seconds behind her, taking up station half a dozen car lengths to her rear. The sedan maintained an even distance as she turned toward Hayward, where she rented a small apartment overlooking the bay, and increased her speed until the little VW was humming along at a steady fifty-five miles an hour. If she had glanced into her rearview mirror and seen the driver of the sedan speaking into a dash-mounted microphone, she might have been driven into a panic that would have had her groping desperately for her bottle of tiny white pills.

Earlier that same day, in an office in the Federal Building in downtown San Francisco, Richard Langtry sat frowning over a stack of reports from fellow agents in the Department of Defense Intelligence Agency, Counterintelligence Division. His dark brown eyes were narrowed in concentration as he studied the reports, and he ran a hand distractedly through a thick shock of unruly dark hair as he shifted position in the uncomfortable government issue office chair. Putting the sheets aside for a moment, he stared into space, drumming his fingers against the gray metal top of his desk.

"Hey, Romeo, got big plans for the weekend?" Jack O'Brien, one of the other agents and an occasional raquet-ball playing partner of Rick's, looked over and grinned as he slammed a desk drawer shut. Without waiting for a reply, he went on, "Barb and I're planning to drive up into the redwoods and rent a cabin." He winked. "Second honeymoon, know what I mean?"

"Umm," Rick muttered, not really listening.

"Man, when're you going to tie the knot?" Jack demanded, a concerned expression on his ruddy, good-natured face. "What are you now, Rick—thirty, thirty-two?"

"What?" Rick glanced over. "Oh, thirty-three. Why?"

"Well," Jack said smugly, "it's a proven fact that married men live longer than bachelors, old man. So I ask you once more: When're you going to get married and settle down?"

"The divorce courts're full of people who were in a big hurry to get married, Jack." Rick grinned as he began stuffing the reports he'd been studying into a manila folder. "Besides, why should I get married? There are so many beautiful women and so little time." Standing, he gestured toward the closed door of the office adjacent to the one he shared with Jack and two other field agents. "The old man in this morning?"

"Yeah, I think so." O'Brien's eyes gleamed with interest. "Why? You got something interesting?"

"Could be. Beginning to look that way."

Scooping up the manila folder containing the reports, he got to his feet, the lithe grace of his movements betraying the years of gymnastic training as surely as the slender but well-muscled physique he'd kept in the peak of condition since he was a teen-ager. O'Brien, who over the past several years had been ruefully contemplating the slow but steady growth of a distinctive spare tire, glanced enviously at his friend for a moment before turning back to his own work, resolving for perhaps the dozenth time in as many days to begin another diet. A strict one this time, damn it, he promised himself.

"Let me know what's up, will you?" he muttered as Rick headed toward the closed door of the supervisor's outer office.

"Watch yourself," Rick retorted. "You just might wind up missing that second honeymoon, if you go volunteering for anything." Before opening the door, he smoothed down his hair and checked to see that his tie was hanging neatly.

"Morning, beautiful," he said as he stepped through the doorway. Joseph Addison's secretary, Beth Ann Williams, sat at her broad desk, surrounded by an IBM Selectric, a jungle of house plants, and enough framed photographs of her husband and three grown children to fill an album. She smiled, blushing like a schoolgirl as Rick approached. "I'd like to see the old man, if he's available."

Beth Ann's eyes sparkled as she gazed fondly at Rick for a moment. "The 'old man,'" she said pointedly, "was on the phone to Washington a few minutes ago. Let me just pop in and see if he's free, Rick." She tiptoed over to the polished mahogany door and opened it, murmuring discreetly to the unseen presence on the other side.

"Hell, yes, send him right in!" Joseph Addison's deep voice boomed heartily. "Talking to one of the boys'll beat hell out of slaving away on this damned cutthroat budget. Rick, get your tail in here, fella!"

Beaming, Beth Ann gestured at Rick. "He's in a good mood today," she whispered as he brushed past. "Now don't you go getting him all worked up again, you hear me?" Rick winked in acknowledgment, gently pulling the door shut behind himself.

Joseph Addison III, a career civil servant who had spent more than twenty years with Defense Intelligence Agency, bared large, square white teeth in a smile as Rick crossed several yards of plush carpet, coming to a halt two paces in front of Addison's desk. The older man's slate-gray eyes twinkled behind silver-rimmed spectacles as he inspected his visitor for several seconds, then waved him into a chair.

"Damn, boy," he exclaimed as Rick lowered himself into the chair. "How do you keep yourself in such good shape? If half the agents in this office kept themselves in as good shape as you do, we wouldn't lose nearly so

24

much time in sick leave every year! Well, I suppose you still work out on the rings twice a week, eh?"

"Right, chief," Rick said with a wry grin.

"Don't look so sour, lad," Addison said. "After all, it's not every office in the DIA who can boast an Olympic competitor on its staff." He frowned. "And don't call me 'chief'."

"I never competed in the Olympics, in spite of the—"

"Well, you would have," Addison proudly declared, brushing Rick's denial aside with a careless wave, "if Carter hadn't cancelled our participation in the 1980 games. Now then, what can I do for you today? Ask me anything—as long it doesn't cost any money."

"It's about the situation at Livermore, chief," Rick began, opening the folder on his lap and glancing down at the pages inside. "I submitted a report a few weeks ago—"

"Yes. The Linkwell woman." Addison nodded soberly, all trace of humor gone from his eyes. "Have there been any new developments?"

Rick hesitated for a moment, gathering his thoughts. With a lesser man than Addison, he might have been reluctant to present his theory at all, but Addison enjoyed a well-deserved reputation in the agency for possessing an unusually sharp intellect and for backing his subordinates to the hilt in confrontations with higher authority—as long as he believed them to be in the right. He was also, as Rick was well aware, utterly merciless with incompetents.

"Go on, lad," Addison said impatiently. "I'm waiting."

"Right, chief," Rick said, hiding his grin at the quick frown that flitted across the older man's face. "As you know, the Linkwell woman first came to our attention as a possible security risk as the result of a routine spot surveillance by our undercover agent at the lab—"

"Damn it, get to the point," Addison interjected. "I said I was familiar with the case. I know about the gambling debts, the frequent trips to Reno." He paused, then added, "And damn it, quit calling me chief!"

"Right, ch—right." Rick was a little surprised that Addison had retained so much information from his initial report, which had been submitted several weeks ago, when he had first begun to develop the case. His respect for the older man increased by several notches. "Well, since then, Linkwell has closed her checking and savings accounts, run up a truly staggering debt with . . ." he shuffled through the papers for a moment, ". . . one Abdul Aramas, who manages the Lucky Dollar casino in Reno for a consortium of investors. A routine background check on Aramas has turned up some pretty interesting information." He glanced up to ensure that he had Addison's undivided attention before continuing. "Aramas has been in this country for just under ten years, having migrated here from Lebanon in the mid-seventies. At a quick glance Aramas comes up clean as a whistle—had to, of course, to get by the Nevada Gaming Commission as a casino manager.

"However, when we checked with, uh, certain other government agencies, a possible connection with the PLO comes to light."

"Possible connection?" Addison's eyes narrowed at the mention of the terrorist organization. "How possible and what other government agencies?"

"It's all pretty vague." Rick shook his head. "My contacts at the Bureau and the CIA refuse to be quoted at all—not yet, anyway." A quick grin flitted across his face. "And you know how glory-hungry some of those guys are, so if they did know anything definite, they'd be broadcasting it to the world." He paused, sobering. "However, as you and I both know, in this business all too often where there's smoke there's fire."

26

"True, true . . ." Addison stroked his chin with his thumb, a faraway expression in his eyes. "The only reason that's a cliche is that it's so true. So. Where does all this take you?"

"I'm just not sure." Rick drew a deep breath, reluctant to go further out on a limb without more conclusive evidence for support. However, in the intelligence business it was often the intuitive leap that brought spectacular results, rather than the slow, methodical plodding that Addison was known to favor. In this instance Rick's intuition was humming like a tuning fork. Addison cleared his throat, signifying impatience, and Rick met his demanding gaze unflinchingly.

"If you take the facts one by one, they admittedly don't seem to add up to anything that would stand up in court—but my gut instinct tells me that Linkwell has been turned, and turned damned good."

"You know what your instinct is worth," Addison said with a snort. "How about the phone tap?"

"Nothing. Just the usual junk you'd expect from a reasonably attractive single woman."

"Nothing at all?" Addison asked, raising his eyebrows.

"Nothing useful. On Monday, she made reservations for Friday—that's tonight—at the Ponderosa Lodge, on the California side of Lake Tahoe." Rick paused, shaking his head. "Our source inside the lab says she told her coworkers she was going to spend the weekend at her apartment in Hayward. Of course, I realize that lying to your coworkers hardly constitutes a security violation, but when combined with everything else, it does begin to take on a stink."

"Maybe, but not much of one," Addison muttered after a moment's thought. He shook his head decisively. "Rick, you'd better wind this one up for the time being. With our budget cuts—"

27.

"Damn it, chief, wait," Rick interrupted. "We have an engineer with an Ultra Top Secret clearance, working on an extremely sensitive project for the Defense Department. She's run up gambling debts she can never hope to repay on her salary." Rick ticked off the points on the fingers of his right hand, ignoring the slowly gathering storm clouds on his supervisor's brow. "She's closed her personal accounts—savings and checking. And finally, the man holding her IOUs is apparently connected, or was at one time, with a known terrorist organization."

"That's a whole lot of conjecture, Rick. You said yourself if your pals at the CIA were sure of their info they'd be broadcasting it to the world! No, it's just too shaky. We have a budget, Rick. We can't go running up expenses every time an agent gets a hair up his ass!" Addison slapped the top of his desk with his hand. "There's insufficient data here to justify my authorizing the continuation of this surveillance. File it, Rick, write it up and file it. If higher headquarters agrees with your assessment, maybe then we can—"

"Hell, maybe then we can kiss the case good-bye!" Rick exclaimed, his brown eyes snapping with anger and frustration. "And don't tell me about the budget. What's the cost going to be if Linkwell does walk off with a load of STEALTH technology? Are you prepared to take the rap when that happens, Mr. Addison?"

"Me?" Addison squeaked, his complexion mottling dangerously purple. "You'd do that to me?"

"You'd be doing it to yourself," Rick retorted. "All this is in my latest report. It's a matter of record now. If Linkwell takes a walk, I'd hate to be in your shoes."

"And if you're wrong?"

"If I'm wrong, I'll take the flack." Rick paused, then

added, "I just don't want to be known as the guy who let a big chunk of STEALTH technology take a walk."

Addison drummed his fingers against the top of his desk for several seconds, then looked over at Rick and sighed.

"Damn it, man, you've been a thorn in my side ever since you started here . . . the thing is, you've been right too often to ignore." He paused, then nodded. "All right, hot dog, you've got it. Another seventy-two hours of close surveillance. You and one other man, unless things really start popping. Check out a couple of cars from the Interagency Motor Pool—damned if I want to spend twenty-one cents a mile of the taxpayers' money for private cars on a case as shaky as this one."

"Good. You won't regret it, sir," Rick said.

"Oh, I know damned well *I* won't," Addison said, baring his large, square teeth in a sharklike smile. "If it turns out you're wrong, you're fired, Rick, and I come out smelling like a rose for canning an agent who was wasteful with government funds. On the other hand," he said, the smile growing even wider, "if you're right, I share the credit of a spectacular counterintelligence coup. No, I just don't see how I can lose, Rick." Addison leaned back in his chair, linking his hands behind his head and looking very much like a cat who had just devoured several canaries. "Now, you still want to push this case?"

"Yes, I do," Rick said after a brief hesitation, realizing that he'd been maneuvered into putting his career on the line in order to pursue this nebulous case. He felt a brief surge of satisfaction when Addison blinked in surprise at his answer.

"All right," the old man said gruffly. "Do you have anybody in mind to work with you?"

"Oh, yes," Rick drawled as he got to his feet. "I've

29

got just the man, chief." Gathering up his papers, he turned and strolled out of the office, hiding a grin at the angry sputtering sounds emanating from the other side of the desk.

CHAPTER TWO

Saturday morning was cold, crisp, and sunny; the previous day's rain clouds had been wiped from the blue slate of the sky as if by magic. Fran rose early, inhaling deeply of the cool, clean air as she showered and dressed, preparing for the day. She was eager to call Shelly and obtain directions to her house, but first, she realized, she was famished. After slipping her raincoat on against the chill, she carried her things out to the car and locked them inside, then hurried toward the coffee shop just beyond the motel office.

She paused in the entrance for a moment, searching the crowded room for an empty booth. She'd had enough of sitting at counters, and wanted to be able to lean back and relax while she enjoyed a substantial, leisurely breakfast. The crisp, delicious aroma of frying bacon assailed her nostrils, reminding her that she hadn't eaten anything since lunch yesterday. She had stopped once on the drive up from Anaheim, in Bishop, but had had only coffee and a slice of toast at that time.

Ah, there was an elderly couple just vacating a booth about halfway down the length of the dining room. Fran walked quickly to the booth and slid into one of the empty seats, ignoring the irritated frown of the waitress who rushed over to scoop up the tip and carry away the soiled dishes.

"I'd've had this cleaned up in a minute, miss," the waitress muttered under her breath, "if you'd just waited."

"Oh, that's all right," Fran replied. "I just didn't want to take a chance on missing it and getting stuck at another counter."

The waitress departed with the dirty dishes, returning a moment later with a decanter of coffee and a cloth she used to wipe the table. After pouring Fran a mug of coffee, she took out her pad. "Are you ready to order?"

Fran ordered bacon and eggs, then leaned back and sipped greedily at the delicious coffee while she waited for her food to arrive. The dining area was packed; she had been fortunate indeed to get a booth. Even the counter was full, she observed, every seat occupied. With an unpleasant jolt of surprise, she noticed that two rather hard-looking men were studying her with cold, calculating eyes from their stools at the counter. Fran frowned at them, but instead of lowering their eyes and looking away, as they would have if they were staring out of idle curiosity, their stares became even colder, more intense. Fran quickly averted her eyes, suddenly feeling alone and quite vulnerable.

Moments before Cindy Linkwell had stood in her room in the same motel, trying to shake off the feelings of fear and despair at the situation in which she found herself. Finally, she sighed and turned toward the door, reviewing her instructions to enter the dining room at 7:30 A.M. and take a seat alone. She was to wear a tan raincoat to aid in recognition and would be contacted by a person called Stoner. As she left the room, she reflected that things had been going badly almost from the moment she left her office the day before.

The worst of it had been when she'd noticed the car following her, climbing east over the Donner Pass late last night. The realization that the large sedan with one headlight cocked off to the side had been behind her ever since leaving Hayward had come as such a shock that she'd groped in her purse for one of her pills, to ward off a heart attack. She had relaxed only slightly when the big car sped past her on the downhill side of the pass, vanishing quickly in the distance. She'd flexed her hands then, removing them one at a time from the steering wheel and wiping them against her thighs, wiping away the moist sheen of sheer terror.

"Tom was right," she murmured aloud. "You're as big a chicken as he always said you were." At the thought she realized that this was the first time in months she'd been able to remember Tom without tears springing to her eyes. Perhaps thinking of him now was an omen, she thought hopefully. A good omen, signifying new beginnings. She'd been alone much too long.

Tom. She smiled now, remembering. Tom Hankins, her high school sweetheart, the young man who had taught her what it was to be a woman. Big, strong, manly Tom had brought sickly, shy little Cindy Linkwell out of her shell, loving her, adoring her, replacing the love of the father she'd lost when she was six, comforting her in a way that her cold, withdrawn mother never could. If only Tom had lived, she thought, the smile vanishing, she wouldn't be in this mess, wouldn't be driving through the dark night toward Reno with a treasure trove of Top Secret information in her purse. If he had lived, if they had married as they had planned, she would never have found herself signing up for that bus tour of Reno several months ago; would never have discovered the despicable weakness within her, the sick, almost erotic compulsion of the addicted gambler.

Blattt! A huge diesel truck swept past her with a tremendous blast of its air horn, jolting her back to reality.

And reality was that Tom had been killed in his freshman year of college on a freeway in Los Angeles, and that the insurance policy he had thoughtfully taken out on his life with his fiance as the beneficiary had paid Cindy's way through college, paid for her degree in electrical engineering, which in turn had led to the job with the lab, which in its turn had brought her to her current situation. All things were intertwined, she thought fatalistically; all things predestined, predetermined. If it was meant to be . . .

She brushed the memories aside with an effort as she arrived at the dining room and paused near the cash register. Another element of the plan had gone awry, she realized with a sinking feeling. There was not an unoccupied seat in the entire place. Sagging in despair, she fought against a strong desire to simply turn and flee.

"Miss!"

With a jolt Cindy realized that the young woman standing about halfway down the row of booths on the side of the room was gesturing at her. Still, she put her finger on her chest and raised her eyebrows, mouthing silently, "Me?"

"Yes, you!" the young woman repeated just loud enough for Cindy to hear her, beckoning urgently. Cindy moved hesitantly toward the booth, frowning in confusion. Nothing was working out according to Aramas's careful plan, nothing.

"You—you're not Stoner?" she asked, but the young woman cut her off with a shake of her head, killing that hope.

"Who? No, I just thought you'd like to share my booth, since this place is packed and I have all this room." She indicated the empty half of the booth, smiling warmly, and Cindy felt the knot of tension in her stomach loosen just a bit as she smiled back.

34

"Well, thank you," she said, glancing around the restaurant once more, then lowering herself into the booth with a grateful sigh. "It is awfully crowded."

"Memorial Day weekend, I suppose. By the way, my name is Fran. Fran Barnette."

"Oh—I'm Cindy . . . um, just Cindy." Licking her lips, Cindy looked around the room nervously once again. Fran looked at her in concern.

"Are you all right?" Her large hazel eyes narrowed as she looked at the other woman. "You're as white as a sheet."

"I'm—I'll be fine," Cindy said. "It's just—I'm supposed to meet somebody here."

"Well, I'm sure he'll show up," Fran said, looking up with a smile as her breakfast arrived. "Good! I'm starved!"

While the waitress took Cindy's order, Fran glanced over at the counter. The two hardcases whose frank interest in her had triggered her invitation to Cindy to share her table were slumped back at the counter now, expressions of consternation on their faces. They were gesticulating excitedly and glancing back at her and Cindy every few seconds, apparently thrown into a quandary by Cindy's presence at the booth. What a pair of weirdos, Fran decided, then turned her attention to her breakfast.

Cindy leaned back in the booth, sipping her coffee, trying to force herself to relax a bit. If Stoner was among the crowd, he was certainly enough of a professional to improvise, to arrange an accidental meeting later on that morning; perhaps even get a message to her right now while she sat in the booth with Fran Barnette. At any rate, she was all finished with working herself up into a state of uncontrollable anxiety over the morning's events. She looked slowly around the room, wondering if she would be able to pick Stoner, if indeed

35

he was present in the room, from the crowd. He would probably be alone, she decided, and was most likely young. Her eyes traveled past two youngish men in a booth across the room, paused, returned to them, then she gasped in shock and clutched at her chest.

There were two men at the table, one of them ruddy-faced and slightly overweight, wearing a baseball cap and sunglasses. But it was the other man who gave her such a fright: a lean, dark-haired, good-looking six-footer who'd been pointed out to her at the lab just a few weeks ago as a field agent of the Defense Intelligence Agency.

"Oh, God," she groaned, as the pain in her chest mounted. Across the table Fran's eyes rounded in alarm. She got to her feet and hurried around to Cindy's side of the table as Cindy slumped back, gasping in pain.

"Do you need a doctor?" Fran demanded, gesturing helplessly.

"No! Leave me alone!" Cindy cried, reaching for her purse. Her clumsy, numb fingers knocked her purse from the table, spilling its contents on the tiled floor with a crash. Combs, lipstick, mirror, wallet, bits of paper, and change hit the floor and scattered in all directions. The tiny prescription bottle rolled under the feet of the couple in the adjacent booth, out of sight somewhere under their table.

"I need that!" Cindy gasped in desperation, sliding inexorably toward the floor, consumed by the pain in her chest. "Lord, I need that!"

Fran crouched down, groping for the bottle beneath the table, the middle-aged couple occupying the booth gaping at her in consternation. She felt Cindy slumping against her, felt something tugging at the pocket of her raincoat, and pulled away. Just as she retrieved the tiny bottle and turned around, Cindy fell the remainder of the way to the floor, her mouth making little spasmodic gasping motions, like a fish out of water.

"Get a doctor!" Someone screamed, and the dining room erupted into a hubbub of excited conversation.

"I'm a doctor, let me through." Fran felt herself unceremoniously brushed aside as a distinguished-looking middle-aged man knelt and placed his fingers against the stricken young woman's throat. "Back!" he snapped, swinging his arm in an arc for added emphasis. Fran, along with half a dozen others who had rushed over to try to help, took an involuntary step backwards.

"Call for an ambulance—this young woman is in cardiac arrest!" the doctor ordered.

Fran stared in shock as the doctor began to administer CPR—rhythmically pumping Cindy's chest, then pausing to breathe life-giving oxygen into her lungs. After a few moments, Fran observed with a sinking sensation, Cindy's chest seemed to stop moving of its own volition, and her open, staring eyes took on a dull, lifeless glaze.

The doctor continued relentlessly, grunting with effort. In a moment the wailing siren could be heard approaching, dying in a dreadful-sounding moan as it pulled to a halt near the entrance of the coffee shop. Two husky young men in hospital whites trotted in carrying a stretcher, barking orders as they approached the scene.

"Okay, folks, get back! Give us some room, damn it! Okay, pal," one of them said, clapping the physician on the back, "you did good. Now let the pros take over."

"I'm a doctor, man!" Nevertheless, he got to his feet, looking on approvingly as the paramedic smoothly resumed the CPR.

"Excuse us, doc," the other paramedic said. "How's it look?"

"This young woman is dying—will die—unless we get her to the hospital at once. Get her into the ambulance. I'll ride along in case there's anything I can do."

A few minutes later the ambulance departed, carrying the young woman to whom Fran had offered hospitality and the doctor who had just happened to be having his breakfast in the same dining room. Fran glanced distastefully at the eggs slowly congealing on her plate, then picked up the check, which had arrived at some point during all the excitement. She noticed that Cindy's check had arrived, too, and after a moment she picked it up as well, shrugging.

It was the least she could do.

On the other side of the dining room, in a booth against the wall, the pudgy man wearing a baseball cap and sunglasses turned to his companion and shook his head slowly.

"Well, hell, that sure's hell throws a monkey wrench in the works, doesn't it?" He took a sip of coffee, then asked, "So what do we do now, chief?"

"Stow that 'chief' crap," Rick said absently, watching the tall young blond woman who was waiting at the cash register for her change. As the waitress counted the bills into her outstretched hand, her eyes just happened to meet Rick's, and he nodded and raised his coffee cup in mock salute. She lifted her chin and turned quickly away, ignoring him. Rick grinned.

"Oh, she's a tiger, that one," he murmured, and Jack raised his eyebrows inquiringly. Rick shook his head, smiling, then grew serious once more. "Okay, next move. I want you to get out to the hospital. Show your badge, take a look through the Linkwell woman's things. I'll toss her room, then I'm going to call the lab and talk to the security people there, maybe her boss as well."

38

"Yeah, right," Jack said dryly, taking another bite of the huge, sugar-encrusted jelly doughnut he'd ordered in lieu of a more nourishing, if less fattening, breakfast. "Might as well find out if anything's missing—since we've got our necks stuck out about as far as they can go."

"Your neck is not out, Jack," Rick corrected. "You won't get stuck with any kind of bad rap from this job, one way or another. This one is strictly between Addison and me—if it's a bust." Pausing, he smiled and spread his hands. "Of course, if we pull off a coup, then there'll be credit enough for everyone to have a share. Now you'd better get a move on. That ambulance'll be getting to the hospital any minute."

"Hey—lemme finish my breakfast first," Jack protested, an aggrieved expression on his round face as he opened his mouth for another bite. He paused with the doughnut halfway to his mouth. "And don't say it. I know I'm supposed to be on a diet. Did you ever try to diet and pull stake-out work at the same time? No, of course not," he answered himself before Rick had a chance to reply. "You've probably never been on a diet in your whole life."

"Go ahead, finish breakfast," Rick said, grinning. "And since we seem to have a spare minute here, let me say I'm sorry I had to cause you and Barb to miss your second honeymoon. If there had been anyone else—"

"Oh, sure," Jack interrupted, speaking around a mouthful of doughnut. "Tell me another lie. You were tickled pink when I was still sitting there in the office, fat, dumb, and happy, trying to catch up on my paperwork, when you came out of the old man's office looking like something had just taken a good healthy bite out of your ass."

"Well, what the hell," Rick pointed out. "You'd've

been as sore as hell if you'd missed out on all this overtime, all this per diem. Think of the money, man!"

"Think of freezing my tail off in the car half the night, watching Linkwell's room," Jack retorted. "Think of drinking gallons of coffee from styrofoam cups and glomming down hamburgers and french fries instead of eating like civilized people. Great, huh?"

"Really, pal," Rick began, wearing an expression of enormous sincerity. "I'm sorry it had to be you, but—"

"Oh, bullshit," Jack interrupted, snorting. "You like working with me, Langtry, and you know it. If I hadn't been sitting there so ripe for the picking, you'd have called me in anyway, wouldn't you have?"

Rick tried to look indignant, but couldn't quite bring it off. After a moment he gave it up and laughed. "Yeah, I probably would have, at that," he admitted, then sobered. "But not unless I thought we had a hot one coming off, Jack. I want you to know that."

"Ah, hell, don't sweat it," Jack mumbled around another bite of jelly doughnut. "Barb knew what she was getting when she married me." He got to his feet, dropping some money on the table. "See you back in the room in a coupla hours, right?"

"Right." Rick glanced up at his partner and laughed. "For Christ's sake, wipe that jelly off your face, man!"

Jack reached up and wiped the jelly away with his thumb, licked it off, then made an obscene gesture only Rick could see. Rick laughed again, shook his head, and waved the other man away.

"Go on, get outa here," he said, "before somebody calls the cops on you." Fondly, he watched his partner make his way from the restaurant, sipping at the last of his coffee, then he picked up the check and got to his feet.

"You'd better hope to hell Linkwell has something stashed in that room of hers, fella," he muttered to himself as he walked toward the cash register, "or you're just liable to find yourself out of a job . . .

Shelly and Todd Hiller's custom-built, three-bedroom home nestled against the shoulder of a hill overlooking Lake Tahoe from the Nevada shoreline. From the second-story veranda, which soared out from the slope above the lake, the highway encircling the lake was clearly visible, a strip of dark gray between the two towering Douglas firs in the Hiller's front yard. As Fran had approached the house earlier that morning, following the directions Shelly had given her over the phone, her first impression of the house, with its soaring buttresses and broad expanses of glass and unpainted wood, had been that of some huge, antique aircraft poised for flight.

"Another glass of wine?" Shelly asked lazily.

The two women had just finished lunch and were relaxing on folding lounge chairs on the wooden-planked veranda, basking in the afternoon sun. They were each dressed in shorts and halter tops; it was as if the cold rainstorm of the previous day had never occurred, the bright sun beating down from clear blue skies with the promise of summer. Todd Hiller, a tall, slender man with flaming red hair and a distinctive, barking laugh, had left immediately following lunch to meet with business associates in Reno, and the two women were taking advantage of the time alone to catch up on news.

"Maybe later," Fran replied after a moment, lying back with her eyes closed, drowsy in the sun. "Where'd you meet Todd?"

"Old Toad?" Shelly frowned as she sat up and refilled her glass from the crystal decanter on the table between the two chairs. "At a new products show my old boss sent me to." She glanced over at Fran and raised her eyebrows. "I thought I wrote you about him at the time."

"You probably did," Fran admitted. "Refresh my memory."

"Well, as you know, Todd's a top-notch salesman, and he was there at the show representing Dynagraphics, showing off all their new products. You know—film, papers, artist aids, junk like that. Anyway, we got to talking, he invited me to lunch, then out on a date . . . one thing led to another." Pausing, she raised her wineglass, encompassing the house, the lake and all her material possessions with the gesture. "And now," she said with a brittle little laugh, "I have all this."

Sitting up, Fran looked at her friend, surprised at the cynical note in her voice. Shelly averted her face, but not before Fran saw the gleam of tears in her large green eyes.

"And so much more?" she asked quietly. Shelly looked up, nodding and gulping audibly. "Problems, kid?" Fran asked sympathetically.

"Oh . . . no, not really. It's—it's just that sometimes I wish I'd taken you up on your offer to go into business instead of getting married."

"It doesn't look as if you've done so badly," Fran observed lightly, trying to regain the relaxed atmosphere of a few moments ago. Standing and walking over to the railing around the veranda, she looked out over the lake for a few seconds, captivated by the magnificent view. Far out on the shimmering blue surface, a water-skier sped along behind a speed boat, a huge rooster tail of white spray marking his progress. "I certainly couldn't afford anything like this." She turned around, leaning with her elbows propped on the railing. "Have you considered having a baby? Or is that none of my business?"

"Oh, hell, Todd doesn't want children—at least not for a long, long time." She gave an ironic laugh as she sipped at her wine. "Todd wants to enjoy life for a few more years first. At least, that's his story." As she shook her head a strand of brunette hair fell across her brow and she brushed it back impatiently. "He's got all the toys, Fran. Cars, motorcycles, guns, computers—even an airplane. Sometimes I get the feeling I'm just another of his possessions. A little more fun than the computer, maybe, but not nearly in the same class as the airplane."

Fran remained silent for several moments. She and Shelly had been roommates for almost three years at college, confiding in each other the most intimate details of their lives, but this was new, possibly dangerous ground. Fran wasn't sure she should hear any more. The intimacy between a husband and wife went far beyond any closeness she and Shelly had shared in their younger days, and Shelly's present resentment of Todd could quickly become directed at her, if the circumstances changed. She decided to change the subject.

"I'd love it if you could come down to Anaheim and spend a few days with me, Shelly. I could show you the shop, maybe even get you on a board for a few hours and steal some of your creativity."

She launched into a description of the new computer-graphics equipment, speaking with genuine enthusiasm. Shelly listened attentively. "I brought up a diskette and a set of slides I generated on the terminal," she concluded after a few minutes. "I'd love to show them to you later on."

"I'd love to see them," Shelly said.

"Maybe we can put them on Todd's terminal this afternoon, then," Fran said. "I think his equipment is compatible with my software, so . . ." She broke off at the sound of tires crunching over the gravel driveway below the veranda. Looking over the railing, she saw a

43

nondescript white sedan rolling to a halt behind her RX-7.

"Are you expecting somebody, Shelly?"

"No." Shelly got to her feet with a puzzled frown. She walked over and looked down at the driveway where a man in a tweed jacket and tie was just getting out of the car. "I don't know who that guy is. Maybe he's looking for Todd."

Fran nodded distractedly, staring as the foreshortened figure slammed the door of his car and stood studying her RX-7 for a few seconds. Abruptly, he vanished from view beneath the veranda. A moment later, the doorbell chimed.

"Excuse me," Shelly muttered. "I'll see what he wants." Setting her wineglass on the table, she entered the house through the open glass doors leading from the veranda into the kitchen, then down the broad, open staircase to the ground floor.

Fran sipped reflectively at her wine, unable to shake the conviction she'd seen the stranger somewhere. Oddly, she was certain that he was not here to see Todd. She suspected that this visit had something to do with the unpleasant episode of the morning, when the young woman had collapsed at her table in the restaurant.

"Fran?" Shelly's voice floated up the stairs. "Could you come down, please?"

Quickly, Fran traced Shelly's route through the kitchen and down the stairs. At the bottom Shelly was standing beside a tall, handsome, dark-haired man, a curious smile on her face.

"This is Special Agent Langtry, Fran," she said wonderingly. "He says he's come to speak to you."

Fran stared at Langtry for a moment, instinctively drawing back from the arrogant, appraising stare as his sparkling brown eyes raked her up and down with swift expertise. Her bare legs, midriff, and shoulders tingled

44

under the frankly admiring stare, causing her to cross her arms in an attempt to cover up as much as possible. Her reaction seemed to amuse Langtry; his confident smile grew even broader, revealing sparkling, even white teeth.

"Miss Barnette—or do you prefer Miz?" Langtry's voice was a deep, resonant baritone, reinforcing the macho impression that had formed in Fran's mind.

"Miss is fine," Fran replied evenly, lifting her chin as she met his frank stare. "And what do we call you? Special Agent?" A glint of amusement appeared in her large hazel eyes as Langtry's smile wavered just a bit. *So,* Fran thought, *he takes himself very seriously . . .*

"Actually, I'd prefer it if you'd call me Rick," Langtry said. "Though I'm sure my superiors would frown on such informality." Abruptly, he sobered. "Miss Barnette, I'd like to speak with you. In private, if I may."

"Well, wait just a minute," Fran said with asperity. "I am a guest in Mrs. Hiller's home. I can't just—"

"Oh, that's okay," Shelly interrupted, smiling up at Langtry like a young girl with her first serious crush. "I was just getting ready to go outside and, um, water the plants." With another adoring smile she hurried away. A moment later they heard the sound of the back door opening and closing. They were alone.

"All right," Fran said with an angry gesture. "Now just what is this all about? I'm on vacation—"

"It's about national security, Miss Barnette," Langtry cut her off bluntly, his eyes containing a glint of anger. He continued, "As of this moment, you are a possible suspect in a case of espionage. If you want to persuade me of your innocence, Miss Barnette, I suggest you start cooperating with me."

CHAPTER THREE

"Me? A—a suspect?" Fran asked faintly, searching his face for the grin that must soon appear; the announcement that this was all just a joke. No such grin appeared, and the eyes that had seemed to twinkle with warmth just a few moments ago were now flat and cold. "You—you can't be serious."

"Oh, but I am," Langtry replied. He glanced toward the arched doorway leading into the living room and gestured. "Must we stand around here in the foyer?"

"No, of course not." Fran led the way into the living room, waving Langtry to a seat on the sofa. She sat across the room from him in a leather-covered armchair.

"Nice place," Langtry observed, taking in the large stone fireplace, polished hardwood floors, open-beamed ceiling, and Navaho rugs with a practiced glance.

"Yes, isn't it?" Fran took a deep breath. "Now, please tell me how it is that I happen to be a suspect in an espionage case, Mr.—?"

"I meant it when I said I'd prefer you to call me Rick." His easy smile reappeared, and Fran felt a little better.

"Rick, then," she said. "And by the way—how about letting me see some ID? Are you with the FBI, CIA, or what?"

"Nothing so glamorous, I'm afraid," he said, taking his wallet from the inside pocket of his tweed jacket and opening it to display his badge and government identification card. "Defense Intelligence Agency. I'm with the San Francisco office, and we're responsible for guarding against security leaks, inadvertent—as well as deliberate—technology transfer, and so on for the entire Silicon Valley." Fran nodded, and he folded the wallet and slipped it back into his pocket.

"Which leads us to you, Miss Barnette," he continued, "and the young lady who joined you for breakfast this morning. Cindy Linkwell, an employee of Livermore Labs . . . just how well did you know Miss Linkwell?"

"Did? Is that use of the past tense deliberate, Rick?"

"I'm sorry. She was dead before the ambulance got to the hospital." Rick studied her reaction to the news, his dark eyes narrowed with interest. She simply shook her head sadly.

"I didn't know her at all, to answer your question." She frowned, pausing. "Actually, I invited her to share my table only because these two creeps at the counter looked as if they were working themselves up to approach me, and I thought . . ."

"—That if there were two women, they might back off," Rick finished, and Fran nodded. His eyes flashed with interest as he asked, "What did you notice about the two men, Miss Barnette? Can you describe them?"

"Oh, really—if I'm to call you Rick, then please, call me Fran. All this formality makes me tired." Rick nodded and Fran smiled. "I really didn't notice much about them," she said. "Just that they really seemed . . . well, not at all my type. Very hard-looking, macho types. Like ex-boxers, maybe, or football players. Do you know what I mean?"

"I know what you mean, Fran. How were they dressed?"

"Oh, I don't know. Casually. As I said, I didn't look at them very closely. I didn't want to seem to be returning their interest."

Rick took a tiny notebook from his shirt pocket and scribbled some notes on a page. As he replaced the notebook, he glanced over at her and his eyes seemed to twinkle a bit as he said, "Not your type, huh?"

"Not at all." Fran's voice sharpened. "You still haven't told me what this is all about, Rick. If I am to convince you of my innocence," she said with a trace of sarcasm, "it would help to know what I'm suspected of."

"All right," he said. "We've had Miss Linkwell under surveillance for several weeks. We're almost certain she was in the restaurant this morning for the purpose of passing classified information to foreign agents. When she sat down at your table, it had all the earmarks of a prearranged contact."

"This is all so—so preposterous!" Fran exclaimed. "I come up here for a couple of days off, and the first thing I know I'm a suspected spy! It's simply incredible."

"Maybe not as incredible as it seems," Rick said. "Please hear me out . . .

"Cindy Linkwell was employed, as I said, at Livermore Labs in a highly classified program for the Department of Defense. In her job she routinely had access to the highest classification of material and information. After the events of this morning, my partner and I contacted her employers—got them out of bed, apparently—and they discovered that a top secret program diskette she'd been working on was missing. It had been signed out properly, and at first they thought it had been signed back in, but when they checked closer, they discovered that a blank diskette had been checked in in its place."

"Well, I still don't see——" Fran began, but Rick cut her off, his dark brown eyes boring into hers. He went on, "The top secret diskette is missing, Fran. It was not among her things when her body was searched at the hospital, and it wasn't in her room at the motel. It wasn't in her car either." He paused for a moment, leaning back against the back of the sofa and studying her with a faint, speculative smile on his lean face.

"It seems that the diskette was passed on before her heart attack."

"And you—you think *I've* got it?" Without waiting for a reply, she got to her feet and stared out through the window overlooking Shelly's backyard. Everything seemed so normal on the other side of the window. The sky was a deep, rich blue accentuated here and there by a dazzling white puff of cloud, and the trees and shrubbery were a clean, crisp green. It was so ordinary, so peaceful, and yet Fran felt as if her world had suddenly been tilted just a bit, so that everything was just slightly out of kilter, and nothing was what it seemed. A sense of unreality pervaded her mind as she turned back to face her inquisitor. He stared back, unmoving.

"Look at the facts," he said flatly. "The diskette left the lab on Linkwell's person—we know that. Before leaving for Tahoe, she didn't have time to hide it in her apartment, so we have to assume she brought it with her. We've learned she was to make contact in the coffee shop—or she was to be contacted." He shrugged expressively as Fran started to protest again. "Within two minutes of arriving in the coffee shop, she was in your booth, and a couple of minutes later she was dying of an apparent heart attack—and the diskette is now gone."

"But—but that doesn't mean that I——"

"Has it occurred to you that you and Linkwell fit the

same general description, Fran?" She stared at him as the implication of his words struck home. "Further," he said, leaning forward and gesturing with his hand, "you were both wearing tan raincoats this morning. Tan raincoats—even though it was not raining."

"My God . . ." Fran whispered, sinking back in her chair. "No wonder you suspect me . . ." She looked up at him, her large hazel eyes filled with a desperate plea. "I wish I could make you believe me, Rick. She gave me nothing, *nothing!* She sat down, we exchanged half a dozen words, then—then she collapsed."

"I see." Rick was silent for several seconds. "You've changed your clothes since this morning. Did you go through your pockets?"

"I didn't have any pockets. I was carrying a purse—and believe me, I would have noticed if anybody tried to put anything in it."

"Damn." Rick stood, sighing wearily. "I suppose it's possible that we missed the diskette in her room or car, but I don't think so . . ." He took out his wallet and withdrew a business card. He scrawled a number on the back and handed it to her. "Please, if you think of anything—and I mean anything—that might help us, call me at this number, day or night. That's our room at the Ponderosa, where we'll be for another coupla days." He turned the card over to the printed side. "This is my office number, and that's my home number. Call, day or night. If I'm not in, somebody'll know where I can be reached."

"Day or night. Your wife must love that."

"No wife, no live-ins of any kind." He looked at her for several seconds, a glint of purely masculine interest appearing in his dark eyes. "You call, anytime."

"If I think of anything, of course," Fran said, hating herself for the coy, flirtatious note that had crept against her will into her voice. Rick Langtry epitomized

50

the type of man she disliked intensely, arrogant, almost overpoweringly male. Why, then, this inexplicable, irresistable feeling of attraction that had been slowly coming over her, this little tingle that went up her spine at the slow smile creasing his rugged features at this very moment?

"In your case," he was saying solemnly, "call for any reason at all."

"Oh, sure," Fran said at once, a trace of anger in her voice as she reacted to the confident male come-on implied in his words. "You probably say that to all the women."

"No. I rarely say that to anybody." He paused a moment, then said, "At the risk of sounding overly dramatic, don't leave town for a couple of days. We can contact you here?"

"Yes. I plan to be here until Monday afternoon." She looked at him, her thoughts in a quandary. Every time she thought she had him neatly pigeonholed, he produced another surprise. "Am I still a suspect, then?"

"What do you think?" he asked. He laughed and held up his hands when she began to sputter angrily. "Let's just say that I think there's a possibility you might be of some further help to us, okay?"

"Damn it," Fran snapped, "you seem to find this very amusing, but I—"

"Hold it, hold it right there," Rick interrupted. "There's nothing amusing about it, Fran. I don't ask you to stick around because it amuses me, or because I'm more attracted to you than I have been to a woman in a long time. I ask you to stick around because as far as we've been able to determine, you're the only person who spoke to Linkwell after she left her motel room this morning. That makes you at the very least a material witness."

"You . . ." Fran's voice trailed off as the impact of

51

his words struck home. ". . . *More attracted to you than I've been to a woman in a long time* . . ." "Material witness?" she asked, faintly. "I see. I won't leave town without contacting you."

"Promise?" he asked, smiling.

"I promise." She couldn't help smiling back.

She stood on the steps for a couple of minutes after Rick drove away in his white sedan, not quite ready to share with Shelly her reactions to this bewildering man. *Damn it,* she thought, confused. On the one hand, Rick Langtry represented everything she hated about men; on the other hand, there was no denying her almost visceral reaction to the man, the sexual pull he so easily exerted over her. After a moment she shrugged. Whether Langtry knew it or not, she was innocent of any wrongdoing in this espionage case, and therefore he would soon discover there was no reason for continuing contact with her. Good, she thought, tilting her chin. She didn't need this kind of confusion in her life; not now, when things were starting to go so well with her business. It would be a relief when Monday afternoon arrived and she could shake the dust of Tahoe from her boots, along with any memories of Rick Langtry and his slim, powerful body and that irritating, arrogant, supremely male grin of his.

As she turned to reenter the house, she heard the sound of a passing vehicle and glanced back at the highway. A green van was cruising slowly past the house, its driver and his passenger each craning their necks, staring at her. When they saw her looking back, the van's engine surged and it roared quickly away.

"Oh, no," she muttered, entering the house and pulling the door closed and locking it. "Those two creeps again!" The occupants of the van, she was almost certain, were the same two hard-looking men who'd been in the restaurant that morning, and she had a distinctly uneasy feeling about them as she went out back, looking for Shelly.

"So what was that all about?" Shelly asked as Fran appeared in the doorway leading to the backyard. "Not that I'd be complaining, if I were you. Not with a hunk like that giving me the third degree!"

"Oh, it was just about that girl who collapsed this morning," Fran said, unwilling to explain further. "I told you about it. She died, and now they're saying she was some kind of spy or something."

"Spy?" Shelly squeaked, fascinated.

"I told him I didn't know anything." Fran held up her hands in surrender as Shelly began to bombard her with questions. She'd had quite enough of Cindy Linkwell and her problems for one day. This was her vacation, even if it was to last only three days, and she was determined to extract the maximum enjoyment of what remained of it—if Rick Langtry and his troublesome suspicions left her alone. "No more!" she said firmly. "I really don't want to talk about it anymore."

Fran and Shelly spent the remainder of the afternoon taking a short walk along the shoreline of the lake, carrying sketch pads. Fran did an interesting pencil study of a dead tree stump that she thought she might develop into a watercolor at a later date. Shelly merely doodled, but it was obvious to Fran that she missed the world of commercial art.

Todd Hiller returned from his business meeting around four in the afternoon, wearing a huge triumphant grin as he joined them on the veranda.

"Todd's made a sale," Shelly said after glancing up at him.

"You bet your hippy," he replied, bending down and giving her a peck on the forehead. "How about dinner in Reno tonight to celebrate?"

"Sounds like fun to me," Shelly said, after glancing at

Fran to check her reaction. "But first I'd like to see those slides you were telling me about, Fran." Briefly, she told Todd about Fran's new computer graphics equipment, and he expressed polite interest as well.

"Sure, let's see what you've got, kiddo," he said in the jocular, avuncular tone he evidently considered appropriate for his wife's closest friend. He gave one of his barking laughs. "Hell, if it's hot, maybe I can persuade my company to get into computer graphics!"

The bedrooms were on the upper story of the house. Fran hurried to the guest room, where she'd hung her raincoat in the closet. She rummaged in the pocket for a moment, frowning in puzzlement when she withdrew two diskettes rather than one. She stared in confusion for a moment, then her face cleared. As she ran downstairs to the phone, she took the card Rick Langtry had left her from the pocket of her shorts. Her fingers trembled with excitement as she dialed the telephone.

Earlier that afternoon, as he drove away from the Hiller house, Rick couldn't drive the image of Fran Barnette's lovely face and sparkling hazel eyes from his mind. Damn it, she seemed just about perfect—though he realized such a thing was impossible. Not only was she extraordinarily lovely, but she seemed to possess an excellent sense of humor and her large, expressive eyes fairly radiated intelligence. And that body! He couldn't stop thinking about those long, slender, perfectly formed legs and those creamy, ripe-looking breasts that had threatened to spill out of the halter restraining them, making it difficult for him to remember at times that Fran was considered a suspect in the case.

In short, he thought, swearing inwardly, she seemed amply endowed with all the qualities he valued in a woman: good looks, sense of humor, and intelligence. Damn. If only she wasn't a factor in this case, he might have had an opportunity to get to know her a bit better. There had to be a flaw in all that perfection . . .

Rick Langtry had remained single for so many years because he was a faultfinder—or perhaps it was simply because the women he'd become involved with up until now had inevitably evinced, sooner or later, glaring faults which prevented him from considering any lasting relationship with them—to his undying, everlasting relief. In any case, something had always prevented him from becoming seriously involved with a woman. Now, at thirty-three, he had almost resigned himself to permanent bachelorhood—not because he had any prejudice against marriage, he frequently told himself—but because his standards seemed to be impossibly high. At least, that was his rationale.

Jack O'Brien, who often listened to pop psychologists on the radio, had told Rick that the truth was that he feared making a real commitment, and that was why he invariably discovered flaws in the women he knew. Rick sighed, driving intently, ignoring the magnificent scenery on both sides of the road. Maybe the truth was somewhere in between, he reflected. One thing he knew for sure: he would have relished the opportunity to get to know Fran Barnette better—flaws or no flaws.

Impatiently, he thrust such thoughts from his mind. He had an espionage case to run, one in which the lady in question seemed to be involved, and it would require all his concentration if a grave breech of national security was to be avoided. Trying to decide on his next move, he drove on toward the motel where Jack was waiting.

"Any luck?" Jack asked as Rick entered the room at the Ponderosa.

"Nope." Rick glanced at the phone. "Did you get hold of the old man?"

"Yeah. He says stick with it. They've got a team going through Linkwell's apartment on the off-chance she had the diskette stashed there." He paused, looking over at Rick with a dubious expression. "Personally, I think they're barking up the wrong tree. I'd bet a month's salary she had that diskette on her when she got here."

"Yeah? Then where the hell is it now?" Rick laid down on one of the beds, his face a mask of frustration. "Man, I am bushed!"

"Why not catch forty winks?" Jack suggested. "I'm going back over to the hospital to double-check her stuff, then I'll give the car another going-over. I should be back here around four, then we can go round up some chow."

"Sounds good to me."

Rick tossed and turned for over an hour after Jack left, unable to fall asleep in spite of his weariness. Finally, he surrendered and sat up on the bed, systematically reviewing the facts of the case, one by one, until he was tearing at his hair in frustration. No matter how you sliced it, he thought, it always comes back to Fran Barnette. She was the only person who had been close enough to Linkwell long enough to have had access to the missing top secret diskette. Barnette, however, vehemently denied any knowledge of the diskette—and in spite of his natural policeman's suspicion, he found himself wanting to believe her.

He shied away from the direction his thoughts were taking him. Every fiber of his being rejected the notion that Fran Barnette could be involved in this filthy traitorous mess. Furthermore, everything they had learned about her during the past several hours only seemed to strengthen his denial. Why would a moderately successful, apparently honest and loyal, businesswoman from southern California knowingly become involved in what was threatening to burgeon into a major spy scandal? It just didn't add up, he thought.

And yet, there was no denying the fact that nobody but her had had the slightest opportunity to receive the diskette. Angrily, he got up from the bed and began pacing the floor, wishing that Jack would hurry up and return. He was beginning to feel a bit hungry. Perhaps if he ate, his thoughts would become clearer.

When the phone rang, he snatched it from its cradle on the first ring.

"Langtry," he snapped.

"Rick? This is Fran. Fran Barnette."

"Fran! I was just thinking about you."

"Oh?" she asked coolly, and paused for a moment before continuing. "The reason I'm calling is that I think I've found that diskette you're looking for. It was in the pocket of my raincoat. When I went to get my diskette out and found two, well, right away I thought—"

"Do you have it with you now?" Rick asked, cutting her off in mid-sentence.

"Yes, I—"

"Is it marked or stamped in any way, Fran?"

"Well, yes. That's why I was so sure it must be the one you're looking for. It's got 'top secret' on the envelope in white block letters and there's some other stuff in smaller print."

"Never mind," he exclaimed. "That's it! I'll be there in ten minutes."

"Wait—there's something else," Fran said quickly, before he could hang up. "I don't know if it's connected in any way, but right after you left this afternoon, I noticed two guys cruising past the house in a green van. What frightens me is I'm almost positive they're the two guys I told you about who were in the restaurant

57

this morning. Do you remember my mentioning them? Oh, I'm probably being foolish, but—"

"Not at all, Fran," Rick interrupted, his mind racing. It was obvious to him that the two strangers Fran had seen must be the contact men to whom Linkwell had been supposed to give the diskette. If that was the case, he realized, then they were professionals—possibly KGB agents. At the very least, they were working for the KGB on a free-lance basis, and that could be even worse.

"Are you and Mrs. Hiller alone in the house now?" he asked.

"No. Todd's here. Shelly's husband."

"Please get him on the phone."

"Todd? But what does he—?"

"At once, Fran," Rick snapped. *"Now!"*

While Rick was waiting for Todd Hiller to come on the line, Jack O'Brien walked into the room. Placing one hand over the mouthpiece, Rick made a circle of thumb and forefinger with his free hand. O'Brien's round, ruddy face was immediately wreathed in a broad, delighted grin.

"Hot damn!" he exclaimed, doing a little hopping dance step on the carpet. "When—?" Rick cut him off with a shushing gesture as Hiller came on the line.

"Yeah? This is Todd Hiller," he said, a little truculently. "What can I do for you, pal?"

"Mr. Hiller, this is Special Agent Rick Langtry of the Defense Intelligence Agency. Mr. Hiller, do you possess a firearm?"

"What?"

When Rick and Jack rolled onto the gravel driveway at the Hiller's house fifteen minutes later, they were greeted by the sight of a tall, grim-faced, red-haired man standing on the doorstep with a long-barreled semiautomatic shotgun held at the ready.

"Mister, you'd better be Langtry," he said, lowering the shotgun until it was aimed loosely in the direction of the two men exiting cautiously from the white sedan.

"I'm Langtry," Rick said, watching the shotgun warily. "And this is Jack O'Brien, my partner. Mr. Hiller, I'm going to take my identification card out now, all right?"

"Slowly! Put it on the hood of the car, then back off." Todd tensed as Rick reached inside his jacket, and the barrel of the shotgun came up and steadied on Rick's chest. Ever so slowly, Jack removed his identification as well, never taking his eyes from Hiller's face. They stepped back several paces from the car as Hiller gestured with the shotgun. Hiller came over and peered closely at their identification, then sighed gustily and lowered the shotgun.

"*Sheesh,*" he exclaimed. "I haven't been so damned scared since my first day of junior high." He shrugged, a sheepish expression on his face, as if embarrassed by the weapon in his hands. "Sorry about the dramatics, but—"

"Don't apologize," Rick interrupted warmly. "You did exactly the right thing, Mr. Hiller."

"Well, I suppose we ought to go inside, then." Opening the front door, Todd stood politely aside. Rick and Jack stepped across the threshhold, and Todd locked the door behind them.

"Fran, Shelly," Todd called, "it's all right. You can come down now."

Rick's eyes were drawn to the top of the stairs. He inhaled sharply as Fran appeared on the landing, as lovely as he remembered. His memory had played no tricks on him this time. He stared, transfixed, as she gracefully descended to the ground-floor level and handed him the classified diskette.

"Here," she said with a shudder. "I can't tell you how glad I am to be rid of that thing."

"Thanks, Fran." Rick slipped the square black envelope into the inside pocket of his jacket. "You've done a great service for your country today—not to mention for yours truly," he added with a relieved grin.

"Does this mean you no longer consider me a possible spy?" Fran asked, raising one finely shaped eyebrow.

"Well, I don't know," Rick said with a smile. "This could be part of a very clever scheme to disarm me . . ." He laughed. "Of course not, Fran," he said, then turned to Jack, still smiling. "Fran, Mr. and Mrs. Hiller, this is Jack O'Brien, my partner."

"Pleased to meet you," Jack said, staring at the two women with frank admiration. He shot Rick an amused glance. "I'm beginning to understand why Rick sent me to the hospital today and came here himself."

"Yes, well," Rick said quickly, clearing his throat, "I really think we should call in, Jack, and get this thing off our hands as soon as possible. Mr. Hiller, may I use your phone to call my office? I have a government charge number for the call."

"Of course," Todd said. "You can use the extension in my den."

"Mr. O'Brien, would you like a cup of coffee or some tea?" Shelly asked as Rick followed Todd into a room just down the hallway a few steps.

"Thanks, Mr. Hiller," he said, when Todd had pointed out the telephone. After Todd left the room, Rick picked up the phone and placed the call, using the number Jack had given him back at the motel.

"Addison," came the curt reply after just three rings. "This better be damned good, because I was just getting ready to go out to dinner with my wife."

"Rick Langtry, chief. And it is good news—you can tell the people out at the lab to relax. We've recovered their property for them."

"Relax, hell," Addison grumbled. "I'm going to go over the security procedures out there with a fine-toothed comb, starting Monday morning. Damn it, Rick, this should never have happened!" He paused, then continued in a milder tone of voice. "But I am relieved. Good work, young man. You and O'Brien can expect letters of commendation for your personnel jackets. Tell me—how did you happen to make the recovery?"

Briefly, Rick sketched in the events of the day, beginning with the abortive contact attempt in the restaurant that morning and ending with Fran's report of the two suspicious men in the van.

"I see," Addison said thoughtfully when he was finished. "So you figure that Linkwell somehow got the diskette into Barnette's pocket before the heart attack occurred?"

"Chief, the only alternative would be that Fran—Miss Barnette—was involved, and that wouldn't make sense, would it? Especially now, since she's turned the diskette over to us. It was only when she went in the pocket of her raincoat for something else that she discovered the diskette."

"Hmm." Addison was silent for so long that Rick was beginning to think they'd lost the connection, then he spoke again. "The thing I don't like about this whole damned mess is that we've lost the opposition, Rick. If this Aramas fellow was running Linkwell, how many others might he be running as well?"

"Damn good question," Rick said thoughtfully.

"Tell me, what's your evaluation of this Barnette woman?"

"Evaluation? In what way?"

"Well, how does she strike you?" Addison said impatiently. "Good citizen? Flag waver? Flake? Some kind of radical?"

"She seems like an average good citizen to me," Rick said after a moment's thought. "Why?"

"Rick, I've got an idea. Just a possibility, and it all depends on just how willing this Barnette woman is to help her country. Now what do you think . . ."

When Rick left the den and joined the others in the living room a few moments later, his thoughts were in a quandary. On one hand, he was in favor of anything that would afford the opportunity to get to know Fran Barnette better; on the other hand, he knew that what he was about to ask of her could place her in great danger. He paused just outside the living room for a moment, then his expression became firm. There was no choice, and in spite of the danger, he knew he would use Fran Barnette to nail the treasonous bastards who were attempting to steal his nation's secrets. He would use Fran Barnette or anybody else in a position to be useful, no matter what the danger.

After passing along Addison's expression of appreciation to Fran and the Hillers, he looked over at Fran. "I'd like to speak to you in private for a moment, if I may."

"Seems to me that's how this all got started," Fran said, smiling, but got to her feet and left the room with Rick. He led her back to the den, where he closed the door firmly behind them.

"Okay," Fran said, perching on the edge of Todd Hiller's leather recliner. "What's the big mystery?"

Standing near the door, Rick gazed at her for several seconds before replying. "Fran, I've got to take this diskette over to Reno tonight. The agency's flying a guy in to pick it up so they can get it back under lock and key where it belongs."

"Yes." Fran said, frowning. Rick's heart accelerated a bit as their eyes met and held for an instant.

"Have dinner with me tonight," Rick said gruffly. "I've got some questions to ask you about the case, and something very important to discuss with you. We can eat dinner after we dispose of the diskette."

"I've got plans," she said with a smile. "Sorry."

"Cancel them. This is more important."

She stared at him, a look of disbelief in her eyes. "Every time I start thinking maybe there's something to you after all, you come on like some he-man. No, thanks, Rick. As I said, I've got other plans." She stood and started to turn away, but Rick gripped her upper arm, holding her securely. A shiver of fear and delight ran up her spine at the strength she felt in his hand and arm. He leaned close, so close she felt the heat of his breath on her cheek and neck.

"This is a matter of national security," he said firmly. "As a representative of our government, I'm asking you for a favor."

"Oh, really?" she asked mockingly, hating herself for the sudden feeling of languor, the watery weakness in the backs of her knees. "And all this time I thought you were interested in *me.*"

"Damn you," he muttered hoarsely, pulling her even closer, until the nipple of her left breast burned with contact with the tight, hard muscle of his upper arm. "I *am* . . ." His eyes blazed with a passion that made it difficult for her to think clearly, and she yanked herself away from him, gasping for breath and trembling, inexplicably angry at him.

"I know what you're doing!" she exclaimed, her hazel eyes hot with fury. "It won't work, mister!"

"Really?" he asked, his voice trembling a bit as he

wiped his mouth with the back of his hand. "I'm afraid I don't . . . But to get back to business—"

"Yes, please do," she said, refusing to look at his face.

"When that plane lands in Reno, it's not only picking up the diskette Linkwell stole; it's bringing in a replacement—on the surface, exactly like the genuine article."

"Oh, let me guess the rest of it," Fran said when he paused, her voice dripping with sarcasm. "You want to use me to try to establish contact with the people Linkwell was trying to turn the diskette over to, right?" He lowered his eyes, flushing darkly, and she rushed on: "It's hardly what I would have expected from a macho guy like you, Rick, but I suppose I should have known better. Gallantry, as well as chivalry, is apparently dead and buried in this country."

"You'd be protected every step of the way," he said raggedly, the expression in his dark eyes a confusing mixture of shame, anger, and a dogged determination to persuade her. "Believe me, if there was any danger—"

"I'm sure you'd never ask me if there was danger," she said sarcastically, snorting in derision as he refused to meet her eyes. "That's what I thought!"

"Listen, any danger would be minimal," he protested. "We'll have more men now, around-the-clock surveillance teams." He broke off abruptly, spreading his hands in defeat. "Ah, hell, forget it. I'll call my boss and tell him you're not interested. Why should you be? You're just like everybody else in this country. Patriotism is for the other guy. Let the civil servants do it, right?" Shaking his head, he turned toward the phone, his contempt for her perfectly expressed by the way he turned his back on her.

"Wait! I'll do it," she blurted as he picked up the phone. He looked back sharply, a whole range of emotions flitting across his face as her words struck home: first, the disbelief; followed quickly by acceptance; and

64

finally, a deep concern for her. The last emotion she thought she detected was fear.

"Are you sure?" he whispered, and she felt warmed by the intensity of his gaze.

"You said it, didn't you?" she asked with a lightness she was far from feeling. "My country needs me."

However, as he nodded slowly in reluctant acceptance, she found herself wondering if she'd agreed to help for the sake of her country or because she wanted to get to know him better. He was a devastatingly attractive man who possessed the ability to evoke powerful emotional responses from her; and to move her from almost overpowering desire for him one instant to something approaching hatred an instant later. He was staring at her now, a deep, unfathomable expression in his dark eyes, and she felt as if his gaze stripped away all of her surface and penetrated to the depths of her very soul.

"I'll take care of you, Fran," he vowed. "I give you my word. Nothing will happen to you."

CHAPTER FOUR

When Fran had packed her bag for the long weekend in Tahoe, she had thought it necessary to bring only two stylish outfits—one for Saturday evening, in case the opportunity to go out arose, and another one for Sunday evening. For Saturday she'd decided on her favorite new outfit which was a pleated white skirt, a soft, short-sleeved pullover, and a classic navy blazer with shining brass buttons, topped off by matching white shoes and purse. Now she frowned over her choices for a moment, wondering if they were too casual. After a moment, she shrugged. She was going to Reno, not the White House, for dinner. The outfit she'd brought for Sunday, a smart pants suit and accessories, she never gave a second glance; she was wishing she'd brought something really dazzling for her first outing with Rick Langtry. She sighed, making up her mind: the skirt and blazer outfit would have to do.

At the realization she was hoping to impress him, she grimaced impatiently at herself, frowning and fluffing her blond hair, still damp from the shower, before beginning to dress. Still, she couldn't shake the sensation, as she toweled dry and slipped into a sheer, lacy bra and panties, that she was preparing for a first date with the most exciting man she'd met in a long, long time.

"You're being silly, girl," she chastized herself aloud

as she sat down in front of the dresser in the guest bedroom and began lightly applying makeup. She'd been blessed with a wonderfully clear and smooth complexion; she wore only a dab of lipstick and some eyeliner. "This is business—and maybe a dangerous business—so you'd best keep your mind on what you're doing."

"Knock, knock," Shelly said from the other side of the door. She entered the guest room carrying two tall, frosty glasses. "Thought maybe you'd like a toddy to tide you over until dinner, and when I heard you muttering to yourself through the door, I knew you would. Better watch it, kid. Next you'll be answering yourself."

"Not a chance, Shelly." Smiling, Fran gestured for her to put the glass on the dresser next to her cosmetics. She had no intention of drinking anything alcoholic for a while. Certainly not until she'd learned precisely what she'd gotten herself into when she'd agreed to do this undercover work for the Defense Intelligence Agency. She glanced up at Shelly's reflection in the mirror and smiled ruefully. "Listen, I'm really sorry about missing this evening with you and Todd, but—"

"Are you kiddin' me?" Shelly interrupted with a lopsided grin. Fran realized with a feeling of dismay that her former roommate was beginning to show the effects of drinking steadily throughout the afternoon. "You'd have to be nuts to pass up an evenin' with a hunk like that Langtry guy so you could lissen to ole Toad braggin' about his sales quotas all night long. Nuts," she repeated sourly, staring down into her drink and shaking her head slowly. "Believe me."

"Shelly," Fran said, turning from the mirror, "are things so bad for you?" Shelly shook her head, but her lashes were gleaming with sudden moisture. Fran got to her feet and put her arms around her friend's shoulders, her hazel eyes dark with compassion. "You and I will have a nice long woman-to-woman talk tomorrow, okay? Really talk, the way we used to. Okay?"

"Okay, fine," Shelly said, then gulped at her drink. She started to add something, but they were interrupted by the ringing of the telephone. Shelly picked it up, holding it out to Fran after a moment.

"It's for you. It's him."

"Yes, this is Fran." As she took the phone and spoke softly, her chest swelled with an odd, tight feeling of anticipation. The deep, resonant voice on the other end was like a caress when he spoke, sending a delicious shiver up along the sensitive skin just below her ear.

"I'm going to be a little later than I said, Fran. Jack's car gave up the ghost, and I've got to help him arrange a rental before I can get away, so it'll be awhile yet. I just wanted to let you know you weren't being stood up when I didn't show up on time." He chuckled, sounding somewhat uncomfortable.

"Why don't we take my car?" Fran suggested.

"Are you sure you wouldn't mind?" His voice quickened with relief. "That would solve the transportation problem for the moment, and of course you would be reimbursed for your mileage."

"Don't worry about all that," Fran said warmly. "I was planning to drive up to Reno anyway."

"Fine, then you can do it at government expense." He paused briefly, then said, "Well, that's settled, then."

"Yes," Fran said, "all settled."

"Um, the thing is, could you, uh, pick me up here at the motel?" he asked, sounding embarrassed.

"Sure," Fran replied, surprised. "Did you think I was expecting you to meet me way out here?"

"No, I guess not. It's just—oh, hell, see you when you get here. We're in Room 122. Just pull up out front and tap the horn. I'll be right out."

"Oh, I don't have to come in and meet your parents?" Fran laughed when Rick muttered something unintelligible. She gently replaced the telephone. Shelly raised her eyebrows curiously and smiled when Fran explained.

"He sounds like a real old-fashioned guy," she observed. "I suppose you'd have to call him a male chauvinist, if that expression hadn't become rather passe."

"Mmm, maybe," Fran murmured, carefully applying eyeliner. "But I kind of like my men on the old-fashioned side . . . as long as they don't carry it too far."

Fran was glad she'd taken the time to hose down the RX-7 with clear water and chamois it dry that afternoon. As she pulled off the highway onto the parking lot of the Ponderosa, the glistening hood of the car reflected the sky and clouds and trees like a mirror, and the leather interior still gave off a "new car" smell. The car looked good, and if Rick knew anything about cars, he'd be impressed, she hoped, then winced at the realization she was still worrying about impressing him. What did she care what he thought? She barely knew him, and since his job was in northern California and hers in the south, chances were they wouldn't get to know each other much better.

Still, she admitted with an inward sigh as she pulled up in front of Room 122 and tapped the horn, she knew she wanted to impress him. He must have been watching from the window; he emerged from the room at once. He was wearing the same tweed jacket but had on a fresh white shirt and a different tie and trousers. Fran smiled as she looked at the sharp crease in the brown trousers and the gleam of fresh polish on his shoes. It seems, she said to herself, that she wasn't the only one who had taken pains over appearances on this occasion.

"Hi," he said, smiling as he came over to the car on the driver's side. "Thanks for coming." Opening the door, he stood aside, an expectant expression on his face. She looked up in confusion for a moment, then felt a burst of irritation when she realized what he was waiting for.

"I'll drive," she said.

"I think it would be better if I did," he said, meeting her glare unflinchingly.

"It's my car," Fran bit out. "I'll drive."

"I must insist," he said, bowing slightly and gesturing for her to get out from beneath the steering wheel. "Please."

"Look," Fran began, sputtering angrily, "I'm perfectly aw–are—"

"Really?" Rick interrupted dryly. "Are you aware that you were followed here? By our friends in the van." Without moving his head, he glanced to the side and the rear of the RX-7. Fran glanced into the rearview mirror and sucked in her breath in surprise at the sight of the green van she'd seen earlier that day parked on the other side of the street and half a block down from the motel's parking lot entrance.

"But—that van might have been sitting there for hours," she protested weakly. Rick just shook his head.

"That van was just pulling up and stopping as I stepped out the door of my room," he said. "I'd be willing to bet any amount of money that they followed you all the way from the Hiller's place."

"But I didn't see it behind me."

"Exactly my point," he snapped, gesturing again for her to get out of the car. "You didn't see it. Why should you have, really? You haven't been trained to watch for surveillance. And you probably wouldn't have the faintest idea how to ditch a tail either." He paused, his chin set stubbornly. "Now, are you going to let me drive this vehicle, or not?"

"Oh, I suppose so," Fran muttered. "I wouldn't want

70

to deprive you of the opportunity to play secret agent!"
Chin imperiously high, she swung her long legs out of
the car and exited. Rick stared boldly, his eyes gleaming
in frank admiration as her skirt parted briefly, permitting a flash of thigh. She glared, but he grinned and
gave a little mock bow.

"Very nice legs," he murmured as she swept haugh-
tily past on her way around to the other side of the car.

"You just had to look of course," she snapped, glaring across the roof of the car.

"Of course," he agreed. "I noticed them this afternoon, when you were in shorts, but there's something
infinitely more sexy about legs when they're covered by
a skirt . . ." Before getting in, he removed his jacket,
folded it carefully, and placed it in the small area behind the driver's seat which was euphimistically referred to by the manufacturer as "the back seat." "Want
to take off your blazer?" he asked. "It'll be warm in the
car, and it's over an hour's drive."

"Yes," Fran said shortly, still smarting over having
lost the argument about driving. She carefully folded
her blazer and placed it on the small rear seat, then sat
down in the passenger seat and fastened her seat belt.

Rick slid into the driver's seat and scanned the controls while he adjusted the seat. Then he put the car in
gear and they moved smoothly out of the parking lot
and onto the highway.

Casually, Fran glanced back toward the green van,
half hoping it would remain where it was parked,
thereby proving Rick wrong, but it was pulling out into
the traffic lane behind them and accelerating to catch
up. She could tell by the expression on Rick's face that
he was aware of their pursuer, but for the moment, at
least, he seemed content to let the van tag along behind.

"By the way," Rick said after a few minutes, looking

over and smiling at her. "I meant to tell you, you look really terrific this evening."

"Thank you." She felt a flush of pleasure spreading up her neck and onto her face, and turned away and stared out the window on the passenger side, marveling at her reaction. *What is the matter with me?* she wondered. *I've had plenty of compliments in my life—why does one kind word from this male chauvinist have the power to make me blush like a schoolgirl?*

When she felt the heat on her face subsiding, she turned back to the front, studying him surreptitiously, watching the way the corded muscles of his forearm flexed and rippled at the slightest movement as he effortlessly controlled the car. His stomach, she saw now that he had removed his jacket, was flat and firm, and the long legs stretching out to the gas and brake pedals were well-shaped and padded with long, smooth muscles that rippled whenever he moved his foot. Shivering, she looked away, feeling a different kind of warmth spreading throughout her body. *Cut it out!* she told herself. *You're acting like a fool!*

"I understand you run a graphics business," Rick said pleasantly.

"Yes, that's right. I always loved art, drawing, painting, things like that. But when I was in college I realized that it was the everyday application of art that fascinated me, rather than what people would call the 'fine arts.' Advertising, illustration, visual presentations of all kinds." Rick smiled encouragingly, and she went on, flattered by his interest. "So I decided to concentrate on commercial art, and—and here I am," she finished.

"And here you are?" Rick gave a little shake of his head, one eyebrow arched skeptically. "You say that like there's nothing exceptional about you. I'm sure that

72

most young artists don't own their own agencies at your age."

"Perhaps not."

"Maybe," Rick suggested, his teeth flashing white against the tan of his face, "you just have to be in control."

"No, I—" Fran started to argue, then she subsided, considering it. There was an aspect of wanting to be in control to her personality; undoubtedly that was one of the reasons she'd opened her own business before reaching thirty years of age, instead of working for someone else as the vast majority of commercial artists did. "Maybe you're right," she admitted after a moment.

"Sure I'm right," Rick said, laughing. "Look at the way you reacted when I wanted to drive. You didn't want to give up control of this car, even for the relatively short drive to Reno. That says volumes about your personality, lady."

"To someone with your high degree of training in psychology, of course," Fran said. She shot him an exasperated glance. "I think we've been discussing my shortcomings long enough. Why don't we talk about you for a while.

"For instance, how did you end up working for the government? I thought only gray little men and women who were willing to trade their whole lives for cradle-to-the-grave security wanted careers working for the government." She cocked her head, enjoying his discomfiture as she studied him. "You don't seem to fit that mold somehow."

"Mold? What a lot of bull." His mouth flattened into a straight line, and his hands flexed on the steering wheel. "I know a lot of damned good people who work for the government. If there weren't, this country would've gone down the tubes long ago, because the average Joe out there couldn't care less about the government, as long as he's making his buck. Hell," he added with a derisive snort, "the average citizen doesn't even bother to vote! The only time he pays any attention to the government is when his taxes go up or some government service he's always taken for granted suddenly comes to an end. Then he screams to high heavens."

"I find your attitude very cynical," Fran said coolly. "Do you really think we're all out here chasing the dollar with such single-minded devotion we've never a thought for our country?"

"Do you really think most government workers are gray little men and women willing to trade their entire lives for security?" He slowed the car for a long, winding curve, glancing in the rearview mirror to check the location of their tail. Still there, he observed, a quarter of a mile back, separated from them by a pickup truck and a pair of motorcycles.

"I didn't realize I'd stung your pride so," Fran said, pleased. "But I did say you didn't seem to fit the mold . . . but really, isn't that the way with most of them?"

"No, it isn't," he declared. "There are plenty of damned good people working for Uncle Sam. Oh, sure, I suppose there are some who sign on only for the security of a civil service job, but they don't rise very far in their fields. Most of the people I work with are just damned good people who would do well wherever they decided to work, in government or out in private industry."

"There," Fran said excitedly, "that's exactly my point. These good people you keep talking about—if they really are so good, why aren't they in private industry where they could earn a whole lot more money?"

"Does everything in your life have to have a dollar value assigned?" He shot her a distasteful glance before turning his attention back to the highway. "This'll

74

probably sound old-fashioned as hell to you, but doesn't anybody do anything out of plain old patriotism anymore?"

"Well!"

"Sorry, Fran," he said quickly, cutting off her angry sputtering, looking mortified. She was too angry to be mollified when he added, "I meant present company excepted, of course," he said. "That is a given."

"Oh, really," she said coldly, then turned and stared out the window on her side of the car, ignoring him for the next several miles.

It's a beautiful drive, Rick thought, glancing over at Fran's rigid form with a shrug, *so I'll enjoy it.* The highway winding down from the mountains near Tahoe was smooth and well-paved, just curved enough to make it an interesting, pleasant drive, and he knew that if the van hadn't been nagging at the back of his mind he would have been enjoying himself immensely. Fran had chosen her car wisely; the RX-7 was a fine, responsive driving machine, and this was precisely the sort of road for which it had been designed.

As they descended from the mountains and rolled out across the high desert floor, the highway arrowed straight north toward Reno. Rick pressed his foot down on the accelerator, glancing into the rearview mirror. Their speed rapidly climbed, and the headlights of the green van gradually diminished in the mirror. Fran glanced over at him as the speedometer needle hovered near ninety.

"We need to shed our tail for a while," he explained. "We don't want 'em around when we make the switch at Reno International, do we? We want these jokers to think they're after the genuine article when you make your pitch."

"Well, sure," Fran agreed, trying not to be frightened by their speed, hoping that he knew what he was doing.

He certainly seemed confident enough. His strong hands rested lightly, surely, on the steering wheel, and his face betrayed none of the tension or excitement most people would have felt as their speed climbed past one hundred miles per hour.

A moment later they rounded one last curve, a long, gently sloping turn that Rick took at ninety, the RX-7 gripping the road as firmly as if they'd been traveling at sixty. As the highway straightened out once again, Rick suddenly hit the brakes several times, slowing the car quickly, then turned off onto a narrow dirt road which led back into the row of pine trees a hundred yards or so from the highway. As the towering evergreens closed in over the car, he killed the headlights, then twisted in his seat to look back at the highway. It was becoming darker by the moment as the twilight deepened, but after a moment he grunted with satisfaction.

"There they go," he muttered. "With any luck at all they'll be all the way into Reno before they realize what's happened."

Fran had also twisted in her seat to look back at the highway, and when Rick started to turn back toward the front, their eyes met and locked, their faces separated by less than five inches. For a moment they both froze, the silence so thick she thought he must hear the pounding of her heart. She met his gaze with a cool detachment she was far from feeling, and when he finally blinked and turned away, she sucked in her breath in relief, as if she'd been literally unable to move until he did so first. Of course, she realized, that was ridiculous.

"Do me a favor," Rick said gruffly as he put the car into reverse and began maneuvering it around, "Don't look at me like that again unless you're ready to get kissed. Because, lady," he added, craning over his shoulder as he backed the RX-7 off the narrow dirt roadway before turning back toward the highway, "that is just exactly what will happen to you the next time you use those eyes of yours on me like that."

"Is that so?" Fran murmured, wearing a half smile as she averted her face from his challenging stare. "You're certainly sure of yourself, aren't you?"

She continued smiling as he drove back out to the highway, and when he pulled out and accelerated toward Reno, she was still smiling. He glanced over and lifted an eyebrow, half in irritation, half in admiration, and gave his head a little shake. She laughed aloud, shivering as her body was suffused with an unaccustomed warmth.

"We're almost there," he announced a few minutes later, just as Fran noticed the sky above the northern horizon appeared to be illuminated by some unearthly light. When she looked to him for an explanation, he said crisply, "Neon. Neon lights reflected on the cloud cover."

"Clouds?" she exclaimed. "Since when?"

"Don't you listen to the news?" He jerked his chin upwards, as if to indicate the sky. "Weatherman says we're in for another rainstorm before the weekend's over. Clouds've been building up ever since we left the motel. Ah, here's our turnoff."

"Reno International Airport," Fran read softly as Rick slowed for the turn. They merged with the flow of airport traffic circling the parking lots, moving slowly. There was an astonishing amount of traffic, Fran reflected, then hastily corrected herself. After all, Reno was a major holiday mecca for the western half of the country; it was not surprising that the airport should be busy on one of the first three-day weekends of the season.

"Where're we going?" she asked, surprised that Rick was turning away from the public parking lots, heading down a narrow side street behind a row of huge hangar-like buildings. A sign at the side of the street read Authorized Personnel Only. "Aren't we going to park?"

"Sure, but our boy'll be coming in over here on this side of the airport, Fran. He's not flying commercial. He'll be in a twin Beech the agency keeps for situations like this." He smiled at her. "We'll avoid the crowds this way—and we'll be able to make our switch away from prying eyes." A moment later he pulled into a parking slot against the wall of a long, multistoried building with official-looking signs painted here and there. U.S. Government Property, one read.

As Fran got out of the car and pulled on her blazer against the chill, she shivered and looked up at the now completely dark sky. There was only blackness above; clouds had completely hidden the stars. Rick donned his jacket, then took her arm and led her through a metal door into the building, showing his identification to a bored, unimpressed, uniformed guard.

"Miss Barnette's with me," he said when the guard looked at Fran. "On official business. Can you tell me where Jerry Whitworth's office is?"

The guard turned and wearily studied a floor plan on the wall behind his booth, then showed Rick what he needed to know. As they headed down the long corridor, Rick turned to Fran and spoke out of the side of his mouth. "Now there," he muttered, "just might be one of those gray little men you were referring to earlier."

Fran smiled. "Is this one of the DIA's buildings?"

"No. There are several government agencies sharing office space here. For example, the air traffic controllers for northern Nevada have their administrative offices here. Customs and INS, of course, since this is an international airport." He shot her a sidelong glance as he continued, "Several other agencies have branch offices here as well. Ah, here we are—Jerry Whitworth."

78

He tapped on the door with the backs of his knuckles, then opened it for Fran and followed her inside. It was a tiny room, furnished in government drab—gray metal desk, gray metal swivel chair, and gray metal filing cabinet. Two straight-backed gray metal chairs stood in front of the desk for visitors. A door in the wall behind the desk evidently led to an office or room deeper in the recesses of the building, Fran thought, but nothing indicated this was so; it could have led to a broom closet, for all she knew.

"Rick! Damn, it's good to see you, fellow!" A tall, middle-aged man with thinning sandy hair and the ruddy complexion and burst capillaries of a hard drinker rose from behind the desk and hurried forward, hand extended in welcome.

"Jerry, it's been too long." Rick shook the older man's hand firmly, then turned and indicated Fran, smiling proudly. "Fran Barnette, this is Jerry Whitworth, an old and dear friend of mine. Jerry, Fran Barnette, the lady I told you about."

"Miss Barnette, it's a privilege to meet you," Whitworth said, pumping her hand. "If only for the opportunity to thank you personally for the help you're giving our agency. If more folks had your sense of patriotism, were willing to risk—"

Rick interrupted with a discreet cough. "Uh, Jerry, what time is the plane from San Francisco due?"

"What?" Whitworth turned from Fran, frowning at the interruption. "Oh, the plane. We've got about fifteen minutes, I think. How about letting me treat you and the lovely Miss Barnette to a cup of our lounge coffee. Believe me, it's an experience you'll never forget." Rick nodded, and Whitworth opened the door Fran had been wondering about and said, "We'll be down in the lounge, Kathy. Buzz me on the house phone if you need to get hold of me."

They followed Whitworth down the concrete corridor another thirty or forty feet and entered a large room containing several battered vinyl and chrome chairs and sofas, as well as a refrigerator and an electric coffee urn. A coffee table in front of one of the sofas was covered with a scattering of magazines and newspapers as well as what appeared to be the remains of someone's lunch.

"Mmm, peanut butter," Fran murmured as she glanced at the scraps.

"Damn it," Whitworth grumbled, rummaging in a cupboard beneath the coffee urn, "I've told those guys and told 'em, to pick up after themselves! Buncha prima donnas, think they oughta have the janitor to pick up their lunch bags for them." He made a disgusted noise as he handed styrofoam cups to Fran and Rick. "Cream 'n sugar's right there," he said, indicating the encrusted containers with a gesture. He filled a cup from the urn and handed it to Fran, taking her empty cup in return.

"Wow." Fran choked when she had taken her first sip of the thick black liquid. "I see what you mean about it being an unforgettable experience."

"Yeah, it's pretty bad." Whitworth chuckled and shook his head, his good humor apparently restored. "But it'll sure keep you going when you need to stay awake." He paused and glanced fondly at Rick. "Still staying in shape, I see? Gonna try it again in '88?"

Rick shook his head. "No, I'll be too old, Jerry. My only shot would've been in '80, but it just wasn't in the cards."

Fran looked from Whitworth to Rick and back, a bemused expression on her face. Whitworth noticed and pointed proudly at Rick.

"Guess nobody told you our boy here is an Olympic-class gymnast, Miss Barnette. He probably would've won a gold medal in '80 if Carter hadn't pulled us out of the Olympics. Why—"

"All right, Jerry," Rick interrupted, a tolerant grin on his face. "Don't lay it on too thick. I might've competed, but a gold medal? The best gymnasts from all over the world might've had something to say about that."

Whitworth opened his mouth to argue, but he was interrupted by the harsh jangling of the wall-mounted telephone. He snatched it up, muttering into the mouthpiece for a few seconds, then hung up and nodded soberly at Rick.

"Our boy just touched down. He's taxiing up out back right now."

"Good." Rick touched his jacket pocket, as if to reassure himself. "It'll be a relief to turn this thing over to somebody else."

They followed Whitworth down the corridor to an intersection where they turned in the direction of the runway, judging from the sounds emanating from the other side of the double doors at the end of the hallway. Whitworth nodded to the guard at the end of the corridor, then led them out onto a sort of loading dock that stretched away in both directions along the length of the building, interrupted every fifty feet or so by short metal ladders. A small twin-engined airplane, white with red and blue trim, was just coming to a halt on the asphalt area adjacent to the loading dock, rocking slightly as its pilot applied the brakes. With a baritone whirring noise the engines idled back, the propellors slowing until the individual blades were distinguishable. The pilot slid open the window on his side of the small craft and waved at Rick, his hair blowing wildly in the prop wash.

"Howya doin', Langtry?" he yelled. "Just like you to have all this soft duty—and with a good-lookin' honey like that to help you pass the time!" He looked over at Fran, who was standing on the dock, and winked and waved, so open and cheerful it was impossible for her to take offense at his words. She smiled, brushing her blowing hair back out of her eyes, watching as Rick hopped down from the dock, ignoring the ladder, and trotted over to the plane.

"Smitty, it's good to see you!" he yelled at the pilot. He withdrew the small, flat, black package from his inside pocket and handed it to the pilot. Smitty glanced at it, nodded, and put it down somewhere near him in the cockpit, then thrust his hand back out the window holding an apparently identical diskette. "Thanks, pal," he said.

"My pleasure." Smitty waved again at Fran and Whitworth, then slid his small window shut and reached toward the controls. Immediately, the baritone note of the engines deepened and the propellor blades disappeared to the naked eye. The small craft began moving away from the loading dock area, back toward the runways, bobbing awkwardly as it picked up speed. Fran watched until it vanished from view behind another building.

"Hungry?" Rick asked as he hopped back up onto the dock. His jacket flapped open in the stiff breeze and Fran couldn't help noticing the checkered walnut grips of a small revolver on his hip. She felt oddly reassured by the sight as she nodded enthusiastically.

"Famished."

"You're in luck, then." He grinned and nodded his thanks as Whitworth held the door for them to reenter the building. When the door closed behind them, shutting out the runway noise, they spoke in normal tones again. "Part of the deal is that Uncle Sam picks up your dinner tab tonight," Rick went on. He paused and gestured expansively. "Now, is there any place special you'd like to eat? After all, we are in Reno. Loads of fancy places to eat, complete with live, big name entertainment, and all the slot machines your little heart could possibly desire. What do you say, Fran?"

"I think I'd like someplace quiet." She gave him a worried look. "I think I need to hear once more just how we're going to proceed with this thing—especially the part about how I'm in no danger."

"Er, right," Rick muttered. He and Whitworth exchanged a quick, almost furtive glance, then Whitworth cleared his throat and said, "You know, I like to take the wife to dinner every now and then at the Bum Steer. It's a damned nice place, enough off the beaten track so you don't have all the noise and glitter, but the food's great and the atmosphere is very pleasant. It's a steak house, but they do have some seafood as well."

"How's that sound, Fran?" Rick asked.

"Does it have slot machines?" Fran asked.

"Honey," Whitworth replied with a laugh, "this is Nevada. They even have slots in supermarkets here."

Fran shrugged in resignation. "Okay with me, I suppose."

After Whitworth gave them directions to the Bum Steer, they said good-bye and left, Whitworth and Rick vowing to get together soon. Five minutes later Rick and Fran were in the RX-7, turning off the airport road back onto the main highway. Before ten minutes had passed, they were pulling into the parking lot of the restaurant.

"I hope the fact it's so close to his office isn't the only reason Whitworth's so high on this place," Rick muttered as he switched off the ignition and opened his door. He glanced around the crowded parking lot and brightened a bit. "From the look of the crowd, the food must be pretty good."

Fran tucked her hand inside the arm he offered as they made their way across the parking lot toward the main entrance, experiencing a thrill of pleasure at the

83

touch of the firm muscle beneath the fabric of his jacket. She felt flushed with pride as they entered the foyer of the restaurant and several people looked admiringly at them. She knew they made a handsome couple; Rick with his dark, slender, powerful good looks and she with her blond hair, fair complexion, and hazel eyes. Rick stepped over to put their names down on the hostess's seating list, and Fran looked around, studying the decor with a designer's eye.

The restaurant, like so many in the western half of the United States, had chosen the Old West as its decorating theme. The knotty pine walls were festooned with ropes, spurs, saddle blankets, hats, and various other cowboy paraphernalia. There was a large reproduction of a Frederick Remington oil painting hanging above the fireplace in the bar, which they entered to have a drink while they waited for a table.

"Pretty corny, eh?" Rick muttered in her ear as he pulled her chair out for her.

"Actually, I kind of like it." Fran settled in her seat, smiling as she looked around. "It's so overdone that it's almost camp—and yet, somehow, it's very pleasant." Her voice trailed off as a waitress dressed in a cowboy hat, mini-skirt, and white boots came over to take their drink order. "I'll have a glass of white wine," she said.

"Mineral water for me," Rick said.

Smiling politely, the waitress went away.

Fran leaned forward, elbows on the table, chin resting on her hands, and studied her companion with a thoughtful expression. "Mineral water?" she asked, raising her eyebrows.

"I'm driving—and working," he replied, just the hint of an edge to his voice. "And as of this moment, you and I are very much on our own."

"But I thought you said we were going to have a lot

84

of help," she protested, glancing around in alarm, as if spies and terrorists lurked behind every chair and table.

"We are," he reassured her. "But you have to remember, this whole operation just got underway a few hours ago. It takes time to get the men over here from the San Francisco office, to get the operation set up, organized . . ."

"Bull." She sat bolt upright, putting her hands flat on the table, staring at him in disbelief. "Why couldn't some men have flown over here on that plane we met awhile ago? It looked to me as if there were at least three empty seats!"

"Good question," Rick muttered, flushing. They were silent as the waitress arrived and deposited their drinks on the table, then he looked at her and went on, "As a matter-of-fact, I had the same idea, but I work for a man named Joseph Addison III, and Mr. Addison almost always gets his own way when it comes to decisions involving money and time. They'll be sending some men over in the morning. They'll meet us at the Ponderosa in time for breakfast."

"I suppose that'll have to be all right then." She stared into his dark eyes, seeking the reassurance he seemed able to impart so effortlessly, but now there was nothing but a vague disquiet in those brown depths, a glint of uneasiness mixed with a spark of interest in her. "If . . ."

"If nothing happens between now and tomorrow morning," he said dryly, completing the thought for her. He cocked his head slightly, studying her. "Do you have any more questions about just what it is you're supposed to do?"

"Yes. If I'm supposed to just walk into that casino and tell this—this Abdul Aramas person I have his diskette to provoke a reaction from him, why can't we do that now while we're right here in Reno and get it over with?" She shuddered, shaking her head. "I don't mind telling you, I'm not looking forward to that, not one bit."

"Don't get in a hurry." He reached out and covered one of her hands with his own. She felt a pleasant tingle of warmth at the contact, and the knot of uneasiness and fear that had been tightening in the pit of her stomach for the last several moments began to loosen a bit. "When you walk into that place you're going to be surrounded by DIA men—me among them." He closed his hand, giving her a squeeze. "I'm not going to let anything happen to you, Fran."

"How gallant you are." Raising her wineglass, she took a sip, peering at him over the rim of the glass. "Why so protective all of a sudden?"

"Because, lady, I've got plans for you, when all this is over."

"Ah." She put her glass down, gazing at him in silence for several seconds, then said, "What makes you think I want to have anything to do with you once this is over?"

"If you don't, I'll have to change your mind," he countered, smiling.

"You're very . . . self-confident," she said softly.

"I know what I want." The smile left his face, and his dark eyes glowed, seeming to devour her. Flustered and shaken by the intensity of desire in his gaze, she lowered her eyes, and was grateful for the diversion of the P.A. announcing that their table was ready.

"Langtry, party of two," she said softly. "That's us."

"Yes." He got to his feet, came around and helped her out of her chair. "That's us."

When their waiter came, they each ordered steak, then went to the salad bar. The food was excellent and the service was fast; by the time they finished their salads, the steaks were arriving at the table, sizzling from the grill. Strangely, as hungry as Fran had been when they entered the restaurant, her food seemed somehow tasteless. She ate with excellent appetite and agreed with Rick's observation that the meat was delicious and perfectly cooked. But something had changed, charging the atmosphere with an appetite that had very little to do with food.

Their conversation had become general, impersonal, as if they'd tacitly agreed to avoid the subject of the dangerous assignment they were embarked upon, at least for the moment. They talked the way any two people would on a first date, getting acquainted, searching for areas of mutual interest, sparring carefully when differences were discovered. They spoke of movies, music, books, sports, and other forms of recreation, finding many mutual likes and dislikes, but they consciously avoided subjects that might have been too personal.

And yet, during their casual conversation, Fran had the distinct sensation that communication on a deeper, more subtle level was occurring, and that volumes were being spoken by the caressing expression in their eyes and the affection in their voices when they laughed or spoke. It was as if the rest of the restaurant had receded in a mist, leaving the two of them enveloped in an aura of enchantment where nothing could intrude. Their eyes became bolder and more searching as they sat there, and though nothing was said, the sexual tension between them was growing by the moment. She had never desired a man so intensely in her life, and when his fingers would occasionally brush the back of her hand or her arm, it required a physical effort of will for her to resist the impulse to seize his hand and put her lips against it.

He was describing his collection of old movies on video tapes when the busboy began clearing their dishes away noisily and clearing his throat. Rick frowned at him, then glanced at his watch.

"Good grief, no wonder they want us out of here," he exclaimed, "we've been sitting here almost three hours!"

"I don't believe it!" Fran said.

"It's almost midnight," Rick said unhappily. "We've got an hour's drive ahead of us, and I've got to be up at six in the morning." He glanced at her and smiled sardonically as he dropped some bills on the table, leaving enough for a generous tip as well as the check. "See how you are? If you weren't such a fascinating woman, we'd've been gone hours ago."

"I'm fascinating?" Fran asked, raising her eyebrows. "It seems to me that I've mostly been listening the past couple of hours. You've been doing all the talking."

"I thought our conversation was sort of mutual," he said, his expression flattening out into impersonal lines. "But then I'm often wrong—especially when dealing with women like you."

"Women like—oh, let's stop, please," she said wearily, "before we really get angry. Please?"

"Sorry," he said curtly, opening the door for her, then following her out into the night. The temperature had dropped several degrees, as if in response to the change in their mood, and the stars were hidden by the thick cloud layer. "Smell that rain in the air," Rick said, trying to lighten the dark mood that had descended. "We'll hit squalls before we get back to the Ponderosa, or I miss my guess."

"And I'll bet you don't miss too many of your guesses," Fran said, taking his arm as they started across the almost empty parking lot toward her car. Rick didn't respond to the feeble attempt at levity; she felt foolish as she glanced at him. There were just a few cars left in the lot—a couple of subcompacts, two or three pickups, and a van. Something was nagging at her subconscious as they arrived at the car and Rick came around to the passenger side to unlock her door for her, something she knew could be important, but it remained just out of reach, tantalizing her. As he straightened up with the key in his hand, it dawned on her what had been troubling her.

"Rick," she blurted, "there's a van over there. Do you think—?"

"Fran, there're lots of vans in the world," he said. "Let's don't start getting para—" Before he could finish the sentence a dark shape loomed up behind him. An arm swung in a vicious arc that ended with a sickening crunching sound at the back of his head. Without another sound, Rick crumpled to the ground like a broken toy.

Fran opened her mouth to scream, but her voice was choked off by a gloved hand across her mouth, crushing her lips against her teeth, while another powerful arm wrapped tightly around her and lifted her off her feet, reducing her frantic struggles to nothing more than a few ineffectual leg kicks before she felt a stinging sensation on her neck and all her muscles suddenly turned to jelly.

"Get 'er?" a gruff voice asked.

"Help me, please . . ." Fran tried to scream, but her voice emerged as nothing more than a whisper, while the earth began to spin beneath her feet, faster and faster, until a black hole shot up from the ground at her feet at the speed of light and swallowed her up, and then there was nothing.

CHAPTER FIVE

Gradually Fran became aware of a sound which had been resonating in her subconsciousness for the past hour or more; a high-pitched, roaring hum that seemed to emanate from the very floor upon which she was lying, reverberating through her head with a steady, irritating persistence that was no longer possible to ignore. In that same instant came the realization that she was moving, and she opened her eyes with a mild sense of shock to see Rick Langtry's face, less than a foot away from hers, pressed hard against the corrugated metal floor they were both lying on. It all flooded back —the restaurant, the men who'd been following them in the green van, and the shape looming up in the parking lot, knocking Rick unconscious, followed by the pinprick against her neck and then the darkness.

As the memories returned, it was easy to identify the roaring sound that had been puzzling her: the whine of tires spinning against the hard surface of a highway, drowning out most other sounds here within the metal body. The other element of noise which had been puzzling her also became clear—rain, beating down against the metal roof a few feet above her head. They were traveling down a highway at a high rate of speed through a rainstorm, trussed up like a pair of turkeys on the uncarpeted metal floor of the van, undoubtedly, she thought, the green van which had been such a factor in the events of the last twenty-four hours.

As her eyes widened in understanding, Rick cautioned her with his eyes, indicating with an almost imperceptible shake of his head for her to remain silent. She frowned, then reluctantly nodded agreement. The movement, slight as it was, brought home forcefully to her that she was bound so tightly she could move only a tiny bit. Her eyes widened even further in incipient panic, but Rick caught her eye and wriggled over closer to her, placing his mouth as near as possible to her ear.

"I can move my right hand just a bit," he whispered so softly she could barely distinguish his words. "Turn over. I'll see if I can untie your hands. If I can get you loose, maybe you can do the same for me."

Nodding agreement, she immediately rolled over, glancing up toward the front of the van as she did so. As he had indicated, it would be best not to alert their captors that they had regained consciousness. There might be an advantage to be had in keeping the fact concealed for the moment. Moving cautiously, she backed up, edging herself closer to Rick's waiting hands. In the occasional flash of light from oncoming traffic, she could see the silhouette of a large man slouched in the passenger seat, but the driver's seat was concealed from view by what appeared to be a kind of partition. The large man in the passenger seat appeared relaxed, his posture loose and at ease. She scooted a bit further, relaxing when she felt Rick's hands at her bonds.

As they lay there back to back, he began plucking at the knots which had been tied with a length of nylon climber's rope, struggling with what he couldn't see. Each time he would twist around in a futile attempt to see the knots, she could feel his breath warm on the back of her neck; in spite of their predicament, it was vaguely arousing.

"I'm sorry as hell about this," he whispered. "It was not supposed to go down this way at all. It's my fault. I should never have assumed we'd ditched them for good just because we got rid of them long enough to make contact at the airport. They probably picked us up out there and followed us to the restaurant. From then on it was just a matter of waiting for us to come out, fat, dumb, and happy." He made a disgusted sound as he picked at the knots. "I oughta have my tail kicked!"

"How's your head?" she asked, twisting around enough so she could see part of his face. "They really gave you a good smack."

"A good smack is right." He gave a bitter little chuckle, grunting with effort as he tugged at her bonds. "Whoever hit me was a real pro. I was out like a light and I don't even have much of a goose egg from the blow, as far as I can tell." He paused. " 'Course, all I can tell is the skin on my head doesn't feel stretched or swollen anywhere. Umf—there!"

"Umm." Fran sighed as the bonds on her wrists fell away, followed almost immediately by a stinging sensation as blood rushed back into her hands and fingers. The restoration of circulation hurt for only a moment, then she glanced up at the front of the van to assure herself nothing had changed. She rolled over and faced Rick's broad back. She could see his bonds clearly now, and gasped in dismay. The nylon rope cut so cruelly into his skin it was a wonder he'd been able to undo the knots binding her. If he wasn't released quickly, she realized, there was a very real possibility of permanent damage to his hands.

"Damn," she muttered fiercely as she began struggling with the first knot, breaking a fingernail. "I—I—can't . . . umph!"

"You sure's hell can," he whispered over his shoulder, glaring at her from the corner of his eye. "Don't you dare quit on me now!"

Muttering imprecations at the man who'd tied them, she exerted an extra burst of effort and felt the rope beginning to slip free at last. Triumphantly, she pulled it the rest of the way out, and then it was simply a matter of working the rest of the knots loose—an easy task once the first one gave way. Groaning with relief, Rick rubbed at his wrists and hands, wincing as the circulation slowly returned to his numb fingers.

"Now what?" Fran asked eagerly.

"Ssh," he cautioned, placing his lips so near her ear that their skin touched. She felt a little tingle of pleasure at the contact, and was sorry when he moved back a bit. "Our only chance now is to play possum. I'll arrange your ropes so it looks like you're still tied up, then try to do the same with mine. And then, if we get a chance . . ." A grim expression came over his face, and Fran shivered, barely able to envision what he might be able to do if given the chance.

"Where's your gun?" she whispered.

"Hell, that was the second thing they took," he said with a grim smile.

"What was the first?"

"The diskette, naturally." He stiffened alertly as the whining note of the tires against asphalt changed abruptly. The van was slowing down and pulling off the freeway. "Ssh!" he hissed. "Pretend you're still out!"

Heart pounding with fear, Fran placed her cheek against the cold, hard, corrugated metal floor, involuntarily stiffening her body against centrifugal force as the van swung in a wide turn. She squeezed her wide, staring eyes shut, certain that if anyone bothered to look they would know at once she was faking, spotting the involuntary little twitches she remembered from when

93

she was a child and trying to fool her parents into believing she was asleep. She gave a little gasp as the van jolted crossing a bump, then she felt herself slide forward a bit as the brakes were applied.

The van stopped and the engine was switched off. The silence was thunderous after the long period of engine and tire noise, and Fran was certain that her captors would be able to hear the pounding of her heart, if they simply stopped for a moment and listened.

"You want some coffee or not?" The driver of the van said in a low, raspy voice.

"I'll take a cup. Black with one sugar," the man in the passenger seat replied. "And Redwing—don't hang around in there flirting with the damned waitress. Got it?"

"Waitress? Hell, if I want something good, I'll take a crack at the honey we've got tied up in the back." Fran felt the van shift minutely as the driver twisted in his seat and glanced back into the cargo area for a moment. "Did you notice what a looker she was when we took them?"

"Yeah, she's a good-looking woman," Stoner agreed with a trace of weary disgust. "What's the matter, Redwing? Aren't you satisfied with women Charonsky buys for you? Never mix business with pleasure, that's what I say—and this woman is business, pure and simple."

"Yeah, Charonsky tries," Redwing muttered. "But those bitches are paid to fight me. I want the fun of a real fight. It's the only thing that really satisfies me."

Stoner made a disgusted noise, shaking his head. "You're a weird one, Redwing. Go on—get the lousy coffee. And don't be all night, either. I want to be in 'Frisco by sunrise."

"Want some pie, maybe a doughnut?" Redwing asked as he opened the door. A gust of cool air filled the cargo compartment; Fran shivered in spite of her resolve to remain motionless.

"Nothing! Just coffee. C'mon, man," Stoner snapped. "Move it!"

Redwing snarled a curse then slammed the door, rocking the van on its springs. Stoner settled back in his seat muttering to himself and shaking his head. After a moment, he sighed and reached out and switched on the ignition key, then turned on the radio. As the sound of an announcer's voice filled the interior of the van, Fran opened her eyes and saw Rick staring at her, his eyes bright with hope and subdued excitement.

"*. . . Rain continuing on through most of the night, clearing by morning in the mountains,*" the radio announcer said in his smooth, polished baritone. "*And now, here's an oldie for you . . .*"

Stoner grunted and reached toward the radio to switch stations as the sound of a saxophone emanated from the speakers.

"Ssh," Rick cautioned Fran, moving with exaggerated caution. In the front Stoner was punching the station selection buttons, going from soft rock to country western to hard rock to all news, growling in disgust at each one. Any minute, Rick knew, he would simply turn the radio off; obviously, he was not a music lover.

Rick wavered a bit as he crouched low in the cargo compartment, wincing as the circulation returned to his legs, then he recovered and moved stealthily forward, freezing each time Stoner leaned back to listen briefly to one of the stations, moving again while Stoner punched out selections, taking full advantage of the bursts of sound and static and the movements of the van caused by Stoner's leaning forward in his seat and punching at the radio dial.

Fran stared, her heart in her throat, as Rick crouched directly behind the big man's seat. She could see Rick's

chest fill as he took a deep breath and made his move.
With the grace and swiftness that bespoke of years of
gymnastic and martial arts training, he wrapped a powerful arm around Stoner's thick throat, cutting off his
oxygen supply as well as preventing him from crying
out for help. The van rocked with the violence of Stoner's struggle, but Rick hung on, his face a grim mask of
determination, until Stoner's movements became more
and more feeble as he was denied oxygen. The big feet
drummed against the floor of the van with a desperation
that made Fran feel almost sorry for him, but she
steeled herself against pity, remembering what the two
captors had done to her and Rick. Stoner deserved
whatever he got, she decided.

"Damn!" Rick exclaimed, withdrawing a small, flat
object from Stoner's jacket pocket and placing it inside
his own. "Here comes Redwing. We've got to make a
run for it now, while we've got the chance! Now, out!"

"But can't we—?"

"Damn it, move!" he cut her off, raging in frustration
as he dragged Stoner out of his seat and reached for the
front door handle. "Redwing's right there—if he just
looks he's going to see what's going on here. Damn it to
hell," he fumed, "if we just had another minute—!"

Fran followed Rick across the empty passenger seat,
crawling across Stoner's inert but breathing body to get
to the door. She stumbled as she hit the ground, snapping off one of her heels. She squinted against the cold
rain, trying to see everything she could before they had
to run. The van was parked at the extreme edge of a
large, paved parking lot in the middle of which was a
huge truck stop. There were dozens of diesel fuel pumps
and broad lanes for the passage of the big rigs, and on
the other side, so tantalizingly close and yet so far out of
reach, was the brightly lit restaurant, festooned with
welcoming signs. "We love hungry truckers," Fran read

out loud with a dizzying sense of unreality. "Tourists, too!" She turned away, toward the eight lanes of freeway that stretched out of sight over the mountains in both directions; four west-bound lanes nearest the truck stop, the east-bound lanes across the way humming with weekend traffic headed for Tahoe and Reno.

"Hey!" The angry shout came from the direction of the restaurant, and she spun around to see what Rick had seen several seconds ago; the approaching figure of Redwing, a white paper bag in one hand. "Get back!" Redwing shouted, dropping the bag and pulling a large handgun from beneath his jacket. "Damn you, I'll blow you away!"

Rick drew back and fired the egg-sized stone he'd found on the ground. It struck Redwing on the thigh. Redwing cursed and howled, lowering the gun and hopping on one leg.

"Come on!" Rick seized Fran by the hand and started pulling her toward the restaurant. Redwing recovered quickly and snapped off a shot, driving them back toward the freeway.

"Damn it," Rick cried in a rage, but as Redwing regained his composure and moved to cut them off, crouching and aiming for another shot, he knew there was no other choice. He dragged Fran out onto the wet surface of the freeway, ignoring the blaring air horns of a big-rig diesel truck that roared by inches away, drenching them with spray thrown up by the huge tires. They darted between the swiftly moving traffic, causing a din of screaming brakes and tires and blaring horns as they dived onto the grassy median strip that separated the east-bound and west-bound lanes. Rick immediately rolled over onto his stomach and peered through the cold, slanting rain back toward the truck stop. He was rewarded almost instantly by the muzzle-flash of the pistol, followed by the faint popping sound of the shot, barely audible above the steady roar of traffic, but the sound of the ricochet as the bullet spanged into the pavement just inches from Rick's nose and caromed off into the night was loud and clear.

"Get down for Chrissakes!" he exclaimed, jerking Fran down beside him and pressing his face into the wet grass and weeds. "He's shooting at us!"

Fran could see Redwing now, crouching on the far side of the traffic lanes, the weapon extended before him the way she'd seen hundreds of actors do when portraying police officers on television. This, however, was not television; it was real, and she was amazed that somebody didn't stop and investigate the sight of a grown man shooting across the freeway. There was another flash then, and the sound of a bullet whizzing past her head, humming like an angry hornet.

"Down, I said!" Rick yelled. "Keep your head down, unless you want to get it blown off!" He pulled her after him as he jumped down into the lowest part of the median strip, crouching low and moving away from the truck stop. "We'll work our way down the highway, then double back. If we can just get to a phone, we'll be okay."

Fran followed him, glancing back from time to time. If they continued to crouch down low, they'd be invisible to their pursuer. The only problem with that, she realized, was that they couldn't see him either. Still, for just an instant it seemed like an incredible luxury to her. That they were out of sight and were not being shot at was intoxicating, even though they were cold and soaked to the skin.

As she crawled along behind him in the six-inch high wet grass, she suddenly butted against his thigh. He'd stopped and got up, staring across the traffic lanes back at the truck stop. He swore, pounding his fist into his open palm.

"Stoner's regained consciousness," he explained when he caught Fran's inquiring glance. "I should've killed the son of a bitch when I had the chance. Now there's no chance of doubling back to the truck stop. He'll be right there waiting, while Redwing just herds us into the trap like sheep to the slaughter." His face closed up in grim lines as he sat back and surveyed their surroundings for a moment.

"Did you—did you get his gun?" Fran asked, caught up in his anger.

"No."

"No?" Her voice rose in disbelief. "Why not?"

"Hell, you know how much time we had! I had to get this."

He tapped the fabric of his jacket over the inside pocket, averting his eyes from her angry glare as the headlights of an oncoming car illuminated his streaming face.

"The fake diskette?" She stared incredulously, ignoring the cold water streaming down her face as she stared at him. *"Why?* Wouldn't it have made a lot more sense to get his gun? I mean, they're trying to kill us, Rick! Are you so stupid you can't—"

"Shut up! If I'd taken the gun and left this, they'd've tumbled to the fact that it's a fake." With a weary sigh he wiped a stream of rainwater from his brow with the back of his hand, gazing longingly back toward the truck stop. "If I'd left it and taken a gun, the game would be over and we'd be the losers."

"Game? Is that what all this is to you—a stupid game?" She started to climb to her feet, her movements jerky and uncoordinated, shaking with anger, but he seized her hand and yanked her back down beside him in the sodden grass. She glared, trembling with helpless rage. "So we're still in the God damned game, only now

99

we just might get ourselves killed! Those are real bullets they're shooting at us, aren't they?"

"Yeah, they're real, all right," he snapped, weary of serving as the target for her anger. "And unless you want to wind up with one in that lovely posterior of yours, I suggest you shut your mouth and get a move on! Let's get the hell out of here."

"Oh, sure, out of here. Where do we go?" She stared at him, then glanced pointedly back toward the lights of the truck stop, just across the west-bound lanes of the freeway, just a few hundred feet away. It might as well have been on the moon. If they stepped back onto that hundred feet of asphalt again they'd be clay pigeons for the man with the gun. "Not . . . not out there?" she asked, jerking her chin toward the forest on the other side of the freeway, opposite the warm, cheerful, beckoning lights of the truck stop. In the chill rain the towering evergreens loomed like a dark, forbidding wall.

"Yes," he said curtly, "out there. Give me your hand."

As they got to their feet and moved in a crouch toward the east-bound lanes, Fran realized she might as well kick off her shoes. With one broken heel she could move at only a sort of exaggerated limp; besides, she was already soaked to the skin. In her current predicament high-heeled shoes were nothing less than a hindrance. Shrugging, she kicked them off into the wet grass. Barefoot now, except for the sheer layer of fabric of her panty hose, she gripped Rick's hand and watched for a break in the flow of traffic.

"Why don't we just flag somebody down?" she yelled in his ear, pulling back from the swirling aftertow of a big rig sweeping past them at eighty miles an hour.

"Great idea," he agreed, eyes narrowed at the oncoming traffic, alert for an opening. "Only problem is, it'd be more dangerous than facing Redwing's gun. Not only might we get run down, but we could cause a multicar pile-up on the freeway. Bad enough doing what we're doing, without trying to flag somebody down." Pausing, he sucked in a deep breath and tightened his grip on her hand. "Now! C'mon!"

They ran awkwardly across the hard surface, splashing water before them in knee-high waves. She was gasping when they reached the other side, but he didn't seem at all winded. Without pause, he led them through the underbrush that lined the edge of the freeway right-of-way and into the forest. Within five minutes, they were walking through deep woods, the sounds of traffic behind them growing fainter with every step. The rain had been letting up during the past few minutes, but it streamed in rivulets from the trees that towered all around them. She hadn't thought it possible to be more miserable and wet; she'd been wrong, she realized now, squinting up at the dark, feathery shrouded tops of the trees and shivering as another stream of water splashed against the shoulder of her already soaked navy blazer.

"Where are we?" Fran asked after a few minutes trudging along behind him, wincing occasionally as her semibare feet encountered a sharp twig or pebble among the cushion of pine needles on the ground. She gripped his shoulder, leaning down to pluck a sharp twig from the fabric of her hose.

"I figure we're probably somewhere near the Donner Summit." He glanced down, watching while she rearranged her hose. "You lost your shoes."

"Oh, he finally notices." She gave him a sarcastic look, then shook her head. "It doesn't really matter. They'd be useless for walking on this kind of ground— in the dark, anyway. But I would appreciate it if you'd walk a little slower from now on."

He nodded. "I think we've lost them—at least for the moment. We can take our time now until morning."

"I'm soaked to the skin," she pointed out. "And it's cold up here."

"Yes. Our first priority right now is finding shelter." He took her hand and gave it a squeeze; she felt a surge of warmth as she returned the pressure. "Unless I'm mistaken, there'll be a frontage road along here pretty soon, running parallel to the freeway. Lots of people from the cities build vacation cabins along through here. I'm hoping we'll run across one."

"Soon, I hope." Fran's teeth were chattering now; he noticed and put his arm around her shoulders, pulling her snugly against his body as they walked on through the forest. Their clothing was soaked, but after a few minutes she could feel his body heat coming through the wet layers of fabric, and it was not only warming but strangely exciting as well. Her spirits rose a bit as they emerged from the trees onto a well-graded, dirt-surfaced road, and she could once again see the sky overhead instead of a jagged layer of branches.

"There, what'd I tell you?" Rick boasted, gesturing expansively at the road as if he owned it. "A nice, hard-packed dirt road for milady to tread upon, marred only by an occasional puddle of rainwater." Pausing, he glanced up and down the road for a moment, then shrugged and turned in the downhill, or westward, direction. "At least we're headed in the general direction of San Francisco this way," he said as they set out. "And look—the moon's coming out of hiding. Is that an omen, or is that an omen?"

"A good omen, I hope." Fran glanced up over her shoulder. A slice of brilliant silver was peeking through the lacy edges of cloud; the storm was breaking up earlier than anticipated. She trudged along behind him for the next half hour, shivering miserably. The rain had stopped, but they were at nearly seven thousand feet of elevation, and the air was achingly cold. Her breath was a white plume.

"Rick," she asked, breaking the silence. "Do you think it's cold enough to get frostbite?"

He glanced at her in concern. Her teeth were chattering audibly. "Your feet?" She nodded, and he led her to the side of the dirt road and made her sit down on a large rock. Cupping his hands at his mouth, he blew into them and rubbed them briskly for a few seconds, then took her feet in his hands, one at a time, and rubbed them energetically. Fran almost wept as the blissful sensation of warmth returned to her feet and toes. Rick massaged them for several moments, his lean, powerful fingers working the tendons and muscles of her feet until they felt warm and relaxed once again, capable of walking on indefinitely.

"Ready to continue?" he asked, and she nodded happily.

"Thank you, Rick," she said. "It was great."

"Just part of the service," he said lightly, gripping her hand and helping her to her feet. "We'll find something soon, and I'll get you indoors. You've had just about enough for one night, I think."

They walked on for another twenty minutes, and just as Fran was on the verge of saying that she couldn't go on another step, Rick stopped and exclaimed, "Ah, here we are!"

Fran followed the direction of his jubilant gaze and felt her spirits plummet. A small, dark, obviously empty cabin sat fifty feet back from the road, the weeds growing in its driveway ample evidence it hadn't been used in months

CHAPTER SIX

"Wonderful," Fran said crossly, shooting him a disappointed look. "Just what good is an empty cabin?"

"Plenty good, lady." He shot her an amused glance before turning back toward the cabin. "And it's not gonna be empty much longer. You just watch."

She stumbled after him as he hurried eagerly up the narrow dirt driveway that led to the side of the small, wooden A-frame cabin. Rick bubbled with enthusiasm, especially when he discovered the cord of firewood neatly stacked against the side of the house, next to the brick chimney. Fran huddled miserably on the front porch, shivering like a wet puppy, her wet clothing sticking clammily to her freezing skin. In spite of her misery, she watched in dismay as Rick methodically tested each door and window, then returned to the front porch.

"You're—you're not going to break in?" she asked, appalled, as he began crawling around on the front porch.

"Don't have to," he said cheerfully, displaying an object that glittered in the faint starlight. "They left their key under the doormat. Must've known we'd be dropping by." He slid the key into the lock and opened the front door, then bowed mockingly. "Will the lady please enter? Just have a seat in front of the fireplace, and I'll have a roaring blaze within five minutes."

"Thank you," she muttered. As she swept past, Rick tried the light switch next to the front door to no avail. "Ah, well, you can't have everything, I suppose," he said lightly. "Maybe I can find a candle or a lantern after I get a fire going."

Fran sank down onto a thick rug in front of the open stone fireplace, hugging her knees and gazing into the murky darkness, wondering how she'd gotten into such a situation in such a short period of time. As best she could tell, it was sometime in the early hours of Sunday morning. Twenty-four hours ago she'd been resting securely in a warm, air-conditioned room at the Ponderosa, looking forward to a peaceful, relaxing weekend with her old college roommate. Now she'd become involved with secret agents and spies, had been drugged and kidnapped, and was now preparing to spend whatever remained of the night in an abandoned cabin in the wilderness with the most exciting, attractive man she'd ever met. She was cold and wet, soaked through to the skin, and yet . . . Somehow, she did not regret one minute of what had happened. She smiled at the thought as Rick reentered the cabin, his arms filled with a load of firewood and kindling.

He knelt in front of her at the fireplace, working quickly. There was a spark, a flicker, and within a couple of minutes the larger chunks of wood caught fire and blazed cheerily, casting a warm, yellow light over the small room.

"What're you grinning about?" he asked, turning from the fascination of the flames to look at her for a moment.

"Oh . . . I don't know," she said evasively. She scooted another inch nearer the fire. "Oooh, this is heaven!"

"Well, it is pretty nice after what we've been through," he conceded, shooting her an affectionate, amused glance. "But I don't know if I'd call it heaven. Look out—in another minute you'll be telling me it was all worth it just to get here." He had been kneeling on the edge of the hearth; now he stood up and looked appraisingly at the interior of the cabin, which was faintly illuminated by the flickering blaze.

"Looks like a typical two-room A-frame," he observed. "This is the dining room, living room, and kitchen combined. That'll be the bedroom and bath through there. I'm gonna have a quick look around."

"Rick!" she hissed, outraged. "It's bad enough we broke into their house. Don't go picking through their personal things!"

Ignoring her protests, he went through the door into the other room. Fran tried to ignore the sounds of drawers and cabinets being opened, rummaged through, then closed. In a few minutes he emerged from the other room, a lighted candle in one hand, a pair of women's canvas athletic shoes in the other. The glow of the candle illuminated his face from below, lending an eerie, almost ghostly appearance to his lean face, which he played upon as he intoned: "Velcome to de castle, doctor. Chust vollow me . . ."

"You found a candle!" She laughed a bit as he lowered the candle and resumed his normal speech pattern.

"Found these, too." He tossed her the athletic shoes. "They look like they ought to fit you—close enough to wear, anyway." He stepped back into the other room for an instant, returning with something else in his arms. He tossed it to her, and she felt the scratchy warmth of a wool blanket. "Better get out of those wet things before you catch a chill. That fire's only warming the front part of you."

She clutched the blanket against her, hesitating, looking at him in apprehension. He shook his head and laughed as he began stripping off his tweed jacket and unbuttoning his shirt. She caught her breath at the sight of his well-muscled chest and washboard hard stomach, covered with coarse black hair.

"Well, you do what you want, but I'm going to be wearing dry clothes when I leave here in the morning."

Ignoring her shocked gasp, he stepped out of his trousers and carefully draped them with the shirt and jacket across the ledge of the mantel, where they would dry quickly. Clad only in his jockey-style undershorts, he turned and faced her for a brief moment, the flickering firelight carving out the slabs of smooth muscle as it highlighted and shadowed the contours of his powerful body in a fascinating way.

Fran swallowed dryly as she felt his dark eyes boring into hers for a moment, and for an instant it was as if some primeval, atavistic force had moved between them, redefining everything she had come to believe about men and women. Never had she felt so much in the presence of not just a man, but a *male,* and as she lowered her eyes it was almost as if she did so as part of some ancient rite of submission . . .

She blinked as Rick wordlessly turned away, disappearing into the other room. The spell was broken, and her heart slowed back to normal as he reappeared, a blanket wrapped around his shoulders, and sat down next to her before the fire.

"Still in those wet things, eh? Well, suit yourself."

"You'll look," she said accusingly, suddenly wanting very much to get out of the sodden clothing, yet not quite trusting him. There'd been something unfathomable in his dark, staring eyes a moment ago.

"Hell, yes, I'll look," he agreed affably. "If you take 'em off in front of me. You're a beautiful woman, Fran, and I think I've made it pretty clear how I feel."

"If you were a gentleman, you wouldn't look."

"Look," he said with a sigh, "if you're worried about it, go into the other room and take your clothes off. Hand them out to me, and I'll hang them on the mantel to dry. Then you can come out securely wrapped up in your blanket, and I'll have seen nothing."

She hesitated for another moment, then when he groaned in exasperation she rose and went into the other room, her blanket still draped over her shoulders. In the pitch darkness she stripped away the soaked blazer and top, then removed the pleated white skirt. It was heavenly to remove the sodden, clammy clothing, and she realized how foolishly she'd been behaving over a relatively unimportant issue. She handed the wet clothing out through the door, as instructed, but there was no waiting hand to accept the garments. She shook them and called his name, and after a moment she stepped back out by the fireplace.

"Ah," he called from the kitchenette area, where he'd taken the candle and set it on the counter. Systematically, he was going through the drawers and cupboards. "Finally took my advice, I see. Good. Just hang 'em up there on the other side of the mantel, the way I did mine, and I'll have a nice surprise for you."

After carefully arranging her clothing so it would dry, wincing at the filthy condition of her formerly white pleated skirt, she sat down with her blanket tightly wrapped around her, watching the fire and waiting expectantly. A surprise, Rick had said. In their present predicament almost anything less than disastrous would be a nice surprise.

"Would madam care for a glass of white wine?"

She glanced up and giggled. Rick had tied a dish towel around his slender waist to keep his blanket in position, and he was holding out a metal tray on which sat a bottle of wine and two glasses. He bowed deeply, skillfully balancing the tray, and his dark eyes flashed with mischief as he looked at her with one eyebrow arched questioningly.

"Indeed, madam would," she said with a smile. "And then madam would enjoy it very much if her waiter would sit down and join her."

"Ah, most excellent!" Carefully, he put the tray down on the floor in front of them, then sat down next to her, so close their thighs were touching. She thought of moving away a bit, but didn't move. Picking up one of the two glasses, which looked as if they'd probably contained peanut butter at one time, he filled it from the three-quarters-full wine bottle he'd found and handed it to her. The other glass he filled for himself. He held up the glass as if for a toast, and their eyes met and held, and for a moment Fran was afraid he could hear the wild pounding of her heart.

"A toast," he whispered huskily, his eyes resting hungrily on hers. "I'd like to drink to the young woman who's endured such a traumatic experience during the past several hours, and yet has never acted less than a lady through it all." He raised the glass a bit, his eyes filled with admiration. "You're quite a woman, Fran Barnette," he murmured.

"No," she whispered, stopping him from drinking with a touch on his arm. "I'd like it·if we drank to us. We've both had some pretty traumatic experiences today."

He lowered his glass and nodded acquiescence. "To us," he said, and they touched their glasses together. To Fran, their glasses seemed to chime like the finest crystal when they struck, and as she sipped the wine, it was like ambrosia, a heady liquid unlike anything she'd ever tasted. She was tempted to examine the label on the bottle but desisted, realizing that it wasn't a rare and special vintage. The night had suddenly taken on a subtle kind of enchantment, and it seemed to her that she and Rick were the only man and woman on earth. She looked into his eyes and she knew that he felt the magic, too.

"Fran . . ." He put his glass down and moved toward her, his eyes dark with longing. The blanket fell open across his shoulders and chest, baring the muscular chest and hard, ridged stomach. Her eyes were drawn to the thick mat of black hair that covered both sides of his chest, narrowing down to a fine line as it went lower, down his body . . .

"Rick, no—" she began, but her words were cut off by his warm, firm lips as his strong arms gathered her to him, crushing her breasts against the broad, muscular chest she'd been admiring. She felt a searing thrill as their lips joined, but still she struggled, twisting away from his hot, searching mouth and demanding hands.

"Rick—I—no!" she gasped, twisting away.

One big hand gripped the back of her neck, forcing her around to face him, and his mouth once again came down and covered hers, triggering a shower of warm, thrilling sensations that made her gasp with pleasure even as she struggled against surrendering to him. Abruptly, she shuddered and melted against him, her lips parting as their mouths moved together in mutual exploration. When he finally released her and leaned back, she gasped for breath, putting a trembling hand to her lips in wonder. She had never experienced such a kiss, ever.

He took a deep sip of his wine, his eyes never leaving her face, a faint glimmer of amusement seeming to dance in their ebony depths. Still, Fran could see that he was breathing rapidly, too, and that his large strong hands trembled as he raised his glass and drank. *Damn his arrogance,* she thought. *I'll show him! One or two more kisses, perhaps, but nothing further. After all, I've known this man for less than twenty-four hours, and here I am carrying on with him like a schoolgirl with her first crush, feeling things for him I've never felt before for anybody, ever. Maybe something will grow between us in time, but this—this was entirely too sudden!*

"Penny for your thoughts?" he asked, cutting off her chain of thought. "Or maybe I should make it a quarter, since a penny isn't what it used to be." His smile grew even broader, and he drew her closer, gazing into her eyes all the while with a confidence that made her all the more determined that he would not have his way with her; not tonight, anyway.

"I—I was just thinking it would be good to get to know you better," she said. "When this is all over, I mean."

"Yes," he agreed dryly. "After it's over."

She huddled against him for a moment, then looked up at his profile. He was gazing into the fire. "Rick, you don't think they'll catch us again, do you?" she asked with an involuntary shudder. Unconsciously, she scooted even closer to him. He shifted position minutely, allowing her smaller body to fit into the curve created by his own position more snugly. Any closer, he thought with an affectionate smile, and she'd be in his lap.

"I hope not," he said huskily, strongly affected by her nearness. The feel of her supple body through the blanket around her shoulders was tantalizing, and the sweet fresh scent of her hair created a desire stronger than anything he'd ever felt. "But let's don't think about them right now. Let's talk about us. Whatever happens, we've got the rest of the night together, Fran. Don't you think we should take advantage of the moment? There might not be another chance for us."

"Rick, I know how you feel—and how I feel—and I think it might be real. But—and this is a big 'but'—I

111

need to know you better before I can let anything else happen between us." She gazed up at him, her large hazel eyes glowing with sincerity and hope that he would understand. "Don't you see, Rick? I don't want it to happen because—because we just happen to be in the right place at the right time. Or the wrong—"

"Hush, darling," he muttered hoarsely, placing his strong hand over her lips. As he removed it slowly, brushing her swollen lips with his palm, his mouth came down over hers, replacing the hand.

"No, Rick—please!" She twisted away, but he caught her and held her, his superior strength forcing her face around to meet his. She struggled weakly, a deep feeling of lassitude, or languor, coming over her, turning her muscles and joints to warm water. When his mouth came down and covered hers once again, she gave a shudder of surrender and her arms went up and encircled his neck, her fingers entwining in his thick, dark hair and pulling his face down against hers.

When she felt his tongue probing moistly at her parted lips, she felt one last, brief spark of protest, then all rational thought was swept from her mind as a storm of pure, erotic sensation consumed her. Rick's hands, his lips, his body—all combined to close out thought as she pressed herself against him, and his tongue slid into her mouth, crumbling the last of her defenses. Mindlessly, her own tongue wrapped around his, tasting and feeling, triggering bolts of sensation that traveled through her body with the speed of light. She pressed herself against him, her hands digging into his hair and flesh, and she was barely aware of the blankets dropping away and falling to the thick carpet beneath them. She pulled his tongue deeply inside, tasting the sweetness and feeling thrill after thrill as it probed and licked at the delicate, sensitive inside of her mouth, igniting fircs of desire that burned out of control.

"Oh, Rick, Rick," she moaned as he pulled his mouth away for a moment, his lips and tongue searing the skin of her neck and throat and ear. His lips caught her earlobe and held it; a second later he was sucking on it, creating sensations in an entirely different part of her body. "I want you—!" she gasped.

"Baby, baby," he muttered, cupping one of her breasts in his strong, warm hand and gazing adoringly at the pink tip before lowering his lips to taste. "I want you, too . . ." When she felt the warm circle of his lips cover the nipple and his moist tongue traveling around the excited, pebbled flesh, until the nipple felt as hard as a rock, she moaned and lay back on the blankets, unable to speak. The sensations radiating out in all directions from her nipple rocked her with an almost violent kind of pleasure, filling her with a mindless desire that threatened to completely wipe her reason away.

He raised his head and looked at her for a moment, studying her face and body as they were bathed in the glowing, flickering light from the fire. She gazed adoringly into his eyes, her fingers linked behind his neck, trying to pull him down.

"Now, Rick, now!" she whispered, her voice a broken whimper of uncontrollable desire.

"No, not yet," he said hoarsely, his eyes full of her. She could see at a glance that he was as ready and excited for her as she was for him, and indeed, he groaned when she reached down and gripped his firm, throbbing flesh with one hand. "Not yet, baby," he groaned, "I want this to last and last . . ."

He lowered himself until she felt the coarse hair of his chest tickling the smooth skin of her belly, and then his large hands cupped both her breasts, bringing them together until the rigid, pink-tipped nipples were separated by only a couple of inches. His mouth came down and covered one of them, his tongue probing, tasting, searing, sending wave after wave of delicious sensation through her body, and then, without losing contact with her flesh, he dragged his lips and tongue across to the opposite nipple and gave it the same treatment. She was thrashing helplessly on the blankets, moaning and sobbing and crying out with the thrilling sensations that washed over her in never-ending waves, her hands wrapped in his thick black hair as if she'd never let him go.

He shifted position subtly, removing one of his hands from her breasts. It traveled down her side and across her smooth, flat, silken belly, stroking in slow, sensuous circles as it moved relentlessly toward the fiery center of her. Then it moved past the moist, aching center and stroked gently at the insides of her upper thighs, teasing the soft, sensitive skin there for a time before brushing lightly, ever so lightly, at the moist opening that quivered under his touch. Fran moaned, twisting against him until she was able to reach him again. He was unbelievably ready for her, quivering rigidly in her hand, yet he still refused to complete the act. His fingers stroked her with expert knowledge and she experienced the first blinding explosion of sensation.

"Rick, oh, Rick!" she sobbed, quivering uncontrollably as the sensations rolled over her, gradually subsiding now, instead of satisfying, she now wanted him more than before. She could feel his heart pulsating in the flesh she held in her hand, and with that tiny part of her mind that could still think, she marveled at his iron self-control. Again, his fingers danced against that certain place in that special way and she exploded, sobbing in ecstasy as she twisted against him in a mindless frenzy of release. Rick pressed his mouth against her nipple as if trying to swallow her entire breast.

When she finally subsided once again, Rick moved down her smooth, soft belly, tongue licking and probing

114

gently all the way, until at last with a gasp of pleasure he tasted the very essence of her and she exploded at once, this time with such intensity that she almost lost consciousness, her mind filled with such a shimmering, vivid display of exploding lights and stars that she was afraid her vision would never return to normal, but when he lifted his face to hers, a questioning expression in his eyes, she saw him clearly.

"Yes, yes, please!"

Groaning with anticipation, he parted her knees gently and raised himself above her, supporting his weight on his elbows. She reached for him and raised her knees until she felt him probing at the moist, throbbing, demanding entrance to her body. He gazed down into her eyes, his own eyes filled with desire, and moved forward just a bit, enough to probe teasingly into her, then withdrew.

Again, he moved forward, gasping aloud this time as the tiny circlet of muscles caught him and tried to hold him tightly. He groaned aloud as he slipped out for just a brief instant, the victim of his own teasing movement. Then he felt her hand grip and guide him once again, and he no longer had the will nor the desire to hold back. He had satisfied her again and again and now it was his turn to share in the ultimate pleasure. As she removed her hand he slid forward, deeply, as far as he could, emitting a shuddering groan of ecstasy as the silken warmth of body firmly encased his entire length. For just a moment he lay motionless, stunned at the pleasure, then they began to move together in a satisfying rhythm that was almost as fulfilling as the ultimate completion of the act. There was a moment of awkwardness while they got used to the newness of one another's bodies, but they quickly adjusted, eagerly, until they were each obtaining the maximum pleasure.

Rick moved slowly at first, his eyes glazed with pleasure, trembling visibly each time she flexed and gripped him with that secret little ringlet of muscle, and then, gradually, as she strained against him with more and more urgency, rapidly moving into yet another climax of her own, he exhaled gustily and began slamming into her rapidly, almost violently, causing her head to loll insensibly beneath him, her eyes half-closed with ecstasy as their bodies temporarily held sway over their minds. Again and again he slammed against her, the blissful sensations becoming sharper and sharper with each movement, until at last he knew he was out of control, approaching that final crest with a rapidity he knew he didn't want to control. Incredibly, Fran felt him grow even firmer and longer as his body prepared for the ultimate explosion of pleasure, and her eyes widened in appreciation as she groaned with pleasure.

"Aaah!" he sobbed, his voice breaking, then shouted out, "Fran!" and collapsed above her.

"I love you, Rick," she cried, rocking against him, and then all rational thought was swept away by the most overpowering explosion of sexual pleasure she'd ever experienced. Rick rocked against her, pulsating and trembling as he emptied himself into her eager body, shuddering as wave after wave of sensation traveled through his body. It lasted for an incredibly long period, and when it was finally over, they lay locked in one another's arms without moving, still locked in the ultimate embrace.

"That was—I can't describe—that was wonderful." He shook his head, as if words failed him, his eyes moist as he raised his head and looked down into her eyes.

"It was wonderful, Rick," she said when she could speak again. She toyed with the hair over his ears and at the back of his neck, remembering her declaration of love at the height of their passion. Where had that come from, she wondered, lowering her eyes from his direct gaze. "I'm looking forward to a lot more of it in the future," she murmured.

He turned his head without replying. He knew he'd never felt as strongly about a woman in his entire life, but she seemed to be hinting that she was interested in a committed relationship. He didn't know about that. Part of the glow in Fran's eye seemed to fade as he remained silent, and he felt like crying out at the thought he had caused her pain.

"Listen, Fran, I—"

"It's okay," she said, her eyes regaining their sparkle for a moment. "I'm making no demands. Just—just hold me."

After a few moments he felt himself swelling inside her again, and as they made love this time, it was with the slow, luxurious enjoyment of two people who realize this won't be their last time; that they have the rest of their lives to savor such moments. When the ultimate explosion came for them this time, it was no less intense for them, but it was quieter, almost serene. When at last Rick withdrew, Fran's eyes were already drifting closed in deep, blissful sleep. He leaned down and kissed her gently on the lips, then sat on his haunches and sipped at his wine, gazing thoughtfully into the fire for a long time before lying down next to her.

"All right, lovebirds, hit the deck!"

Rick jerked upright, his heart thudding in alarm and dismay at having fallen asleep. The sun glared through the window from a cloudless sky. His heart sank at the sight of Stoner and Redwing standing just inside the door of the cabin, a large pistol of heavy caliber firmly gripped in each of their right hands.

"Rick . . . wha—?" Fran sat up drowsily, the blanket falling away from her. Rick quickly crouched and covered her, but not before Redwing had caught a

117

glimpse of pink-tipped breast. Flushing with anger, Rick met Redwing's eyes as he straightened back up to face the two invaders. Redwing made a gesture toward Fran that caused Rick to stiffen in anger.

"Good, eh?" Redwing leered.

"Get up and get dressed," Stoner snapped. "Redwing —check their pockets first."

"With pleasure." Redwing's eyes never left Fran's as he moved over by the fireplace and began pawing through their clothing.

"Aha," he exclaimed, brandishing the diskette with an air of triumph. "I was afraid you might've had presence of mind enough to destroy this while you had the chance."

"I should've," Rick muttered.

"All right, get dressed," Stoner ordered. "Now."

"Not in front of you," Fran said, her voice quiet but determined. Redwing made a threatening gesture with his pistol, but Rick quickly got to his feet and stood protectively in front of Fran, naked and unarmed but somehow with an air of dignity.

"Don't touch her," he said evenly.

"Pah!" Redwing snapped after a moment, lowering the pistol with an air of disdain. "We could kill you both, now that we have the diskette. What do we need you for, um?" His voice trailed off as his eyes rested with covetous lechery on Fran. "Of course," he added suggestively, "we wouldn't have to kill you right away. There are . . . ways . . . you could prolong your lives, *if* you follow my meaning."

"I'd rather die right here and now," Fran said softly, staring at him with loathing. Redwing, a tall, heavyset man in his mid-forties with a pockmarked, hatchet face, stiffened at the insult, his black eyes narrowing as he swung the gun up again.

"Cool it," Stoner said, interposing himself between

Redwing and the others, gently but firmly shoving his partner's gun aside. Redwing resisted briefly, then twisted away, cursing. As he slammed out through the front door of the cabin, Stoner looked at Rick and shook his head warningly.

"Don't get him riled," he advised. "Just between you and me, he's not quite normal . . . if you follow my meaning."

"I follow you," Rick muttered grimly. He spread his hands in appeal. "Can she step into the other room to dress?"

Stoner walked over, watching them all the way, and pushed the bedroom door open with the barrel of his gun. He turned just long enough for a quick look. "Sure, why not," he said. "But make it quick. We've got a long drive ahead of us, and we're already late, thanks to you two."

CHAPTER SEVEN

When Fran emerged from the dimly lit interior of the cabin into the warm, buttery-gold sunshine outside, her eyes were immediately drawn to Rick. He was slouching near the van, his hands resting on his lean hips, an angry, helpless expression on his face. Redwing stood nearby, watching Rick and lovingly stroking the large, blue steel pistol in his hand. When Rick saw Fran on the porch of the cabin, his eyes glowed with an inner warmth that was somehow very reassuring to her after the night they'd just spent together. She walked over and took his hand, smiling up at him.

"I never thanked you for the shoes," she said. "They might not exactly go with my ensemble, but they're a darn sight better than going barefoot." She glanced with distaste at her wrinkled and mud-streaked, once white skirt, at the patches of dried red mud on the navy blazer. "I look a sight," she muttered, brushing futilely at the jacket with her free hand.

"You look beautiful to me," Rick murmured, glancing around to see if Redwing had approached to within earshot. She squeezed his hand and moved a bit closer to him, leaning up against his broad chest. Even in their present situation, she marveled, she felt warm and safe as his strong arm went lightly around her slender waist.

"My, what a touching scene." Redwing took a long,

thick cigar from his mouth, jabbing at the air with it as he spoke. "Now you've had your little session of grab-ass, get your butt up in the van, Fran." He paused, his ugly face lighted by a sudden grin. "Hey—I'm a poet. Get your butt in the van, Fran. Not bad, eh?"

Rick looked away in disgust, and the grin on Redwing's face was wiped away, replaced by an almost casual malevolence as he said, "We'll tie the lady first, and this time nobody'll be picking the knots loose. I can promise you that."

"Rick, what—?" Fran looked at Rick, who shrugged, his eyes filled with rage and frustration.

"You heard him, Fran," Stoner's voice came from inside the van. The side door opened and Stoner appeared, squatting in the entrance like a carved stone Buddha, a coil of rope in his hand. "Get up here."

"Do as they say," Rick muttered in an undertone when Fran stared at him beseechingly. "They're holding all the aces—for now."

"Aces, my aching butt," Redwing snorted. "There's hope for you yet, man . . ." Quickly, he moved around where he had a better view, eyes narrowing as he watched the graceful movements of Fran's body as she climbed up into the van. Rick glared with impotent rage, reading the openly lustful expression on Redwing's face as easily as if it had been carved in granite in ten-feet-high letters. Redwing understood Rick's expression and laughed, winking. "What'll you bet I have me some of that one of these days, G-man?" he asked.

"That'll be the day you die, Redwing," Rick said quietly. Redwing stepped over, laying the barrel of his pistol on the side of Rick's neck just under his right ear.

"You got a smart mouth, G-man," he said in a menacing voice. "Just when I was starting to think maybe you were getting smart, you gotta go and lip off. Well, bad things happen to people who piss me off, Langtry

. . ." Viciously, he jabbed the muzzle of the pistol into the tender flesh of Rick's neck, then flicked it across his cheek and jaw, the blade leaving a red furrow that quickly filled with blood. "We don't need you, G-man," Redwing said. "Remember that."

"Oh, I'll remember, all right." Rick turned slowly around, watching closely as Stoner tied Fran up.

Stoner took his time with the ropes, working with the skill and patience of one who knew and understood his craft. Though her wrists were not as severely constricted as they'd been the night before, Fran realized with a sinking feeling that these knots were not going to yield to Rick's fingers, no matter how long they had the opportunity to struggle with them. Finally, she felt Stoner give her an almost companionable pat on the shoulder before he rolled her over onto one of the thin blankets taken from the cabin—their captors' one concession to their comfort.

"All right, Langtry," Stoner said, beckoning. "Your turn. Hop up here."

Flushing with embarrassment and resentment at being so helpless before a woman he dearly wished to impress, Rick climbed into the interior of the van and submitted to the indignity of being trussed up like a hog on its way to slaughter. He grunted with pain as Stoner heaved at the bonds, pulling and tugging and checking the knots until he was completely satisfied.

"Now then," Stoner said, resting on his knees and looking thoughtfully at the two of them. "I think those'll hold you . . ." He glanced out through the open double doors on the side of the van, locating Redwing. Apparently reassured that his partner was out of earshot, he leaned a bit closer and addressed Rick in a low voice. "Listen, Langtry, don't antagonize Redwing." When Rick raised his eyebrows questioningly, Stoner held up his hands and shook his head. "I know, I know, but you and I are professionals. Redwing's a fluke, an amateur they hired from the outside because he works so damned cheap." His eyes filled with scorn as he lowered his voice to a whisper, intending his words for Rick alone. "He just wants enough money to get by on, but he also demands a couple of women a week he can give one hell of a going over . . . If you think anything of this lady you're traveling with, you won't do anything to piss him off. Clear?"

Rick nodded, frowning.

"Okay, glad we got that straight." Stoner leaned back, resting his hands on his thighs as he studied them for a moment. "Now then, we can do this the easy way or the hard way. Give me your word you won't yell or try to attract attention, and I'll forget about the gags."

"You'd take my word?" Rick asked, staring skeptically.

"Look, Langtry," Stoner said, cutting off the angry sputter from Redwing, who had just climbed into the driver's seat, "you and I are professionals. I'm willing to keep things on a businesslike basis insofar as possible— if you are. Of course, I know you're duty-bound to try an escape; I'd do the same thing, in your position. However," he said heavily, pulling his jacket open to reveal the checkered butt of a large pistol in its shoulder holster, "right now that would be extremely foolish of you. And it would endanger the young lady."

"Hell, let him try an escape." Redwing laughed as he turned the key in the ignition, starting the motor. "Just as long as we don't lose the girl. Mmm, I got plans for her."

Rick's eyes blazed; Stoner gave a warning shake of his head. After a moment Rick swallowed and said, "All right. You've got my word. For now."

"Sure, for now." Stoner got to his feet, crouching as he moved forward and levered himself down into the passenger seat. "Once we turn you over in San Francisco, it's a whole new ball game. Cut yourself a new deal then." He glanced at Redwing and made an impatient gesture. "What're we waiting for, man? Let's go!"

Rick sank down on the hard floor, trying to get comfortable as the van began to move. Fran stared at him in shocked disbelief as the van backed down the dirt driveway and out onto the graded road. Then, as Redwing shifted into drive and the van began to move forward, gradually picking up speed, she leaned forward and whispered furiously, "Why'd you ever make a promise like that? Are you crazy? I'm not bound by your word, and if I get the chance—"

"Oh, shut up," he interrupted wearily. He looked at her, frowning. "You're not naive enough to think for one minute that Stoner made the deal out of the goodness of his heart, are you? Hell, Fran, there's not a chance in hell they're going to be stopping anywhere between here and San Francisco. I'll lay you any odds you care to name they gassed this thing up at the truck stop last night before setting out to track us down. And I doubt like hell if we'll be stopping for any meals. So, unless you really want a gag, I suggest you go along with me and keep it quiet."

She opened her mouth as if to retort; then, after a few seconds, closed it without speaking. As the van turned off the dirt road a few minutes later and the tires assumed the familiar high-pitched humming note on the pavement, she looked back at him and said resentfully, "I thought we were safe there in the cabin. I trusted you."

"I'm sorry as hell I disappointed you," he said with exaggerated sarcasm. "I guess I really screwed up bad. I hope you won't tell my boss; it would spoil my chances for promotion."

She stared at him, wounded by his seeming indifference to her. Just a few short hours ago, she reflected, she had lain in the ultimate embrace with this man, experienced depths of feeling and sensation with him she'd never felt before, not with anyone, not ever. She'd even gasped out, mindless with pleasure, that she loved him. Now, as she studied his cold, expressionless face from less than a foot away, she was reminded that he had not responded with any kind of declaration on his part. For all she knew, she had been nothing more than a convenient receptacle for his need, a warm, available body for his pleasure. She flushed hotly at the thought that she had been used by him.

"Rick?" she asked, "do you think they're looking for us?"

"Umm?" He'd been on the verge of dozing off and blinked in surprise at her question. She repeated it, and he forced his exhausted mind to remain conscious for another few minutes. "Yes," he declared flatly. "Jack O'Brien's got the machinery in motion already."

"But—how can you be so sure?"

"Because he's my partner." He stared at her. "You don't let your partner down, Fran."

"Oh, sure," she said skeptically, rolling her eyes. "Saving your partner's such a macho thing to do . . . sometimes, Rick, men like you make me ill."

Ignoring her, he turned away, trying to scrunch himself into a comfortable position on the hard metal floor of the van. The one thin blanket brought from the cabin and spread on the corrugated metal floor helped some, but it was still miserable. Closing his eyes, he tried to relax. He'd had very little sleep since Friday, when he and Jack had been involved with the surveillance of the Linkwell girl. Then, last night—well, he wasn't ready to think about last night, not just yet . . . It was enough to say that he'd had less than two hours sleep when Stoner and Redwing had burst in through the door of the cabin, waving guns under their noses and making threats.

Jack will find us, he thought, lulled by the soporofic hum of tires against the freeway, rocked by the slight movement of the van until his eyelids became unbearably heavy. *Good old Jack. He wouldn't leave his partner in the lurch, not for long . . .*

Shortly after sunrise that Sunday morning, while Rick and Fran were still sleeping in the deserted A-frame cabin, Jack O'Brien sat in Room 122 at the Ponderosa, the telephone gripped in his sweaty hand.

"Yeah? What time was it when they left to go over there, Jerry?" He was speaking with Jerry Whitworth, who was still pulling weekend duty at the DIA field office at Reno International airport. "Do you remember?"

"Why, hell, it was a little after nine, I think," Whitworth replied slowly. "You mean to tell me they still haven't showed up back there?"

"No, they haven't." Jack felt a little worm of worry beginning to uncoil in the pit of his stomach. In just about an hour, he knew, if Rick was still unaccounted for, that little worm was going to transform itself into a dragon and begin gnawing rapaciously at the lining of his stomach. It was a cheerless prospect. "I'm starting to get pretty damned concerned, Jerry."

"Ah, hell, I wouldn't worry, Jack." Whitworth gave a comfortable, man-to-man chuckle. "You know how Langtry is, and that was some good-looking babe with him. Unless I miss my guess, they're holed up in a motel somewhere having a high old time."

"Yeah, you could be right, I guess," Jack conceded, while his mind screamed silent denial. "But listen, just for the sake of my peace of mind, how about a favor?"

"Well, sure, if I can." Whitworth was beginning to cool just a bit, Jack realized, crossing his fingers.

"They were driving Miss Barnette's car, Jerry, a new Mazda RX-7. The jazzy little sports job, dark blue." He drew a deep breath before taking the plunge. "Would it be too much trouble for you, or one of your people, to shoot over to the . . . the Rum Steer and check the parking lot. See if the car's there?"

"The Bum Steer," Whitworth corrected automatically, sounding distinctively cooler now. He sighed heavily. "All right, O'Brien, but you're gonna owe me a big one if the car's not there. Damn it, it's Sunday, and I don't have anybody I can send over there. I'm gonna have to go myself, and I haven't even had a chance to open my paper or have my—"

"I know, Jerry, I know," Jack cut him off, rolling his eyes heavenward as if for a sympathetic audience, "and believe me, if there was anybody else to ask . . ."

"Okay, okay," Whitworth grumbled, "I'm leaving right now. At this hour there shouldn't be any cars at all in that lot. Call you back in twenty minutes or so."

Jack spent the next forty minutes pacing the floor, sipping four cups of instant coffee and downing four of the jelly doughnuts from the bag of a dozen he'd purchased earlier. Every few seconds he glanced at his watch, cursed Whitworth roundly, walked over to the window and drew the drape back, hoping to see a blue RX-7 rolling up in front of the room. When the phone finally did ring, he snatched it off its cradle instantly, spilling the dregs of his fourth cup of coffee in the process.

"O'Brien," he snapped.

"Yeah, this is Jerry. We got trouble, pal. The RX-7 was there, all right." Whitworth now sounded alert, interested, all trace of ennui gone from his voice. "Reason I took so long is that I talked to the local cops and asked if anybody'd called in about the car. Thought maybe the manager of the joint might've called it in when he took off last night."

"And?" Jack prompted when Whitworth paused dramatically.

"They had a call all right. Came in at twelve minutes past midnight, according to the police log. Some drunk, claiming he'd just witnessed a mugging in the parking lot of the Bum Steer. The cops know him, a real local character, evidently, so they didn't take him seriously at first. But he kept insisting, so they finally sent a unit over to check it out."

"Nothing there, of course," Jack guessed.

"You got it. Nothing. Zilch. They did notice the RX-7, but at that hour of the morning, there were still a few cars around. Bar was still open; several restaurant employees were still on the premises, cleaning up. Cops figured—" Jack lowered the phone at the sound of a knock on the front door.

"Just a second, Jerry, I've got company." Leaving the phone on the bed, he stood up and cautiously drew back the drape, revealing two casually dressed men in their mid-thirties standing at the door. With a smile he opened the door and waved them in.

"Pete, John, good to see you." Pete Smith and John Simmons were field agents from the San Francisco office; he'd been expecting them, or somebody like them, ever since the phone call to Addison the previous afternoon. "Find a spot and siddown," he said, gesturing expansively as he reached for the phone. "I'll be with you in a minute."

The two big men nodded. Smith, a tall, cadaverous, dark-haired saturnine man, took the room's only chair. Simmons, a rotund redhead, perched on the edge of the bed, grinning happily as he noticed the bakery bag and the remaining jelly doughnuts. He held the bag up and

Smith chuckled and shook his head. Jack frowned as he nestled the phone against his ear.

"Sorry about the interruption. The cavalry just arrived—Smith and Simmons, from 'Frisco. Now, where were we?"

"As I was saying, the cops didn't take the call seriously, but they did take down the drunk's information." Whitworth paused again, and Jack stifled his impatience. Each time Whitworth prepared to impart some fresh kernel of information, there was a dramatic pause, as if he were awaiting coaxing before going on. Jack remained silent, fuming. "It seems there were two men," Whitworth continued, sounding just a bit miffed, as if disappointed that Jack had outwaited him. "They were assaulting a man and a woman in the parking lot. This was just after twelve, of course, so—"

"I suppose he didn't get a look at the vehicle the two men were using?"

"No such luck, pal. The guy was blasted; we're lucky he even bothered to call at all. A civic-minded drunk, I guess." Whitworth paused, then said seriously, "Listen, Jack, if there's anything I can do—anything at all—you call me. Rick Langtry is a damned good friend of mine."

"Thanks, Jerry. You've already been a big help, and I'll keep your offer in mind."

His expression was grim as he hung up the phone. Simmons and Smith watched him alertly, having heard just enough of his end of the conversation to have gathered that something was going on.

"Trouble, Jack?" Simmons asked, his round, normally good-natured face solemn.

"Trouble. It looks like the opposition has picked off Langtry and the civilian woman—Fran Barnette—who's working with us on this one."

Simmons and Smith listened attentively while Jack

129

briefed them on everything that had occurred since he and Rick left San Francisco Friday afternoon, bearing down heavily on the van Fran had reported and that Rick had verified. "I was hoping the witness might've seen the van," he concluded several minutes later. "It would've been confirmation of what I'm almost certain of—that the two guys in the van followed Rick and Ms. Barnette up to Reno and popped them when they were least expecting it."

"I don't see how they could've taken Langtry any other way," Smith commented thoughtfully.

"So, what's our next move, then?" Simmons asked. He hefted the bag of doughnuts, raising his eyebrows questioningly, and Jack gestured permission. Grinning happily, Simmons took a large bite out of one of the red, gooey doughnuts. "Do we stay here?" he mumbled around a mouthful of dough, "or head back to town?"

Jack hesitated for a moment, frowning in thought. On one hand, he was certain that the next several scenes in this drama were going to occur on the stage of San Francisco; on the other hand, if Rick and Fran were able to escape somehow, and make their way back to the Ponderosa . . .

"One of us probably should stay here for at least the next day or so," he decided after a moment. "Just in case Rick shows up. The other two should head back to the main office and get things organized in the Bay area." He paused, smiling grimly as he continued, "Because when they find out they've got hold of a phony diskette, I've got a feeling they're gonna want to talk trade."

Simmons glanced up sharply, the doughnuts forgotten. "Langtry and the girl for the real thing, you mean?" Smith laughed, shaking his head.

"What else? Why else would they even bother hanging onto the two of them, unless they're holding them as possible bargaining chips in case the diskette is unsatisfactory." Jack fell silent, a troubled expression on his face.

"Well, you might as well kiss them good-bye if that happens," Smith said. "You know as well as I do Addison'd never go for a deal like that, not even if his own wife was the hostage."

"Well, I'm not prepared to kiss anybody good-bye, not yet." Jack's jaw tightened grimly at the prospect. "Well, we might as well get moving. Who's gonna stay here and keep the home fires burning?"

"Hey, that's for me," Simmons declared, arranging himself comfortably on the bed, the bag of doughnuts within easy reach on his chest. He looked up at the other two, beaming, a trace of red jelly on the corner of his mouth.

"Okay with you?" Jack asked Smith.

"Fine with me." Smith turned toward the door. "I'd go nuts, just sitting around, waiting. I'll be tickled to go with you, Jack. Hell, I like to drive."

As the two agents left the motel and headed north toward Interstate 80, where they would swing west toward San Francisco, Jack was mouthing a silent prayer for the safety and well-being of his friend and partner, and for Fran Barnette as well. He clenched his jaw as he stared out at the landscape rushing past in a blur while Smith drove with a heavy foot, speeding down the highway at fifteen miles an hour above the posted limit.

"Hey, listen," Smith said, breaking Jack's chain of thought. "You might as well grab some z's, if you can. I'm good for at least eight more hours, myself."

"Thanks, Smitty." Jack glanced over at the lean, dour profile behind the steering wheel with a small smile. He'd been up most of the night, and he realized he was going to need some rest, and soon, if he was to maintain a degree of efficiency. "I think I'll take you up on that."

"Sure, do that." Smith's somber features were lit by a sudden smile, altering his entire personality. "And don't sweat it. I'll wake you in plenty of time before we hit 'Frisco."

Jack took off his jacket and folded it into a square, then stuffed it behind his head. Leaning up against the makeshift pillow, he closed his eyes, but all he could see in his mind's eye, over and over, was the image of the green van.

When Rick finally woke up, the green van was rolling down one of San Francisco's many steep hills. When Rick opened his eyes, the first thing he saw was Fran, sleeping with her cheek pressed against the floor a few inches away; the second, when he raised up and looked toward the front, was the deep, cerulean blue of San Francisco Bay, seeming to fill the entire front windshield with its brilliance. They were headed downhill toward the waterfront.

He lay back down, watching Fran sleep. A wisp of blond hair lay against her cheek; with each breath she exhaled, the tress fluttered, then settled back against the smooth, tanned skin. He experienced a powerful desire to reach out and smooth the hair back for her, but even as he tensed to move he remembered his bonds.

And these bonds are nothing, he reminded himself tensely, compared with the kinds of bonds inherent in a relationship with a woman like Fran Barnette—for he knew instinctively that Fran was not the sort of woman he'd known in the past. She was not the sort to be contented with an occasional roll in the hay. She would demand more, much more, of a relationship, he realized. But in another part of his mind he knew that there would be much greater rewards with her than he'd ever known with anyone else.

The van turned sharply at the bottom of the hill. Fran rolled a bit with the movement of the van and her eyes blinked open in momentary confusion. She stared at him for a few seconds, then comprehension returned, and she looked as if she was going to cry.

"We're almost there, I think," Rick whispered. "We're right on the waterfront."

"I had the nicest dream," Fran whispered, a wistful expression on her face. "We were still in the cabin. You'd found some popcorn somewhere, and we were popping it in the fireplace and drinking red wine."

"Nice dream." Rick smiled, then sobered. "We'll go back there someday, if you like."

She looked at him for several seconds as the cool air from Stoner's open window wafted across her face, restoring her to full wakefulness. She frowned slightly as she looked away. He was such a puzzle! Cold one moment, warm the next; she never knew what to expect of him. Still, he was a wonderful lover, and the time they'd spent together in that mountain cabin had to rank up there with the best memories of her lifetime so far. Suddenly she looked over at him and smiled.

"Oh, Rick, that would be so wonder—" She broke off as the van came to an abrupt halt. The front doors opened and Redwing and Stoner got out, letting in a gust of cool, salty air.

"Okay, folks, we're here," Stoner said, opening the side doors and filling the entrance. Over his shoulder, Rick saw with a sinking sensation, was the bow of a large, ocean-going freighter, Cyrillic letters on the bow reading Vostok. A Soviet ship. Stoner climbed up into the van and knelt beside Fran, a knife gleaming in his large hand. "I imagine you'll be happy to get rid of these ropes," he said as the blade flashed in the afternoon sun.

As Stoner moved over to Rick, Fran sat up and rubbed her wrists and ankles, mildly surprised at the lack of pain. Stoner, she realized with mixed feelings, was an expert at his business.

"Climb down here. Now." Redwing appeared beside the van, gesturing impatiently. Fran glanced back at Rick, who was just sitting up, and he nodded.

"What you looking at him for, damn it!" Redwing exclaimed. "I'm the one with the gun. You do what I say, not him."

"Yes, of course," Fran said, swallowing her fear as Redwing opened his jacket to display the large pistol in its shoulder holster. She felt a bit better as Rick joined her, standing next to her on the pier.

They stood near the van for several moments, Stoner glancing at his watch every few seconds, then peering down the length of the pier, obviously waiting for someone to arrive. Fran experienced a pang of apprehension. Somehow the thought of strangers entering the picture now was terrifying. Having had to get used to Stoner and Redwing had been bad enough.

She followed Rick's gaze toward the activity occurring around the stern of the Soviet freighter. Fifty yards down the pier from where they stood, two large yellow forklifts were busily transporting wooden pallets laden with bags of flour from a warehouse out onto the pier. As soon as the forklifts backed away from their loads, the hook from the ship's deck crane snaked down and two crewmen swiftly hooked cables to the pallets. The crane then raised them into the air and swung them over an open hatch on the ship's deck, then lowered them out of sight into the hold. As they stood watching, one of the pallets suddenly gave a loud snapping noise, scattering the men below on the pier with shouts of alarm. Seconds later the pallet snapped into two pieces and the bags of flour plummeted toward the ground. Two bags burst when they hit, like bombs going off. Everything within a fifty-foot radius was coated with white; the air was blue with curses in at least two languages.

Fran glanced over at Rick and saw a gleam of amusement in his dark eyes. She smiled, then giggled. Rick's mouth twitched, then he was laughing as well. They roared with amusement, clinging to each other, while Stoner and Redwing studied them coldly. The hilarity lasted only a few seconds, but the relief from tension made every second as refreshing as an hour's nap.

"Ah," Stoner said after a moment, eyes narrowing at the sight of a black Mercedes sedan approaching from beyond the stern of the ship. "Let's see how you laugh now."

The glossy black sedan came toward them slowly, its smoked glass windows making it impossible to distinguish the driver or passengers. The car slid smoothly to a halt, and Stoner and Redwing seemed to draw themselves up as the back door opened with an oiled click. A tall, well-dressed man in his forties got out and stood with his hands on his hips, surveying them with a mildly amused expression on his handsome face.

"So, what have we here?" he murmured.

Fran studied the newcomer hopefully, strangely reassured by his impeccable appearance. It was as if she couldn't believe that such a handsome man—so beautifully dressed in a tailored blue three-piece suit, dazzlingly white shirt, red tie, and glossy black shoes—could possibly represent a danger to them. Surely, she thought, such an obviously cultured individual would quickly set matters straight.

"Charonsky," Rick muttered bleakly, and her spirits, which had been soaring, immediately plummeted.

"Charonsky?" she quavered.

"Charonsky, indeed, my dear," the tall man said in flawless, unaccented English, with a slight bow and a flash of perfectly even white teeth. "Anatoly Ivanovitch, at your service." He sobered as he straightened back up. "And you are Miss Francine Barnette, I believe? Ah, yes. And you, sir, are Richard Langtry, one of Joe Addison's most notorious DIA field agents." He held up an admonishing finger as Rick opened his mouth, "No, no, don't deny it, please. You'd be amazed at the extent of our files on you and your colleagues, Mr. Langtry, simply amazed. So please don't insult my intelligence by denying what I know to be a fact."

Rick lowered his eyes, but made no other reply. Charonsky stared at him for a few seconds, then clapped his hands, turning to face Stoner and Redwing.

"You have done well," he stated. "Yes, a fine job indeed, and you shall both be suitably rewarded. Redwing, your reward is already waiting for you back at your room. I'm sure you'll be most pleased."

"Thanks. Can I—?"

"You may go now. Take the van, if you wish. Stoner can ride back with me after our business here is finished." Charonsky smiled indulgently, like a proud father, Fran reflected, watching as Redwing hurried over and climbed into the driver's seat of the van. The engine caught and roared as Redwing put it in gear and drove rapidly away. Charonsky turned back to Rick and Fran.

"Now, to the business at hand . . ." He turned, gesturing toward the gangplank of the ship tied up a few yards away. "If you'll join me, we'll go aboard the *Vostok.* Your quarters have been prepared for your stay. I'm quite certain you'll be comfortable."

"Our stay?" Rick held back for a moment, shaking Stoner's hand from his elbow as Stoner tried to move him toward the ship. "And how long will that be, Mr. KGB?"

"Ah, I see you know a bit more than I suspected." Charonsky's eyes narrowed as he looked at Rick. "How long? That depends entirely on our degree of satisfaction with the diskette, Mr. Langtry—or may I call you Rick?"

"Why don't we just cut all this phony courtesy crap right now?" Rick asked roughly, responding to Stoner's urging with a couple of quick steps in the direction of the ship. Fran, still holding tightly to his hand, was dragged along with him. "You and I both know you people wouldn't hesitate to kill or torture us if it suited you."

"Ah, then I take it you don't mind if I call you Rick?" Charonsky replied, unfazed by Rick's hostility. Fran thought she detected a hint of cruel amusement in his dark eyes, but he persisted in the courtly manner he'd adopted from the beginning. "You may call me Mr. Charonsky, or, if you wish, just Charonsky." He paused as they reached the bottom of the gangplank, and when he looked at Rick all trace of amusement had left his eyes. "It can be easy or difficult, Mr. Langtry. It depends on you."

"No more deals, pal," Rick said, glancing apologetically at Fran as he spoke. "We'll play it as it lays."

"Very well." Charonsky gestured for them to go ahead of him up the gangplank, his lips pressed together in distaste.

As Rick and Fran reached the top of the gangplank and stepped onto the deck of the ship, their nostrils were assailed by a foul mixture of odors unlike anything they'd ever smelled before: a mixture of cabbage, potatoes, garbage, and unwashed bodies. Fran recoiled, leaning out over the railing and gulping down a lungful of relatively clean, fresh air.

137

"I agree," Charonsky said quietly as he reached them. "It's filthy. But the ship is mechanically sound and seaworthy, as are all Soviet ships. Ah, here is the captain. Captain Levinsky, here are your guests."

"Welcome aboard the *Vostok*," Levinsky said in thickly accented English. It was evidently the extent of his English vocabulary, because he and Charonsky began conversing rapidly in Russian. They were following Levinsky through a series of narrow passageways that seemed to Fran to be leading deep into the bowels of the ship, inward and downward, as they climbed down a couple of flights of ladders. At last they came to a halt before a gray steel door, which the captain unlocked and opened with a flourish.

"In you go," Charonsky said jocularly, "both of you."

At least they're letting us stay together, Fran thought, as Rick guided her through the steel opening with his hand at her elbow. He followed her into the room, and they surveyed their grim surroundings for a few seconds. Except for a pair of cots with paper-thin mattresses and a fold-out table on the opposite wall with a pitcher of water and two tin cups, the room was utterly bare. Tears sprang to Fran's eyes as the harsh reality of their predicament descended upon her.

"No deals, Langtry?" Charonsky asked with ironic amusement. "You're sure now?"

"No deals," Rick said firmly.

Charonsky jerked his chin, and Stoner stepped into the small room, something metallic shining in his large hands. Before Fran had recognized the object it was snapped coldly around her wrists: handcuffs. Rick also submitted to the cuffs, his eyes blazing with helpless rage as Stoner tightened them on his wrists.

Stoner stepped back into the passageway, rejoining Charonsky and the freckle-faced young seaman wearing a side arm who had joined them when the captain departed a few moments before. The youth, who appeared to be no more than eighteen or nineteen years old, swallowed as he gaped at Fran, his prominent Adam's apple bobbing comically. Self-consciously, his right hand rested on the butt of his holstered pistol, as if he hoped to impress the glamorous, though decadent, American.

"This is Boris," Charonsky said, a glint of amusement in his eyes as he clapped the youngster on the shoulder. The seaman looked up at the sound of his name and grinned, revealing a steel tooth in the front of his mouth. "He has the key to the door . . . and instructions to shoot to kill if you try anything." He paused for a moment, eyes narrowing, then nodded.

"Stoner will stay for a few moments, while you both are given the opportunity to use the heads. To wash up, of course," he said wryly. "Food will be brought to the room later, when the crew eats . . . Miss Barnette, do you need to . . . ?" His voice trailed off delicately, and Fran nodded.

"Yes, I do. It was a long ride in the van."

"Of course." Charonsky inclined his head slightly. "Boris!" He spoke rapidly in Russian, and the youth blushed as he gestured for Fran to accompany him down the passageway. As she passed him, brushing against him in the narrow passage, his pale blue eyes looked as if they were going to bulge right out of their sockets.

"It seems Miss Barnette has made a conquest," Charonsky observed wryly, watching as Boris and Fran disappeared around a bend in the corridor. He glanced at Rick and shook his head. "Pity she had to become involved in this business, Langtry." Shooting his cuff, he glanced at the thin, elegant gold wrist watch on his arm and added, almost as an afterthought, "However, she'll be quite safe . . . if the diskette is satisfactory, of course." He jerked his chin at Stoner. "I'm going down to the car, Stoner. Finish up here and join me, eh?"

"Right." Stoner waited until the sound of Charonsky's footsteps in the steel corridor had faded away, then looked at Rick and raised his eyebrows. "Well? How about it—you have to go too?"

When Rick returned to the room a few minutes later, Fran was back in the room, seated on one of the thin cots, looking so utterly miserable and dejected that his heart went out to her. She looked up at him as he entered the room and managed a tremulous, brave little smile.

"It'll be all right, babe," he said, sitting down next to her, patting her knee awkwardly with his handcuffed hands. "It'll be okay, you'll see."

However, as she leaned up against him, he glanced around at their steel cage, wondering how much truth his words held. There was no window and only the one door—locked, and with an armed crewman on the other side in any case. They were aboard a foul, stinking merchant ship tied up at the pier in the process of the legitimate loading and unloading of cargo. Complicating matters even further, Rick realized, was the red flag of the Soviet Union flying from the ship's mast.

Although he had no intention whatsoever of pointing this out to Fran, Rick knew that that national banner practically guaranteed that no search or invasion of the *Vostok* in any manner or form would be permitted—simply as a matter of government policy. Joseph Addison III was too experienced a bureaucrat, and had survived the vicious infighting and politics of the upper levels of the civil service for too many years to make a fool of himself now by creating an international incident looking for an agent who had, in effect, made a fool of him. Rick knew there was no chance of Addison launching an operation against the *Vostok,* even if he knew that Rick and Fran were aboard, which, of course, he did not.

No, he thought, awkwardly patting Fran on the knee, trying to comfort her, the conclusion was inescapable: They were utterly on their own.

CHAPTER EIGHT

After a light, unsatisfying supper of watery cabbage soup and a slice of dark bread, Fran lay down on one of the thin mattresses and fell asleep. She woke a few hours later and discovered that Rick was sound asleep on the other cot, snoring softly, as contentedly as if he hadn't a care in the world. Stifling a surge of envy, she twisted on the narrow bunk, trying to find a comfortable position to lie in. With her hands cuffed together it seemed impossible, and she finally gave up and relaxed. With that she slept fitfully through the remainder of the night, waking in the morning with a dull feeling of grogginess and the sour taste in her mouth. It had not been a bad dream, she reflected dully; they were still here, prisoners aboard this Soviet ship.

"Morning." Rick's soft voice startled her out of her glum thoughts. She felt a twinge of pity as she looked at him.

His lean face was covered now with thick dark stubble, and the deep scratch on his neck, inflicted the previous morning by Redwing's gun, had scabbed over, giving him the raffish appearance of the survivor of a drunken brawl. His tweed jacket and trousers were soiled and wrinkled, and his tie had long since been thrown away, adding to his disreputable appearance.

"Good morning." She sat up on her cot and rubbed

her face as much as she could with the handcuffs restricting her movements. "I was hoping this would turn out to be a bad dream . . . but here we still are."

"Unfortunately. Can't hide from reality, though." He sat up, hesitated a few seconds, then walked over and pounded on the steel door with the flat of his hand. The scratching metallic sound of a key in the lock, then the door opened a few inches and Boris's face appeared in the opening. His large blue eyes hungrily sought Fran. He gawked at her for a moment, then looked at Rick and raised his eyebrows questioningly.

"I've got to go to the rest room," Rick said. "Uh . . . toilet, head, W.C.—" At that, Boris's face cleared and he opened the door wide, gesturing for Rick to follow him.

While Fran waited for Rick to return, she ran her hands through her hair, wishing she had a comb or a hairbrush. Her purse had vanished somewhere since leaving the Bum Steer Saturday and she had no idea what had become of her things.

Good grief, she thought, *I've got to call! My credit cards, traveler's checks—just everything!* She got to her feet as if to rush from the room in search of a phone, then sank back down on the cot abruptly. What was she thinking of? In her current situation what became of her credit cards had very little relevance. As matters stood now, it was her very life that was in danger.

At last the steel door opened and Rick reentered the room, looking vastly refreshed. His hair had been combed and his teeth sparkled as he held out a toothbrush and a small tube of toothpaste.

"They gave us each a toothbrush," he said. "But only one comb, so we'll have to share it."

"Thanks." She accepted the items. "I see they didn't offer you a razor."

He self-consciously rubbed the bristles on his jaw.

143

"Probably afraid I'd attack old Boris if they gave me something that'd cut." He sat down on the edge of his bunk and sighed. He glanced over at Boris, who was standing in the open doorway, gazing worshipfully at Fran.

"Well?" Rick snapped. "You going with him or not? He's not going to wait forever—even for you."

"Oh." Startled, Fran turned quickly to the door. "I didn't know he was waiting. Of course I want to go." Boris's face lit up with a huge grin, revealing a stainless steel incisor, and he gave a deferential half bow as she brushed by him. Flushing with pleasure, he turned and escorted her down the corridor.

While Boris stood guard at the door of the heads, Fran brushed her teeth thoroughly, then rinsed her face in tepid water and moistened her hair and combed the tangles out. There was no soap, and the only available towel was soiled, damp and threadbare. She felt it, grimaced, and decided to let the air dry her skin.

"Okay," she said, stepping back out into the corridor where Boris waited. He beamed happily, then said something in Russian, pantomiming eating motions. Assuming that he was asking if she was hungry, she smiled. "Yes, I'm hungry! But please—no more of that yucky cabbage soup, okay?"

"Okay!" Boris bobbed his head emphatically. "Okay!"

"Do you speak some English?" Fran asked hopefully.

"Okay?" Boris said. She sighed; he did not speak English. Boris stopped in front of the door to their room and unlocked it, bowing slightly as she passed him.

"Well, you look like a new woman," Rick observed as she entered the room. He frowned slightly, studying the way Boris gawked at her for several seconds before pulling the door shut and locking it.

"Thanks. I do feel better." She sat down on the cot

and leaned back against the steel bulkhead, sighing. "I wonder if we ought to start scratching off the days on the wall, like those prisoners do in the cartoons." She sighed again. "It wouldn't be so bad if we just had something to read, or even a chance to shower and change into clean clothes. I don't know about you, but I'm starting to feel really grungy."

Rick chuckled softly, nodding. He jerked his head toward the door. "Looks like you've made yourself a conquest."

"Boris?" She wrinkled her nose in disdain. "Why, he's just a kid! He can't be more than nineteen years old. Besides, he's—" She stared at him, her voice trailing off. "Why, Rick," she said after a few seconds, "I do believe you're jealous!"

"I don't get jealous," he said flatly. "No, it's just that I might be getting an idea, that's all."

"Sure, you and your ideas. The last big idea of yours was that we spend the night together in that cabin. If I recall," she said, lifting an elegant eyebrow, "that was where Redwing and Stoner caught us again. So it turned out to be a pretty bad idea, didn't it?"

"Oh, really?" He said in an injured tone of voice. "I seem to recall that you were pretty enthusiastic about the idea at the time. As a matter-of-fact, it seems to me that you were down right . . . um . . . primitive in your enjoyment."

"Oh, wow." She flushed with a combination of embarrassment and anger. "The old male ego rears its ugly head again. What's the matter, Rick, do you always find it necessary to rub your partners' faces in the fact that you've had them?"

"Rub your nose!" He turned away, wounded. "If that's what you think, I'm sorry. And as for my male ego as you so charmingly put it, it has nothing to do with this conversation."

"It does if I say it does." She glared at him, angry now, remembering how, at the height of passion, lying locked together in his arms, she'd told him she loved him, and his lack of a response. "Or doesn't a woman have any right to decide what a conversation will be about? Is that strictly a man's province, in your tiny world?"

"Cut it out, Fran." His skin darkened under the stubble of whiskery growth and she could see the muscles knotting in his jaw. "I don't think I deserve this, not from you."

"Oh, really?" She deepened her voice mockingly, saying, "Oh, we'll protect you every step of the way, Miss Barnette. You'll be in no danger at anytime. I won't let anything happen to you, Miss Barnette."

"All right, rub it in, if it makes you feel better." His eyes were cold and angry now. "We—I—screwed up. I admit it, and I'm sorry as hell about it. If we ever get out of this mess, I'll try and figure out a way to make it up to you."

"Very pretty words. Unfortunately, it doesn't look as if we are going to get out, does it?"

"We might. It depends."

"On what? On your government friends getting us out? Fat chance of that!" With a sniff she turned away. "I hope you're not counting on a bunch of fat, lazy civil servants storming to our rescue, Rick."

"Oh, right—I'd forgotten your contempt for civil servants." He stood and began pacing. There was room for only four steps in each direction, but he felt that if he didn't move he was in danger of exploding. "If they had any brains at all, any moxie or old-fashioned gumption, they'd be out there chasing the bucks with the rest of you, right?" He stared at her, wondering how this stubborn female could possibly be the same soft, bewitching creature who'd spent such an ecstasy-filled morning in

146

his arms less than forty-eight hours ago. How quickly she could change from a loving sex kitten to a spitting, snarling wild cat!

"Rick . . . it's not—oh, look, we shouldn't be fighting this way, not now." She looked pleadingly up at him. "Truce?"

He stared at her for a moment, an unfathomable expression in his dark eyes. He nodded curtly. "Truce."

For the next few minutes they spoke to each other with exaggerated courtesy. Fran glanced over at him and sighed, but he ignored her, or pretended to.

Several times Fran was on the verge of blurting out an apology, even though she was convinced that it was he who was wrong. She wanted to yank him around by the scruff of his neck and demand whether or not he could remember the bliss they'd given to each other. However, something cold and remote in his eyes warned her to keep her distance, at least for the moment. She sensed that he was deliberately creating space between them, distancing himself from her so that he would be less affected by whatever was going to happen to her. At the thought she became even more depressed. To think that he could just—just emotionally dump her that way. Gradually, her depression evolved into anger —damn the arrogant, macho son of a bitch, anyway. Where did he come off, with his snide cracks about the innocent Russian boy who was so obviously infatuated with her, and how about the utterly crass, insensitive manner in which he'd reminded her of their lovemaking? Primitive, was she? She'd show him primitive, if he pushed her any further.

She was working herself into a self-righteous rage that threatened to erupt at any moment—one word from Rick was all it would have taken—so it was a relief when Boris opened their door and stood aside while a swarthy, dark-eyed steward delivered two trays of food.

Her hands shook with fading anger as she arranged her tray on the end of her cot and surveyed her breakfast with distaste. Half an hour ago she'd been ravenous; now the only thing that looked appetizing at all was the heavy ceramic mug of coffee. Nevertheless, she bit off a hunk of the dark bread and chewed on it, then took a sip of the strong black coffee. As she lowered the cup back to the tray, her handcuff bumped the edge of the tray and she jerked the cup, spilling half the coffee into the oatmeal.

"Oh, damn it!" she swore, and held out the handcuffs imploringly. Rick's eyes widened in astonishment as Boris took the key from his pocket and unlocked her cuffs and removed them. When he held out his hands, pantomiming the same request, Boris just smiled and shook his head. Rick nodded wryly; Boris wasn't as dumb as he looked. Fran looked over at Rick, and he just shook his head slightly, but that cold, remote look was gone from his eyes. She felt much better as she looked at her food.

Thoughtfully, she bent over the tray and finished the spartan meal. It was amazing, she reflected as she scooped up the last spoonful of the oatmeal, how hunger improved the taste of even the simplest foods. She set the tray aside, feeling much better.

"Thank you," she said as the steward reentered the room and collected the steel trays. He refilled their mugs from a pot of coffee, then ducked his head in acknowledgment of her thanks and backed out into the corridor and disappeared. Boris smiled softly at Fran as he pulled the door closed and locked it, leaving them alone once again. He hadn't replaced her handcuffs, and she spread her hands delightedly while Rick watched enviously.

148

"Listen," he muttered after a few minutes, "I'm sorry if I made you angry before. I know we called a truce but neither of us apologized." He hesitated, then said, "Well, I'm apologizing now."

Fran felt as if a heavy weight had been lifted from her shoulders, and her face lit up with a smile that made his heart skip a beat. "You're forgiven," she said. "And I apologize for the mean things I said to you, too."

"Oh, what the hell." He shrugged awkwardly. "You didn't say a thing that wasn't true . . ."

Raising his mug, he sipped at the dregs of his coffee, confused and just a bit alarmed at the intensity of his emotional reactions to her. He'd been down in the dumps, filled with a feeling of gloom, but when she'd smiled at him that way, his heart had fairly leapt in his chest, filling him with an inexplicable feeling of elation totally unlike anything he'd ever known. *Damn,* he thought, *we've got to get out of here so I can get away from this bewitching woman before her hold over me gets any stronger than it already is. If there's one thing I've always put a high value on, it's the ability to walk away from any relationship without a backward glance, whenever things got uncomfortable, or the woman got to clinging too hard. But never, ever, have I been involved with anyone who can change my entire mood simply by the expression on her face.*

"I feel so much better, don't you?" Fran asked, her hazel eyes shining as she patted the narrow cot next to her. "Why don't you at least sit next to me, Rick? We don't know what's going to happen to us, so—" She stopped, turning to face the door at the sound of a key turning in the lock.

"Ah, good morning." Charonsky smiled smoothly as he stepped into the room. He was dressed in a brown blazer, tan slacks, and a light blue silk shirt, and a dark blue silk ascot was knotted with artful carelessness around his neck. "I trust you have been enjoying your stay? Accommodations are satisfactory, I hope?"

"Good morning," Fran said coolly. Rick glared.

"Your friend could teach you some manners." Charonsky sobered as he looked at Rick. "She, at least, is courteous enough to return a civil greeting. Perhaps that is the reason the good Boris has seen fit to relieve her of her handcuffs, hmm?"

"Morning, Charonsky," Rick said, deciding there was nothing to be gained by churlishness.

"Ah, that's better." Charonsky carefully hitched up the cuff of his immaculately pressed trousers as he rested a foot on Rick's cot and leaned forward, resting his elbow on his knee. He surveyed them with an amused expression for several seconds, then sighed theatrically, shaking his head.

"I'd been hoping to release the two of you this morning, but . . ." He paused and shook his head. "Alas, 'tis not to be."

"And why not?" Rick demanded.

"Oh, I think you probably know why." Charonsky's charming smile vanished, replaced by a chiseled, flinty expression. "We naturally flew in an engineering expert from Moscow to analyze the data on the diskette. You were very stupid to think we would fall for such a simple ploy. Counterfeit data, indeed." He paused, and when he continued, his voice had taken on a steely edge that sent a chill of fear up Fran's spine. "It didn't work. Now, you and your, um, lady friend are going to be with us a lot longer . . ." He looked at Fran for a few seconds, a calculating expression on his face, then turned back to Rick.

"There are ways to make you cooperate, Langtry. I sincerely hope that it doesn't become necessary to use some of the, shall we say, less savory methods?"

150

"Are you threatening torture?" Fran said angrily, but Charonsky cut her off with a violent, chopping gesture.

"Shut your mouth!"

"Look, don't talk to her that way," Rick said quietly. "She has done nothing wrong. It makes no sense to get rough with her, Charonsky."

"Ah, I see." The Russian's eyes gleamed with satisfaction, looking from Rick to Fran and back again. With a sinking sensation Rick realized he'd just placed a weapon against him in the KGB man's hands, but there had been no way to avoid it. He was not willing to listen to them abusing Fran. He shrugged inwardly. They were going to discover his feelings for her anyway, the first time they touched her in his presence. Still, he wished there'd been some way to avoid letting Charonsky find out how he felt. He couldn't shake the feeling of impending doom that had come over him with the gleam of malice that had appeared in the Russian's eyes.

"Ah, what's the use?" Rick asked, spreading his hands. "Why threaten her? She has nothing to do with all this—nothing at all. She's an innocent civilian, Charonsky, recruited to help some government employees with an operation that went wrong almost from the very beginning. It's not her fault she wound up in this situation. Let her go."

"Sorry." Charonsky shook his head. "Civilian . . . maybe." He leaned forward, brushing an imaginary speck of dust from the toe of his glossy brown loafers with a clean white handkerchief. "Innocent?" He raised his eyebrows. "That remains to be seen."

"In any case, she can't help you."

"We will see, won't we . . ." Charonsky smiled slyly, slanting his eyes over at Rick. "Of course, if you were to help us, Langtry, it's possible we might not even question her."

"Rick, don't!" Fran exclaimed. "He's bluffing."

"Possible, isn't it, Langtry?" Charonsky said casually. "Am I bluffing? Who knows?"

"Stay out of this, Fran." Rick turned back to Charonsky. "My name is Richard Langtry. I'm an employee of the United States government. That is all the information I am required to give you, Charonsky. You are holding us aboard this vessel illegally, and I demand that you release us at once!"

Charonsky clapped his hands in mock admiration, an arrogant grin on his handsome face. "Very good, Langtry! Excellent. In fact, I wish I had it on tape."

"That's all I'm saying, Mr. KGB."

"I see. Then, perhaps Miss Barnette—"

"Leave her out of this!"

"Rick, please," Fran began, "I can take—"

"Would you please just be quiet and let me handle this, Fran?" Rick snapped, staring at her with a plea in his eyes. "This is my job. I know what I'm doing."

She frowned, appalled by the vehemence of his reaction. She'd wanted only to tell him not to worry about her, not to make any concessions just because of her. She stared at him and detected the urgent plea for cooperation in his eyes. She nodded imperceptibly, and she saw him sigh in relief. After all, she told herself, Rick was right: this was the sort of thing he was paid for. This was his field of expertise.

"I just wanted to tell you—"

"Cool it, Fran." He cut her off.

"I will, Rick, but—"

"But nothing. Just please, for God's sake, cool it!" he warned, a frantic, pleading expression in his eyes. Against every instinct, which screamed that she should retaliate, she nodded and lowered her eyes.

"All right," Rick asked. "What do you want, Charonsky?"

"The genuine diskette, of course."

"You must realize that Miss Barnette and I have no idea where the diskette is now. I suppose back at Livermore by now."

"Yes, I would suppose the same." Charonsky cocked his head, smiling. "I want you to help us get it back, Langtry. We paid for it—we want it. You're a capitalist —surely you can understand that. We want you to make a tape recording. A recording we can use to bargain with your superiors. A recording for the ears of Mr. Joseph Addison the third, as it were . . ."

"Forget it, Charonsky." Rick chuckled sourly. "I'm not playing your little game—and Addison'd never deal with you anyway. Not for what you want."

"That's most unfortunate . . . for you." Charonsky walked over and rapped once on the steel door. It was opened at once by the ubiquitous Boris, who craned for his usual peek at Fran. "I think it quite likely that Mr. Addison will be willing to deal with us, Langtry." He stepped through the door and turned back, smiling wolfishly. "Especially after he begins receiving pieces of your bodies in his daily mail . . ."

Without another word he was gone, his footsteps echoing in the corridor. The sound of the key turning in the lock added credence to his threats. Fran stared wide-eyed at Rick and said, "Gulp."

"Yeah."

"Do you—do you really think they would—?" She quavered after a moment of silence.

"Hell, yes, they would." He shot her an angry glance. "And listen, from now on let me deal with Charonsky, okay? I at least know these people. You don't."

"Naturally, you being a man, you—"

"Damn it, get down off that high horse of yours, will you? Being a man has nothing to do with this, and the quicker you get it through your head the better off we'll both be!" He scooted a bit closer to her, speaking in low

153

tones as he continued, "The only thing that matters right now is knowledge, Fran. Charonsky wants the knowledge—the data—represented by that diskette. I have to use the knowledge I have of their methods to keep our skins in one piece until we can get out of here."

He paused a moment, gathering his thoughts. "You see, Fran, there's a—a line in these things, a line that hasn't been crossed yet. That line is physical violence against us—torture, beatings, and the like. Rape." He glanced at her. "Once that line is crossed, very often there is no going back. Something changes . . . a kind of—of acceptance, I suppose—an acceptance of death. Because death is often the result once that line of violence has been crossed. We've got to get out of here before that line is crossed."

"Is that why you were so willing to cooperate with Charonsky?" She stared at him, her hazel eyes huge and solemn. "Because you're afraid to die?"

"Of course not. I'm no more afraid to die than anybody else." He struggled, groping for the right words. "What I am trying to forestall is that—that moment when Charonsky thinks it will be to his benefit to cross that line!" He paused to see if she understood. She nodded, and he went on, "Hell, as far as helping Charonsky goes, what can we do to help him?" He spread his hands expressively. "Face it, kid. All we are now is a couple of chips, bargaining chips. Charonsky wants the diskette; presumably Addison wants us back. You, anyway," he added with a grin. "He'd probably be just as happy to let me quietly disappear . . ."

"Well, then, are you telling me it's just a matter of surviving until they make their deal?" Her eyes glowed with renewed hope.

"Afraid not, Fran. You see, Addison would never agree to a trade if it meant giving up the information on that diskette, so if that's what Charonsky's counting on, he's in for a big disappointment. Of course, he won't be half as disappointed as you and I will be."

"Then what are you saying, Rick?" The hopeful glow faded from her eyes as she gradually accepted the truth. "That we're on our own, nobody out there who can help us?"

"Essentially, yes." He studied her closely. "Can you handle that?"

"What's the difference if I can or not?" she demanded crossly. "So what do we do? Just sit and wait for them to kill us?"

"Not really." He leaned forward and lowered his voice confidentially. "You see, I told you all that so I could tell you this. I've got an idea . . ."

Outside the small steel room in which the Americans were being held, Boris glanced impatiently at his wristwatch. The noon meal would not be served for another two hours; he was already impatient for another opportunity to look upon the glamorous American woman. She was so beautiful that it was difficult for Boris to accept what he'd been told: that she and her companion, the DIA spy Langtry, were dangerous enemies of the Soviet Union, and had been arrested while plotting against the state. They were being held here, on the *Vostok,* while it was decided whether or not to transport them back to the Soviet Union for a trial. Boris fervently hoped that they would be.

He shook his head, thinking of the American woman. *It just goes to show you,* he reflected philosophically, *you cannot tell the contents of a sausage by looking at its skin —the American woman was ample proof of that! Still,* he sighed, *it would be most pleasant to curl up in bed with such a woman, if only once in a lifetime, even if she was a murderer and a spy . . .*

"Boris, help!" The American agent's baritone voice came from behind the door, fraught with urgency. Although he didn't understand the words—except for his name—he did feel the urgency and immediately inserted the key entrusted to him into the lock, his fingers trembling with apprehension. What if something had happened to the American woman? If the DIA agent with her had harmed her—!

"Hurry, Boris!"

He swung the door wide open, his jaw dropping in astonishment at the scene that greeted his eyes. The American woman lay flat on her back on one of the bunks, her blouse unbuttoned down to the third button, revealing a creamy, swelling expanse of cleavage that drew Boris's eyes like a magnet. Her skirt was hitched up several inches above her knees; poor Boris didn't know which direction to look, his Adam's apple bobbing convulsively as he tried to take it all in.

Fran gazed up at the young Russian sailor through half-closed eyes and released a series of moans, clutching her stomach and thrashing wildly on the bunk, sending her clothing into even further disarray. Boris held out his hands as if to stop her, babbling in Russian. His eyes bulged with excitement and panic.

Before the young Russian had time enough to recover his senses and realize he was being had, Rick stepped out from behind the door where he'd been standing, one of the heavy ceramic mugs gripped in his hands. He raised the mug high, then slammed it into the back of Boris's head. The mug cracked into two pieces. Boris dropped as if he'd been pole-axed.

"There, damn it," Rick said, gripping Boris by one arm and dragging him over into the corner of the room away from the door. "One down." He paused, shooting Fran a hurried glance. "Put yourself back together, will you? Then get over here and give me a hand. Get the key to these damned cuffs first of all, will you?"

He went over to the door and pushed it closed, after a quick look in both directions up and down the corridor. Nobody in view in either end. *Good,* he thought—*nobody to come looking for Comrade Boris, at least not right away.*

Fran shot him an angry glance as she buttoned up her blouse and rearranged her skirt to cover her legs. It hadn't been her idea to use Boris's obvious infatuation for her in such a cold manner, playing on his youth and inexperience the way they had. Still, she had to admit that Rick was right; it had worked. Then why was he acting this way toward her now, she wondered, treating her as if she had done something wrong. Then it occurred to her that he was acting exactly like a jealous husband. She smiled to herself, strangely pleased, as she knelt next to Boris and began going through his pockets.

"He doesn't have the key!" she hissed frantically.

"Damn it, he's got to!" Rick hurried over and knelt beside her, staring at the unconscious youth. "He unlocked your cuffs this morning, didn't he?" Fran nodded, staring at her unfettered hands as if reassuring herself that she hadn't imagined the entire episode. The cuffs were gone, and it had indisputably been Boris who removed them.

"Well, he might have had the key this morning," she said dully, "but he doesn't have it now."

"Charonsky." Cursing, Rick rolled the Russian sailor over, searching his pockets as best he could with his hands cuffed together. It was useless; Fran was correct. There was no key. He yanked the heavy pistol from Boris's holster and examined it. Dull blue steel with checkered black plastic grips, it was a Soviet-bloc manufactured 9mm automatic, similar to the Colt .45 auto-

157

matic the U.S. Army had been using for seventy-five years. He shoved the weapon into his belt, confident he could use it if the need arose.

"All right," he muttered grimly. "Let's get the hell off this Russian tub."

"You look like a real desperado," Fran commented, studying him thoughtfully. In the wrinkled and soiled tweed jacket and trousers and the shirt he'd been wearing for the past two days and nights, he was indeed a disgusting sight. Then she realized that her own clothing didn't look any better than his; worse, if anything, since so much of hers had been white to start out with.

"Yeah, well, you don't look a hell of a lot better," he said, grinning. He ran the back of one of his hands over his jaw. "But at least you don't have a world record case of five o'clock shadow." He held up his hands, displaying the chrome-plated cuffs. "These things aren't going to be a bit of help, either," he added, the grin fading. "I'll try to keep my hands out of sight as much as possible, once we're off this rust bucket."

They left the room then, creeping up the corridor until they came to the steep staircase that led up to the next deck. Awkwardly, Rick climbed a few steps, looked around, then beckoned for her to follow when it was safe. Another corridor, another flight of stairs, and they emerged onto the main deck, blinking in the glare of sunshine. They could see the warehouse across the pier from the ship from where they stood, and for the first time in almost twenty-four hours Fran was able to breathe deeply of air that didn't reek of cabbage, unwashed bodies, or oil.

"The gangplank is right over there," Rick muttered, pointing and indicating a direction with a jerk of his thumb. "There's almost certainly a guard."

"What'll we do?" she whispered, staring longingly at the side of the warehouse. It was less than fifty feet away, but it might as well have been a hundred miles. That warehouse was on American soil, she reflected, and for the first time, she had a glimmering of what it must be like for people who longed to set foot in the United States but who were prevented from doing so by their own governments or by American law. Freedom had never been so precious, she realized, as it was now that she had lost it. More than anything in the world, she wanted to be back secure in her own country, off this alien ship with its alien smells and alien ways.

Rick pulled out the gun he'd taken away from Boris. "Drape my coattail over this as well as you can," he said. "Then if I need to I'll stick it right in the guard's nose. He'll get out of our way then, I promise you."

"Right." She pulled his coattail up and over his right arm, arranging it so it covered all the gun and most of the handcuffs. She studied him critically for a few seconds. Sloppy, she decided, definitely sloppy, but with the gun and the cuffs out of sight he didn't look nearly as threatening or alarming. They might, she thought, even be able to approach a stranger without sending him into a fit of panic.

Boldly, they stepped out onto the main deck, strolling toward the gangplank as if they hadn't a worry in the world. A couple of sailors passing by with buckets in hand glanced curiously at them, but didn't speak. A uniformed sailor stood on guard at the head of the gangplank with a clipboard in his hand, looking very stern and official. As they approached, he turned and stared at them in confusion.

"Good morning." Rick stepped past the sputtering Russian, ignoring his frantic gesturing, then bowed slightly while Fran preceded him down the gangplank. The Russian's jaw dropped in astonishment, and he began blowing a loud silver whistle that hung from a chain around his neck. The sound of footsteps approaching across the steel deck told them the alarm had been heard.

"Run, Fran!"

She ran down the gangplank as fast as she dared, Rick a step behind. He ran awkwardly, both hands out in front, clutching the big Russian automatic. At the bottom of the gangplank, he turned and looked back. It looked as if half the Russian navy was after them.

"Fran, hold it!" he yelled, skidding to a halt and facing the ship. She stopped, gaping in disbelief, then hurried over to him.

"What is it?" she demanded. "Why'd you stop?"

"Pull this slide back—quick," he snapped, ignoring the question. He indicated the top part of the Russian pistol with his chin, gripping the gun in both hands. After a second's hesitation, she understood what he wanted, and tugged on the top part of the barrel. The gun slid smoothly, and when it slid forward again with a businesslike, oiled click, the small hammer stood out from the firing chamber.

"Okay, go!"

He gave her a little shove, then pointed the gun in the general direction of the ship and squeezed the trigger several times in rapid succession. The loud, flat, shots sounded nothing like shots Fran had heard on television or the movies. The Russian pursuers were in no doubt as to the authenticity of the shots, however; two of them dived off the gangplank into the murky waters next to the pier, the rest of them disappeared at once behind railings or whatever cover was available. With a grunt of satisfaction, Rick tossed the weapon into the water.

"Why'd you do that?" Fran gasped.

"If you were a cop," Rick puffed, catching up to her, "and saw me waving a pistol around, how would you react?"

Fran nodded in understanding, saving her breath for

160

running. They ran along the dock away from the *Vostok* for several minutes, until they passed under a huge bridge. The rumble of traffic overhead was deafening, but he leaned close and yelled into her ear. "This is the Bay Bridge! If we keep heading in this direction, we'll soon be down at the Fisherman's Wharf area. There's bound to be somebody there who'll help us—the place is packed with tourists almost every day of the year."

"I—sure—hope—so," Fran panted, sucking down great gulps of air, leaning forward, resting her palms on her knees. "I'm not cut out for this running stuff, I can —tell you!"

"You're doing great so far," he replied, with a warm encouraging smile that sent a warm feeling through her. "But if we can just get to a phone, we'll be out of this. My office is less than ten minutes from right here."

"Oh, God," Fran moaned, staring back in the direction they'd just come from. "You'd better find that phone quick! Unless I'm mistaken, that's Charonsky's car—and it's headed right toward us!"

CHAPTER NINE

Rick spun around and looked in the direction she was pointing. His heart sank at the sight of the gleaming black Mercedes approaching from the direction of the docks. Charonsky's car. The driver had spotted them; the car surged forward, accelerating. In just about ten seconds, Rick figured, they were going to be recaptured. He cursed himself for having thrown the Russian automatic pistol in the bay too soon—a couple of well-placed bullets would have postponed the inevitable for at least a few minutes—and as he knew, much can happen in a few minutes.

"Look! A bus!"

He felt renewed hope as he turned in the direction she indicated and saw a San Francisco city bus slowing down for a stop less than a hundred feet from where they were standing, its air brakes hissing and snorting flatulently. The destination plate above the windshield read FISHERMAN'S WHARF.

"C'mon!" They ran toward the intersection, Fran gesturing frantically as the bus rolled to a halt and an elderly man tottered down the steps and onto the sidewalk.

"Wait!" she screamed as the driver started to pull the doors closed. The driver, a fat, middle-aged black man, stopped the bus, throwing up his hands in disgust, waiting for them with ill-disguised impatience. The instant they were both aboard he yanked the door closed and accelerated roughly away from the bus stop with a string of muttered curses.

"Stuff some quarters in the box, pal," he snapped. "Ya don't get no free rides in this town."

Bracing herself against the acceleration, Fran peered down the length of the half-empty bus and out through the rear window. About fifty yards back, the black Mercedes hung on tenaciously, like a bulldog with a bone, its blacked-out windows seeming to glint with malevolence in the sun. She nudged Rick and gestured toward the car with her chin. He nodded, watching the bus driver.

"Look driver—" he began, but the driver interrupted.

"C'mon, pal, put your fare in the box! This ain't no charity, y'know. It costs money to ride in this—" Suddenly he stopped, his eyes widening in alarm as he caught sight of the handcuffs. "Jesus, mister, what'd you do? Please don't hurt me! I got a wife and kids at home."

"Hurt you? What the hell're you talking about?" Rick snapped, preoccupied with trying to plan his next move. It was imperative that he contact his office, and quickly, before they were recaptured.

"Ain't—ain't those cuffs on your wrists, mister?" the driver quavered. He glanced quickly up at Rick, then back at the street ahead. "Listen, mister, you just forget the fare, okay? You can ride free for as far as you want to go. Hell, it's no skin off my neck, if you know what I mean."

"Hey, check it out," a lanky, bearded young man wearing granny glasses in one of the front seats called over his shoulder. "The dude with the whiskers is tellin' the driver he's a Fed! And get this—he's wearin' hand-cuffs!"

"Handcuffs?" someone yelled in alarm. Several passengers erupted in an excited clamor, craning their necks to get a glimpse of the drama taking place in the front of the bus.

"Hey, the kid's right!" somebody yelled. "The guy does have cuffs on!"

"Driver," Rick continued doggedly, leaning close in order to speak without being overheard by the passengers, "I am a federal agent. If you'll just get me to a pay phone, or flag down a policeman—"

"You want me to stop a cop?" the driver stared incredulously. "You're kiddin', right?"

From her perch on the second step of the entry to the bus, Fran peered out through the vast windshield, watching traffic and street signs. On the right side of the street, there was an apparently endless row of large, industrial-looking concrete buildings; on the left, several lanes of traffic going in both directions, separated from them by a concrete divider, and frequent intersections with narrow streets leading up steep hills into the main part of San Francisco. She saw no phone booths or police cars.

Turning, she stared out through the back window, ignoring the fascinated faces of the passengers staring back at her. The black Mercedes was still there, as if attached to the bus by invisible threads.

"No, I'm not kidding," Rick said impatiently. "Get me to a phone booth or a cop."

"Hey, the chick's been watching the black Mercedes behind us! Must be fulla Russian spies, huh!" With a guffaw of laughter, several of the passengers turned and craned their necks at the car following them.

"That's exactly what it's full of!" Fran yelled. "Those people have been holding us prisoners on a Russian ship!"

The Mercedes wavered, as if the driver was pumping

164

the brakes, and veered off, alarmed by the scrutiny of the busload of passengers. Fran turned excitedly to Rick, who had already seen what had happened. Out through the windshield of the bus she saw that they were rapidly approaching the Fisherman's Wharf area, one of San Francisco's most popular tourist attractions. Little shops, restaurants, and bistros specializing in seafood lined the narrow streets beside the bay for several blocks. Several piers jutted out into the bay, featuring shopping malls and entertainment areas alive with performers of all descriptions, from jugglers to mimes. A pair of gaily painted tour boats nosed up against a dock, a line of passengers waiting to board. They passed a parking lot glittering metallically with cars. Beyond, the sidewalks teemed with people: people walking, running, dancing, riding bicycles, and even one or two unicycles. Fran spotted a man on stilts in the crowd ahead, dressed like Uncle Sam.

"Let us off here," Rick snapped.

"But my regular stop's just—"

"Now, damn it," Rick repeated. "Stop this bus!"

"Yessir!" The air brakes squealed and belched as the bus swung in against the curb. The door opened and they quickly stepped down and surveyed the street in both directions. Traffic crawled through the district at five miles per hour; the Mercedes had gone from being an invincible foe to a helpless behemoth, Rick reflected with a grim smile. The car's superior speed would be of little avail in these crowds.

"Let's see if we can find a phone!" He was forced to raise his voice in order to be heard above the hard rock blasting from a suitcase-sized radio around which several teen-agers were dancing. In the center of a small circle, a boy was spinning rapidly on his head, his legs in the air, kicking in time to the music.

"Rick, look!" Fran pointed in the direction from

which they'd come, and he cursed as he saw what she was pointing at. Stoner was fifty yards behind them, moving through the crowds on the sidewalk like a battleship through a fleet of yachts, shoving smaller people aside without a second glance, ignoring the howls of protest and curses in his wake.

"Damn," Rick muttered, "I think he's spotted us."

Even as he spoke, Stoner whooped triumphantly, his hoarse yell audible even above the rock music, and gestured broadly, signaling to someone across the street. Rick looked and saw Redwing on the other side of the street. Redwing grinned wolfishly when he saw that he'd been spotted, and began loping toward them, ignoring the angry horn blasts and screeching brakes.

"Let's run for it," Rick said resignedly, and they began thrusting against the crowd, moving as rapidly as they could away from their pursuers.

"Let's cut in there," Fran suggested, as they approached a sign advertising Pier 39. "Maybe we can find a place to hide for a while."

"Why not?"

Shrugging, Rick bent low in an attempt to blend in with the crowd as they turned right onto Pier 39, hoping Stoner and Redwing would miss their turn and continue on toward the main section of Fisherman's Wharf. They trotted down the wide plank boardwalk and through an alleyway between two rows of two-storied buildings. They emerged into an open square, surrounded on all sides by the two-story buildings, which housed a wide variety of shops and restaurants. They ran down the boardwalk, barely glancing at the lovely, old-fashioned carousel that occupied a prominent spot in the center of the square. Ornately carved and beautifully restored wooden horses from another era pranced once again on polished brass poles, ridden by laughing children and adult tourists to the accompaniment of a calliope blasting out traditional merry-go-round music.

They darted off to the right, footsteps echoing on the boardwalk, until they had to stop to catch their breath. Rick spotted a recessed doorway in front of a shop called Mandrake's, and pulled Fran in after him, holding her against his chest as they both heaved for breath.

"Hold—it—for a—minute," he puffed. "I think we might have given them the slip."

"I sure hope so." She slumped against him, then tensed as Redwing appeared on the opposite side of the square, running with his head low and on the move, like a bloodhound casting about for spoor. He paused, and for an instant it seemed to Fran his ugly face looked directly at them. She shuddered as Redwing looked away, then moved on.

"That means Stoner's gotta be on this side of the square."

Pulling Fran around in front of him, they slipped quietly inside the shop and walked quickly into the dimly lit interior. They knelt in front of a display case, where they wouldn't be easily seen from the boardwalk, watching the window.

Fran hissed in alarm as Stoner's profile appeared at the window, and she clung to Rick until he moved on by. With a sigh of relief, Rick started to get to his feet, then froze alertly at the sight of the merchandise on display in the glass case before which they'd been kneeling.

"Hey," he exclaimed, nudging her on the shoulder. "Look at this." In the display case were several pairs of handcuffs, identical to the ones around his wrists. "Mandrakes . . . of course," he said. "A magician's shop! Maybe—"

He broke off as a slender young man dressed in black approached them, a helpful smile on his face. A wary expression came over his face as he observed the condition of their clothes and the stubble on Rick's face.

"Yes, sir, how can we help you today?"

"You can help me plenty, I hope," Rick said, a rueful expression on his face. "Somebody gave me these yesterday, and just as a gag, I put them on. It wasn't til then I found out the rotten so-and-so had lost the key! Big joke, right?" He glanced at the young man's face, who appeared to relax slightly as Rick went on, "Hell, I couldn't even get my clothes off or shave this morning, because of these damned things. The thing is, her brother—" he nodded at Fran—"said he bought them here, so I was kinda hoping . . ."

"Ah, of course. You want the key. No-o-o problem!" Kneeling behind the display case, the young man unlocked the display case and took a key from one of the sets. Rick held out his wrists and sighed with relief as the cuffs fell away. The young man beamed at them. "Say, I hope I'm not going to find out tomorrow that you're some kind of escaped criminal or something!"

"Far from it." Rick glanced over his shoulder; the boardwalk out front was clear, no sign of Stoner or Redwing. He turned back to the clerk. "As a matter-of-fact, I'm a federal agent. I'd appreciate it if you'd let me use your phone."

"I see." The clerk frowned and backed up a step. "Well, our only phone is back in the office, and . . ."

"Just give me two minutes with the phone, and I'll see you get official thanks from the Defense Intelligence Agency! Okay?"

"I dunno . . ." The young man shook his head uneasily, taking another step back. "You have any ID?"

"It was taken away from me! Look—" But the young man had turned and hurried through a door leading to the inner part of the building. They heard a click as he locked the door behind himself.

"Damn it!" Rick slammed his hand down on the counter, an angry, frustrated expression on his face. "You're crippled in this society without an ID!" He sighed in resignation. "Well, let's see if we can find a pay phone somewhere."

They turned toward the door, then froze as Stoner pushed into the shop, wearing a broad, triumphant grin. He strolled toward them, the picture of confidence, reaching lazily for the weapon Rick knew rested in an armpit holster under his jacket.

"Well, well," Stoner drawled, "It's just like the old saying, isn't it? You can run, but you can't hi—oof!"

Rick had moved with lightning speed, his right leg shooting up and out, his heel catching Stoner squarely in the middle of the solar plexus. Fran gaped, almost as astonished as Stoner, who hit the floor with a thud that shook the building. He stared up at Rick in shock, slowly turning purple. Rick reached down and plucked the pistol, a snub-nosed .38 revolver, from the holster in Stoner's right armpit. After jamming the small pistol into the waistline of his trousers in the small of his back, he took Fran by the elbow and led her around the gasping, heaving Stoner. Stoner reached up and grasped Rick's trouser cuff in a feeble attempt to stop them, but Rick shook him loose with ease and stepped over him.

Outside, Fran stared at him in admiration, thrilled and impressed by the manner in which Rick had dealt with a much larger opponent—and who was armed as well. Maybe there was something to this old-fashioned macho stuff, she reluctantly concluded, smiling dreamily.

Rick stood on the boardwalk, looking in both directions for a sign of Redwing or any other pursuers. Charonsky had not made an appearance, yet they knew he had to be nearby. He frowned at the thought. It would do no good to continue on toward the end of Pier

39; there was nothing in that direction but the San Francisco Bay. They had to head back toward the street outside, which led down into the Fisherman's Wharf district. They would just have to keep their eyes open and hope to spot Charonsky before he spotted them.

"What're you grinning about?" he asked as he took her arm and moved her along the boardwalk. They began walking past the row of tiny, expensive specialty shops, pretending to be part of a group of chattering tourists a few paces in front of them. They passed a glassblower, who was working on public view, behind a plate-glass window.

"Oh, nothing," she said, feeling a surge of admiration for the glassblower, who was putting the finishing touches on a tiny glass butterfly that looked as if it could fly away. "I was just thinking . . ."

"Well, save your happy thoughts until we're out of this, okay? We've got rid of my cuffs, and we've got a gun, but we're a long way from being safe." He looked around, leaning out to look beyond the group in front of them. "Damn. Where'd they put all the pay phones? China?"

They paused in the alleyway that opened up out onto the street while Rick looked for any sign of Charonsky. He saw nothing, not even the Mercedes, no sign of Redwing, either. A chill stirred the hair on the back of his neck: it was too damned easy all of a sudden.

"See anybody?" he asked Fran softly, one hand resting on his hip, inches away from the butt of the .38 they'd taken from Stoner. She shook her head. "Me either," he muttered, "but unless I'm mistaken, that's a row of pay phones over there by the ticket booths for the harbor tours." He took another careful look around, then stepped out into the opening.

"Gotcha!" came a loud shout, and Rick spun around to see Redwing leaning over the railing on the second story of the building they'd just stepped away from. He'd been waiting on the second-story boardwalk, confident that they had to come back this way. Rick swore for having overlooked something so obvious.

Redwing vaulted lightly over the railing and clung to the second-story boardwalk for an instant by his fingertips, then dropped lightly to the ground. By the time he turned to face his quarry, Fran and Rick were running pell-mell toward Fisherman's Wharf.

"Why didn't you use the gun?" Fran gasped as they reached the street and ran through the mob of pedestrians as fast as they could.

"I wouldn't shoot in these crowds," Rick replied, speaking in jerky bursts. "But Redwing wouldn't hesitate. It was too dangerous."

Up ahead a crowd had gathered around a pair of jugglers who rode in tiny circles on unicycles, all the while keeping half a dozen shining knives aloft. They dodged through the crowd, jostling the gawking onlookers as they hurried on. The aroma of fried shrimp suddenly assailed their nostrils, and Rick felt almost faint with yearning as they ran past an open-air sidewalk cafe specializing in fried seafoods. A well-dressed man was crossing the sidewalk up ahead of them with a paper basket of shrimp. Rick tried to avoid him, but as they ran past he jostled the man's elbow, causing him to spill his food. He looked up in outrage and Fran gasped.

"Charonsky!"

Already Charonsky was hurrying across the narrow street to the parked Mercedes, gesturing furiously. At his beckoning the two rear doors of the black car sprang open and two burly-looking men leaped out and took up the chase. Fran groaned inwardly as she heard an encouraging yell from behind. Redwing was back there, pounding tirelessly after them.

It seemed futile to her to continue running. Three

large armed men against the two of them seemed almost insurmountable odds to her. Still, she reflected, there was the way Rick had dispatched Stoner, back in the magic shop; make that four large men after them, if Stoner had sufficiently recovered to resume the chase.

"This way." Rick jerked her around a corner and turned toward the bay, the gleam of sunshine on the water in the near distance. The street was short and narrow, less than a hundred yards long. They came to an alleyway between two rows of restaurants, and he cut swiftly into it, glancing over his shoulder. Halfway down the alley was a large, industrial Dempsey dumpster of the kind used by restaurants and stores to hold trash.

"Inside," he said after glancing inside.

"In—there?" she asked incredulously.

"Damn it, there's no time to argue!" Unceremoniously, he scooped her up in his arms and lifted her roughly to the lip of the dumpster. He pushed her over and dropped her, ignoring her squeal of protest.

"Get down and lie still!" He vaulted inside with her and pulled the steel half-lid down, enclosing them in blackness. She leaned back against him, trying to still her racing heart, wrinkling her nose against the odors that assailed her nostrils. At least, she thought grumpily, the dumpster is almost empty. A few cans and boxes and some papers were piled near the opposite end, but that was all.

She snuggled close against his wide, firm chest, enjoying the closeness with him in spite of their dangerous predicament. All in all, she decided, if you had to be in such a situation, you couldn't pick a better person to be with than Rick Langtry.

"Sssh!" He tensed at the sound of running footsteps in the alley outside, just inches beyond the thin steel wall of the dumpster. The steps skidded to a halt, and she could hear Redwing's voice.

"They must've headed down this way, damn it! Probably went in the back door of one of those joints! C'mon!" There was a grunt, then the footsteps hurried away.

"That was at least two of them," Rick whispered. "That'll leave at least two more out there looking for us." He shifted position, getting comfortable. "We're probably just as well to stay right here for a while—at least until they give up searching in this area. Do you have any idea what time it is?"

She shook her head. Her watch was with her purse and other things, which had been missing since Stoner and Redwing had taken them prisoner back at the Bum Steer in Reno.

"But it must be afternoon by now," she said tentatively. "Seems like we've been running for hours and hours."

"Yeah, it seems that way, but you're probably overestimating it." She felt his arms go around her waist and pull her up against him. She laid her head back under his chin, thinking that they couldn't possibly have selected a less romantic spot in which to hide out for a few hours. Still, she thought with just a trace of smugness, it wasn't the locale; it was the company that made a situation romantic.

Rick leaned back against the steel side of the dumpster, trying to relax. The unremitting tension of the last several hours had taken its toll; his body was as tense and keyed up as if he had been preparing for a gymnastics competition. His lips curled in the darkness as he felt Fran take one of his hands and squeeze it. As he returned the pressure, he felt a renewed surge of admiration for her. She was some woman, this Fran Barnette. When he compared her to the other women he'd known in his lifetime, he couldn't think of one who would have responded to their situation with the grace and aplomb that Fran had displayed since the very beginning. Most of them, if not all of them, would simply have given up in despair long before now, he reflected—hell, most *men* he knew would have given up by now, for that matter.

Yes, she was quite a lady. If she had a serious fault, Rick mused, it was probably her attitude about ambition—the personality and disposition that had made her a successful businesswoman at such a young age was undoubtedly part of the reason she seemed, at times, to look down on him and his choice of a career. That, along with her occasional reluctance to let him be in control sometimes, as when Charonsky had been making his threats and it was so difficult for her to remain silent and let him handle the situation. He shook his head slightly, a bemused smile on his lips. The paradox was that the very things he did not like about her—at least on a conscious level—were also among the things that attracted him so strongly. And that, he admitted to himself, was a major hurdle that would have to be gotten over, sooner or later.

Sooner or later? Whoa, boy, he told himself with a stab of alarm. You're thinking like there is a future to this relationship! Slow down, Langtry, he told himself, shifting position slightly, trying to relax.

Slow down.

Fran was beginning to relax a bit, feeling warm and secure in the circle of his strong arms and legs, which enfolded her like a child. Her head was pillowed against his chest and her elbows rested lightly on his knees. His strong arms were like a safety bar around her waist. Her eyelids began to sag a bit as they huddled together in the stygian darkness, listening to the faint street sounds outside.

174

He was some kind of man, she thought admiringly, managing to hang onto his sense of humor and keep his spirits—and hers—no matter what the situation seemed to be. Not once had he seemed to be on the edge of despair, and the only time he seemed ready to crumble was when Charonsky had threatened her.

There must be some fairly deep feelings she reflected happily; more than just the concern one would normally expect from a government agent for the well-being of a cooperative civilian in such a situation. Of course, she realized that their morning together in the cabin in the mountains had colored their relationship, making it, if nothing deeper, extremely personal. She felt a little shiver of delight as she remembered the long hours of ecstasy on the rug before the fire. She'd never experienced such a powerful, exciting, and utterly satisfying lover. Was that the way it would be every time with a man like Rick Langtry, she wondered, or had it been caused by the aphrodisiacal effect of the danger and excitement? She shook her head slightly, and felt him nuzzle her hair a little in response.

Her heart skipped a beat as his arms tightened almost imperceptibly around her, and she knew beyond any doubt whatever that whether what she felt for Rick was love or simply overwhelming physical attraction, she'd never felt anything like it, and her future, at least the immediate future, was irrevocably bound to this fascinating, exciting man. She knew one thing: that what she was sure she felt for Rick, even on the basis of having known him for only a matter of days, was stronger than anything she'd ever felt for Bill Munroe, to whom she'd been engaged for over two years and had almost married.

She wasn't about to let this one get away, she promised herself, not until she was certain of her feelings for him. Of course, so much depended upon their successful escape; nothing could be decided about her future, or his, while they remained fugitives like this. Her chin sunk to her chest, and after a little while, in spite of the danger and their incongruous surroundings, she began to doze off. Soon, she was sleeping peacefully.

"Hey, time to wake up," his voice whispered against her ear. "I think maybe we can try getting out of here now—it's been over an hour."

"Mmm." She yawned and shifted position, stretching as much as possible in the narrow confines of the dumpster. She moved out from between his legs so he could stand and push the steel cover up. More than anything in the world at that moment, she decided, she wanted a long, hot bath, followed by a complete change of clothing.

"Looks like we're in the clear," Rick muttered, after raising the lid a couple of inches and peering in as many directions as he could. Cautiously, he raised the lid the rest of the way back, dropping it and letting it slam against the side of the dumpster as it fell. He stood erect, nodding in satisfaction after a moment.

"C'mon." He held out his hand to help her. When she was on her feet, he vaulted lightly over the side of the dumpster, landing on the surface of the alley. She climbed awkwardly to the lip of the dumpster, where he took her in his strong arms and lowered her gently to the ground. They paused in that position for a moment, their eyes locked together, and she leaned forward a bit as if to receive his kiss. Rick looked away and released her, and the moment was lost.

"Damn," he said, leaning back and rubbing the small of his back. "That pistol about wore a hole in me."

"Why didn't you move it? You could've shifted it to a pocket or something."

"You were asleep." He looked back at her, his eyes

seeming to caress her for an instant before hardening again. "I didn't want to bother you after you nodded off. No telling when we'll get to put our heads down for a good night's sleep." Briskly, he stepped toward the mouth of the alley, where he paused and looked up and down the street.

"C'mon. There's a little cafe up there with a public telephone inside. We'll call in from there." He turned to her, a warm smile on his face. "Maybe, with a little luck, we'll be able to sleep in nice clean beds tonight."

"Mmm." She fluffed her hair with her hands. "After a nice hot bath, of course."

"Oh, but of course," he said in a terrible, phony French accent that made her smile. Hand in hand they walked across the narrow street and entered the small cafe. Across the plate-glass window in front was a large painting of a deep-fried shrimp in full color, above which the words LUIGI'S SEAFOOD were neatly lettered. When they stepped through the door, the delicious aromas that wafted out from the kitchen were almost more than they could bear.

"Help ya, pal?" A burly, middle-aged man wearing a chef's tall hat stood behind the counter, eyeing them with a frown. Fran blushed, realizing what an unappetizing picture the two of them must be. She tried to smile reassuringly, but it didn't faze the big man's suspicious scowl.

"Just want to use the public telephone," Rick said, emphasizing the word public.

"Yeah, well, don't hang around, okay? Unless you're buyin', that is. I'm tryna run a business here, not soup kitchen."

Rick headed for the pay phone, which hung on the wall between the doors of the rest rooms. Fran entered the women's room to freshen up while he made the call. The counterman glowered, but said nothing.

"This is DIA field agent Richard Langtry," he said when the operator came on the line, "calling the Federal Building, Joseph Addison's office. Collect." He gave the number, then waited until the connection was made.

"Mr. Addison's office," Beth Ann's voice said. "May I help you?"

"Richard Langtry calling collect, will you pay?"

"Rick—! Yes, of course!" Beth Ann exclaimed delightedly. Rick was grinning so hard it hurt his cheeks. "Rick, where are you? We've got half the agents in this district out scouring the town, looking for you!"

"Hi, Beth Ann. Right now we're down on Fisherman's Wharf, believe it or not. Is the old man there?"

"I'll put him on at once. He's been simply out of his mind with worry over you two. Just a second, Rick."

"Rick, boy, how the hell are you!" Addison's voice boomed into his ear a moment later. "And where the hell are you?"

"We're fine, chief. We're down here on Fisherman's Wharf, in a little place called Luigi's Seafood. We're hungry and dirty and tired as hell, and the sooner you get somebody down here to pull us in, the better I'll like it."

"Um, yes, well . . . where've they been holding you, son?" Addison asked. "I told them, if anybody could escape, it'd be you."

"Thanks," Rick said wryly. "We've been aboard some Soviet rust-bucket called the *Vostok*. The *Vostok*'s tied up down at one of the docks, taking on a cargo of flour and wheat. I don't know which dock, but the harbor master'll know. Right now, all I want is a shower and a shave and a change of clothes—and something to eat. The smells in this place're driving me nuts!"

"Well, let's think about things for a minute, Rick. We don't want to forget our original reason for enlisting the services of this Barnette woman now, do we? We set out to catch a nest of spies, and that's what our top priority must remain, don't you agree?"

"Look, chief," he snapped, "they didn't fall for our little ploy. They knew in less than twenty-four hours they had a counterfeit diskette on their hands. And besides, we never even got near this Aramas character in Reno. Charonsky's boys picked us up and brought us back here. So what's to be gained? Hell, we've known Charonsky was KGB for a long time, no matter what kind of fancy title they put on him at their embassy." He looked up and nodded as Fran emerged from the rest room and stood next to him, smiling tentatively. "Now would you please quit stalling and have Jack come down here and pick us up?"

Addison cleared his throat uncomfortably. "I'm afraid that's not possible. A decision has been made at a much higher level than myself. It was decided that if you managed to bust out and make contact, that you should be instructed to permit yourself to be recaptured. Now, hold on, damn it!" he snapped, when Rick began sputtering in protest. "I've got a man on his way down there right now to put you under surveillance, and we've got another team heading for the *Vostok*. They won't be able to get an ant on or off that ship without us knowing about it." Addison paused, then added, "this call is coming in on my speaker phone, and I had an office full of agents in for a staff meeting when you called. I've been sending them out of here as fast as you've been giving me pieces of info—"

"Is Jack there?"

"Hi, buddy," Jack's familiar voice echoed slightly, as he was standing a few feet from the speaker phone. There was no mistaking the relief and tension in his voice. "I tried to talk these people out of this thing, but it's no go. Look's like you're stuck, at least for now."

Rick pressed the phone to his temple, thinking. He

179

could understand the strategy Addison was proposing; having a man on the inside, under surveillance, could result in the accumulation of important intelligence. They already knew about Stoner and Redwing. How many more might be uncovered if he went along with Addison's plan?

"Okay, then," he said, "but what about Fran—Miss Barnette? We've no right to ask anything further of her. She's done what she signed on to do. Now let's cut her loose while we have the chance." Fran was tugging his sleeve urgently, he shook her off impatiently. "Wait a minute, damn it," he snapped. "I'm trying to save your butt!"

"All right, Rick," Addison's voice came back on the line. "I've made a command decision. The Barnette woman can come in now. As I said, we've got a car on the way down there right now—it should be there in less than ten minutes. Just keep her out of harm's way until then, and she'll be out of this with the grateful thanks of Uncle Sam."

"Rick," Fran hissed, tugging at his sleeve with frantic urgency now. Turning, he frowned.

"What the—?" he turned pale at the sight of Redwing standing just inches away, holding a large blue steel .357 magnum in his hand. Rick tensed, as if preparing to make a move. Redwing gripped Fran by the arm and placed the muzzle of the revolver at her left ear.

"Go ahead, try it, Langtry," he snarled. "Just one of your cute moves and I'll splash this chick's brains all over the wall! Huh? Wanna try me?" He grunted when Rick relaxed. "Yeah, that's what I told Stoner—you're not so damned tough. Say 'bye-bye' now," he said, gesturing at the phone.

"Rick—? What's going on?" Addison's voice could be heard piping thinly from the handset until Rick re-

180

placed the receiver. He moved slowly, hoping that the DIA agent on his way to pick up Fran would arrive in time to help.

"Let's all walk outside together now, okay? Stoner's anxious to see you, Langtry. I think he has something that belongs to you . . ."

"Any trouble?" the man behind the counter stared alertly, wiping his hands on a towel.

"No trouble at all." Redwing stepped back slightly, revealing the revolver. The counterman's eyes bulged with excitement and curiosity. "San Francisco PD—just a routine arrest. Nothing to get excited about, pop. Just sit down and relax."

Rick stared at the proprietor, trying desperately to convey the truth with his eyes, but he knew the only thing the cafe owner was seeing now was the huge handgun in Redwing's fist.

"He's lying," Rick said. "He's not a cop—he's a Soviet agent." The counterman's eyes sparkled with excitement as he looked from Rick to Redwing and back.

"Oh, sure," Redwing said with a relaxed chuckle. "Last week I busted a guy who squawked that I was an alien from another planet when I took him in. What'll they think of next, eh?"

"Yeah, I guess they'll try anything." The counterman leaned forward eagerly. "What'd they do, kill somebody?"

Redwing's eyes glinted with amused malice. "Worse than that, pop. These two tried to sell some of our top secret defense secrets to the Russians. How do you like that?"

"Hang the bastards, that's what I say!" the counterman gestured angrily. "Get those traitors outa my store before I take this cleaver to 'em myself!"

Outside Stoner stood next to the all too familiar van, a thoughtful expression on his face as he watched them

181

approach. As he pulled the side door open, his eyes never left Rick's face.

"That was a pretty smooth move you put on me back there on Pier 39," he said with grudging admiration. "Just to show you there's no hard feelings—" He pivoted on one foot, a huge fist moving with lightning swiftness upward into Rick's solar plexus. The air rushed out of Rick's lungs and he bent forward in reaction. Stoner's knee slammed up and caught him flush on the chin. There was an instant of dazzling, flashing light, a tremendous burst of pain, then darkness.

CHAPTER TEN

A pale, watery light penetrated the high, dirt-encrusted panes of the window at one end of the attic, creating an ambience of gloomy unreality in this, their new prison. This place, Fran thought with a shudder, made the malodorous old *Vostok* seem like a palace by comparison.

She glanced over at Rick, frowning in deepening concern. It had been hours since Stoner struck him, but he still hadn't stirred, not even to roll over. It was as if, she thought with incipient panic, he'd sunk into a coma. She'd read of people remaining in comas for months, even years, following injuries to the head.

Rick lay on his back, hands at his sides, his chest rising and falling with metronomic regularity. The lower part of his face was badly swollen and discolored; blood from the split lip had caked and dried in the whiskery stubble of his chin, giving him more than ever the aspect of a bum from skid row. She grimaced in sympathy as she looked at the split lip; it was a miracle that he had lost no teeth. He'd gotten off lightly, as far as permanent injuries went, but he was going to have a pretty sore lip for the next few days.

She looked up at the small, filthy window, up high, near the apex of the steeply pitched roof, and tried to estimate the time of day. From the angle of the sun's rays, she guessed, it must be shortly before sundown—

maybe seven thirty or eight o'clock, at this time of year. She'd glimpsed a digital clock on a bank sign through the windshield of the van, just before they'd blindfolded her, and the time then had been three fifteen. She frowned as she looked at Rick. That meant he'd been out for at least four hours.

"*Uunngh . . .*" He groaned and opened his eyes, and Fran almost wept in relief.

"How do you feel?"

"Like hell," he said, slurring his words a bit through the swollen lips. "Where are we? We're not on the *Vostok?*"

"I think it's a house," Fran said. "I was blindfolded when they brought us here, but we came up two flights of stairs, and then a ladder up into this attic. They had to carry you, of course. You should've heard them swearing when they carried you up the ladder." She shook her head, grinning. "Whew! Talk about turning the air blue."

Groaning, he sat up and looked around for a moment or two. Tentatively, he reached up and touched his face, wincing as his fingers grazed his swollen, protruding upper lip.

"What makes you think it's a house? Could it be some kind of warehouse or barn?"

"No, I'm sure it's a house. When we came in, we were on a carpeted floor, and I bumped against a sofa on the way through one of the rooms." She paused, a thoughtful expression on her face. "It just had the—the feel of a house."

He nodded. "Look at the pitch of this roof. You don't see too many houses in California with roofs like this unless it's up in snow country." He paused, thinking. "Two stories, plus a full attic. Makes me think this is an old house, Fran, maybe built around the turn of the century."

"Yes," she said eagerly, nodding. "Yes, it has an old feeling to it."

"How far did we come from Fisherman's Wharf? Do you think we're still in San Francisco? There're lots of old houses like this in the city."

"We drove for a long time, Rick. And a lot of it was on a freeway."

"About how long?"

"Well, it's hard to say." She frowned in thought. "But I'd estimate it was at least forty-five minutes, maybe even an hour. And it was fast driving, too—not city driving through traffic." She paused, then added, "And we went across a long bridge, just a little while before we arrived here. I heard them paying the toll."

He was silent for a few moments, then said, "In order to cross a long bridge, after driving fast for half an hour or forty-five minutes from San Francisco, you'd have to have been coming south, Fran. The only long toll bridge in that direction is the San Mateo, which crosses the bay into Hayward. If you're right, and I'm right, then we could be in Hayward, Fremont, San Leandro, or Castro Valley. Hell, half a dozen small cities, for that matter. The east side of the bay is solid with them."

"Whatever." Fran shrugged disinterestedly. "I'm not familiar with this—"

"Ssssh!" he cut her off, a finger to his lips. They cocked their heads, listening to the low, rumbling sound for a few seconds.

"What do you think?" he asked. "A train?"

"Yes, that's it. A fast passenger train, maybe an Amtrak. It was much too fast and too short to be a freight train."

"No," he declared. "It's BART." At her questioning expression, he explained, "BART—Bay Area Rapid Transit. We're narrowing it down, Fran," he said excitedly. "Give us a couple more clues and we'll know just where we are. About how long would you say it took to get here from the end of the bridge?"

"Oh, what good is all this doing us, anyway?" she snapped, suddenly weary of the game and feeling inexplicably cranky toward him. "Look around you, for Pete's sake! We're locked in this damned attic, we can't even see out it! So what's the difference what town we're in, anyway?"

"How long, Fran?" he asked. "From the end of the bridge to here?" He stared patiently at her until she lowered her eyes.

"I don't know," she said disspiritedly. "Maybe five, ten minutes. Something like that."

"That means we're almost certainly in Hayward."

"Wonderful. We're in Hayward. So what?"

"Well, damn it, doesn't it make you feel any better, knowing where in the hell you are? Come on, Fran, use your head. Knowledge is important."

"Yeah, I remember you going on about how important it is once before." She turned her back on him, leaning up against one of the posts that ran from the floor of the attic up to the rafters. She crossed her arms.

"Damn it, I wish I'd never agreed to work with you on this case," she muttered. "I almost wish I'd never met you."

"Oh, hey, come on, lady." He walked around to face her, stooping in order to avoid scraping his back on the sloping rafters. He was hurt and a little angered by her last remark; he'd flattered himself that she had deeper feelings for him. "One of the things I've admired about you is your refusal to let things get you down." He paused, his split, swollen lip stretched in a crooked half smile. "And remember—if you hadn't agreed to work with us on this thing, we would never have—"

"Never what?" she demanded, her hazel eyes snapping. "Made love? Fallen in love? Become lovers? Just what the hell are you trying to say to me? Because you've been very careful to never say the one thing—" She broke off abruptly, closing her mouth almost with a snap. She shook her head and looked away from him. She would not grovel, would never nag a man for a declaration he was reluctant to make of his own free will.

"What the hell did I say?" he asked, eyes wide with innocence. "What did I do? I'm just trying to keep our minds occupied in a constructive way and you turn all female and emotional on me!"

"That's right, you—you chauvinistic, macho so-and-so—make me look like a fool because I happen to be a woman!" She turned her back on him, her body rigid with anger. Her hands were trembling with rage. "Listen, if I want to play mental games with you, I'll let you know. In the meantime, how about a little privacy?"

With a disgusted snort, he turned on his heel and moved away. Women. If he lived to be a hundred, he'd never understand them.

However, his problem at the moment was not that he did not understand Fran; it was that he did. She craved some kind of commitment from him, a declaration she could cling to and use as justification for the things she'd done with him. He glanced across the space separating them. She sat rigidly, her back stiff and cold. He shook his head wonderingly. He'd have been willing to bet anything he owned that Fran had never been physically intimate with a man she didn't believe she loved at the moment; now, having made such passionate, uninhibited love with him, with no such declaration by which she could rationalize her behavior, had obviously been troubling her. In Fran Barnette's world, he thought, people did not make love just for pleasure— they did it only for love.

Love. He stared at the unrelenting figure seated there

on the dusty floor in the gathering gloom. The sun was down now, and it was almost completely dark in the attic. Did he love her? He did not know. He knew that he would do almost anything to prevent harm from coming to her—but was that love?

Once, when he'd been a teen-ager, he'd asked his father, "Dad, how did you know you were in love with Mom? Enough so you knew for sure you wanted to marry her?"

Instead of some well-worn platitude about love and commitment and the sanctity of marriage, his father's reply had been shockingly blunt. "Son, when you just can't stand the thought of another man making love to her, then there's nothing for a guy to do but marry the lady. Because then, son, you are in love."

Okay, then, he admitted to himself, by his father's standards, he was in love with her, because it was certain that he hated even the thought of another man invading that body of hers, of knowing the thrills and sensations with her that he had known. The thought was unbearable, and he thrust it away with a feeling almost of panic.

At the realization of how vulnerable he had become, a cold knot formed in the pit of his stomach. He hardened himself against her, deliberately making an effort to distance himself emotionally from her. He refused to become so much at the mercy of another human being that he could be crushed by a word or a cross glance. If that was the sort of thing that happened when you fell in love and wanted to marry the object of your love, then it was sure as hell not for him. If Richard Langtry was certain of anything in this life, it was that you had to look out for number one. And part of looking out for yourself was to never, ever lay yourself open to the whims of another or expose yourself in a way that made you vulnerable and open to pain.

To hell with all that. He sat down near the other end of the attic and leaned back against one of the rafters, forcing his mind onto less personal subjects. Such as trying to figure out an escape plan, or working himself into a position to learn more about this nest of spies and agents provocateurs. Something useful, for Chrissakes —anything but moping over a woman like some damned high school boy in love for the first time.

The strained silence in the attic was broken by the sound of the trap door slamming open, followed a moment later by the appearance of Redwing's head in the opening. He took in the scene for a moment, observing the distance separating the two of them, and grinned lewdly.

"Ah, lover's quarrel, eh?" Without waiting for a reply, he hoisted himself up onto the attic floor, beckoning to someone behind to come as well. An instant later Stoner appeared, carrying a white paper bag from a fast-food outlet somewhere nearby. Fran almost fainted at the aroma of hamburgers and french fries that permeated the air.

"Hungry, folks?" Stoner asked. "Got cheeseburgers and fries and chocolate shakes here." He grinned as Fran stood up and eagerly reached for the bags. "Course, we know you'd probably rather have the cabbage soup they serve aboard the ship, but what the hell —ya got to improvise, right?"

"How long are you going to leave us up here in this damned attic, Stoner?" Rick accepted one of the cheeseburgers from Fran with a nod of thanks. She ignored him, pointedly turning away to bite greedily into her own sandwich. "No water, no furniture, no toilet facilities? We're not animals. We could use a chance to take a shower and wash our clothes." He began wolfing down

189

one of the cheeseburgers, watching the two men alertly as he ate.

"You'll each have a chance to use the john after you eat," Stoner said with a placating gesture. "And we're gonna bring up some blankets and pillows for you to use tonight. As for any other, uh, luxuries, I'm afraid that's gotta depend on your cooperation, Langtry."

"Your boss already knows I've done all the cooperating I intend to," Rick said, wiping his mouth with the back of his hand. "If you're smart, you'll let us go before this thing goes any further, Stoner. It's not too late to chalk it all up to a diplomatic misunderstanding, you know . . . but if somebody gets hurt, well, then it gets real serious."

"Ah, I gotta hand it to you, Langtry," Stoner said with a chuckle. "You're good—real good. You could almost talk me into letting you go—if it was up to me."

"Let him go if you want," Redwing said with a giggle, "but don't let her go—not yet."

Stoner's eyes came up and met Rick's in an instant of mutual understanding and disgust, then Stoner's eyes turned cold and impersonal once again.

"You're disgusting," Fran said quietly, staring at Redwing with hatred. "Disgusting and sick."

"I'll show you how disgusting and sick I really am, bitch," Redwing muttered, moving purposefully toward her. "I've been waiting for this since I first laid eyes on you!"

"Redwing!" Rick shouted, dropping the remains of his second burger to the floor and gathering himself to attack. Stoner stopped him with a massive hand on his arm.

"Hold it, Redwing," Stoner said softly, his voice heavy with menace. "If you touch that girl without permission, Charonsky'll make you wish you'd never been born."

Redwing stopped as if he'd run into a brick wall, blinking slowly as sanity returned to his staring eyes. He looked at Stoner for several seconds, then nodded. "Right," he muttered huskily. "Right. Gotta wait for permission."

As Redwing moved over and through the trapdoor to the main part of the house below, Fran shuddered visibly, making a disgusted sound. "I'd rather be dead," she said quietly, "than to let him touch me."

"Yeah, well, I'm afraid that sometimes the two sort of run together," Stoner said, glancing pointedly at Rick. "He ain't the kind of guy you'd want going out with your daughter or your sister, if you get what I mean." He gestured at the bags of food. "Lotsa stuff left in there," he said. "You guys haven't touched your milk shakes."

"I'm not hungry anymore," Fran said.

"Suit yourself." Stoner shrugged. "This stuff won't keep. It's eat it or throw it out."

"Throw it out, then!" Fran snapped. "I'm not hungry."

"Suit yourself," Stoner repeated, shrugging. He glanced at his watch. "Anybody ready for the john?"

Fran got to her feet, nodding, and followed the big man down the ladder. The instant they were out of sight, Rick hurried over and yanked at the handle of the trapdoor. Damn. It was locked or fastened on the other side, and after Boris's misfortune aboard the *Vostok*, it was unlikely that anyone would be careless about checking it frequently.

When Fran returned, she marched over to her section of the attic and sat down with her back to him. Rick stared at her for a moment, then followed Stoner down the ladder to the main part of the house. He tried to observe everything, his eyes swiveling from the floor to

191

the ceiling to the walls to the hardware on the doors. It was an old house, that much was clear.

Countless layers of paint were caked on the doors and trim around the doors, and the carpet on the floor, obviously of high quality, was threadbare and worn. Wainscoting of dark wood panels covered the walls to shoulder level, and then wallpaper ran to the ceiling; an old-fashioned, muted pattern that hadn't been popular in fifty years or more.

An Edwardian home, Rick decided, walking down the hallway as slowly as possible. At least two stories high, with a full attic, steeply pitched roof and, he would have been willing to bet, a cellar or basement. He could almost see the gingerbread trim and curlicues on the exterior of the house, especially when he stepped into the large bathroom and noted the huge, claw-footed tub and the flush tank suspended from the ceiling above the toilet, brass flush chain hanging down, a smooth wooden handle on the end. The heavy porcelain handles on the faucets and the sturdy cabinets all reinforced the image of a house built at least eighty years ago.

"Nice old place, isn't it?" he commented lightly as he stepped back out into the hallway after using the bathroom. "Are there lots of these old Edwardian homes here in Hayward?"

"How would I—" Stoner broke off and shook his head, chuckling. He glanced at Rick, an expression of reluctant admiration on his face. "Not bad, Langtry, not bad at all. They told us to watch ourselves around you, and it looks like they knew what they were talking about."

One of the doors between the bathroom and the ladder leading up into the attic opened abruptly. Charonsky, immaculately dressed as usual, stood in the opening, smiling as Rick and his escort approached.

"Ah, Langtry," he said pleasantly. "It's good to see you again. A word, if I may?" He stepped aside, indicating that Rick should enter the room. His attitude was that of a social superior encountering a neighbor in a shopping center, and inviting the lesser individual for a drink.

"Oh, sure," Rick said dryly, stepping into the room and looking around. It appeared to be an ordinary bedroom; a double bed, large, six-drawer chest and a well-worn easy chair comprising the furniture. "Have a word, by all means."

"Please, sit, sit." Charonsky indicated the easy chair with a gracious wave. Rick sat down and crossed his legs, watching the other man warily. This was their first encounter since his and Fran's abortive escape, and he was uncertain of the Russian's reaction.

"Now, then," Charonsky said, sitting on the edge of the bed and carefully hitching up the cuff of his trousers to preserve the knifelike crease. "I hope you've had your fill of this foolish resistance, and are ready to cooperate with us."

"If that's what you want," Rick said, getting to his feet and wearily shaking his head, "we have nothing to discuss."

"Sit!" It was the first time he had heard the Russian raise his voice, and he looked at him in surprise. Charonsky's handsome face was grim.

"The time for games is over, Langtry. You're going to cooperate with us or you are going to regret it very much."

"You know," Rick said after a few seconds, "I've often wondered about myself. How much could I take if I was tortured? Hell, I suppose everybody—at least everybody in our line of work—wonders about that from time to time. Know something? I don't really care how much I could take. I just know I'm not going to cave in

193

and help you . . . not because you're a Russian and I'm an American, but because I just can't stand assholes like you who dress like dukes and have the mind of thugs." He crossed his arms and leaned back, his mouth dry with expectation. *Now it begins,* he thought, *I've provoked him into action for sure this time.*

"Clever, very clever." Charonsky stared at Rick for several seconds, then stepped over and opened the door leading into the hallway. "Stoner, get Redwing up here, will you please? Thanks." As Stoner's heavy footsteps hurried down the hallway and clattered down a flight of stairs, the Russian turned back to face Rick, an impassive expression on his face. He shot his cuff and glanced at a thin, elegant gold wristwatch.

"What's the deal?" Rick asked, his palms beginning to perspire in spite of his determination not to show fear. "Need your toadies to do your dirty work for you?"

It was as if Rick had not spoken. Charonsky reacted only when the sound of footsteps pounding down the hallway heralded the arrival of Redwing. There was a single rap on the door.

"You wanted me, Mr. Charonsky?"

"Ah, very good," Charonsky looked pleased when he looked up from his watch. "Twenty-seven seconds flat. Yes, please step in here, Redwing."

The door opened and Redwing's bulk filled the opening. His dark eyes glittered with malice as he looked unblinkingly at Rick for a few seconds, then turned his attention to his employer.

"Yeah, Mr. Charonsky?"

"Please, Redwing," Charonsky held up a hand, a pained expression on his face. "I've asked you to not use that honorific with me. It's not 'mister'—it's 'comrade'. *Comrade!*"

"Yes, uh, comrade." Redwing shot Rick a poisonous

glance, embarrassed at being rebuked before their prisoner. Rick watched expressionlessly, wondering what Charonsky was planning.

"You've been a rather naughty boy again, haven't you?" Charonsky said quietly. Redwing fidgeted and slowly turned a dull, brick red, the color spreading upwards from his neck. His pockmarked features flamed with color under the Russian's direct questioning stare. He swallowed like a schoolboy called on the carpet by his principal.

"Wha—whaddya mean, Mi—Comrade Charonsky?" he asked hoarsely.

"Comrade Stoner informs me that he had to—dispose of the body of a young female early this morning. Seems she had been invited around to your apartment and things got a little out of hand." Charonsky looked at the big man with a chiding expression, *tsk-tsking.* "What saddens me is that the young lady was at your place at my invitation, Redwing. Is that any way for you to treat a guest provided by your employer?"

"But—you know how I am. I thought that was the whole idea, mi—comrade!"

"Tell our guest, Langtry, what you did to the young lady," Charonsky said. Redwing gaped at him, and Charonsky compressed his lips into a flat, uncompromising line. Redwing swallowed and nodded.

"Okay, if . . . if you're serious." He turned and stared at Rick for a moment, twisting his big, calloused hands together, cracking the knuckles repeatedly as he spoke.

"Well, first off, I tied her hands and feet to the corners of the bed . . ." He paused, licking his lips, a light coming into his eyes as he thought back. "Then I took my knife and cut her clothes all away, till she was stark naked. Then I—"

"All right, all right, I get the picture!" Rick interrupted, glaring at Charonsky. "What's the point of this anyway?"

"The 'point,' as you put it," Charonsky said with a smile, "is that when Stoner cleaned the place up—well, let's just say that even though he has seen many things in his life, he was shocked at the things that had been done." He paused, staring at Rick to ensure that he understood, then raised his voice. "Stoner! Are you there?" At the gruff reply, he said, "Come in, please."

Charonsky studied Rick with a half-smile on his lips until Stoner entered the room. Stoner glanced at Rick, a hint of sympathy in his eyes, then looked back at the KGB man. "Yeah?"

"Just stand by for the moment." Charonsky's smile grew wider as he turned to Redwing and said, "Redwing, you'd like to have the woman in the attic—Miss Barnette—to yourself for a few hours, wouldn't you?"

"Hey, wait just a damned minute!" Rick started to get out of the chair. Stoner shoved him roughly back into the chair, giving a little warning shake of his head.

"Don't get yourself hurt, Langtry," he muttered. He stepped back and drew a pistol, and aimed it loosely in the direction of Rick's left knee.

"Ever seen a man kneecapped, Langtry?" Stoner asked conversationally. "Ugly. Damned ugly."

"You can't do this, Charonsky!" Rick subsided back into the chair, a sick sensation spreading through his middle at the avid expression on Redwing's face.

Charonsky lifted an eyebrow. "Go get her, Redwing," he said. "She's yours." With a soft moan, Redwing moved toward the door.

"No!" Rick yelled. He started up out of the chair, subsiding when Stoner took careful aim and pulled back the hammer, cocking the pistol. Rick was sick with horror at the way Redwing ran from the room, his footsteps pounding down the hallway now, moving toward the end of the hall where the ladder leading up into the attic was located.

"Charonsky!" he yelled, twisting in agony. "No!" Squeezing his eyes shut, he imagined the horror and revulsion Fran would feel when she realized that the big, ugly, pockmarked pervert had finally come for her, that there was really nobody there to stop him, not this time. He pictured those big, calloused hands ripping her clothing from her body, pawing her, invading her, forcing her—

"Stop him, Charonsky," he said, when he realized that the Russian was not, had never been, bluffing; that he was perfectly willing to sacrifice Fran to Redwing's perverted, sadistic pleasures in order to secure Rick's cooperation. "I'll do whatever you want."

Lazily, Charonsky inspected the perfectly manicured fingernails of his right hand, then buffed them against his lapel. "Are you quite certain, Langtry?" he murmured. "We wouldn't want you to feel you were helping us against your will, now, would we?"

Stoner snorted with a combination of derision and amusement, but the pistol aimed at Rick's knees never wavered. From down the hall came the sound of Redwing beginning to pull down the ladder leading up to the attic. Rick groaned aloud.

"Oh, is that a yes?" Charonsky asked.

"Stop him!" Rick roared, his face twisted with anguish. "I'll do anything you say! Just stop him."

"Very well." Charonsky looked at Stoner and lifted his chin in a signal. Stoner hurried from the room, cursing under his breath. Charonsky studied Rick through narrowed eyes. "Stoner has stopped him, Langtry, before he got up into the attic, because you have agreed to cooperate." He paused to allow that time to sink in, then went on: "There is one other condition, my friend. You are to tell the Barnette woman nothing of this conversation, nothing. If I learn that she has discovered what transpired here today, I will turn her over to Redwing and there is no power on this earth that will drag him away a second time. Listen!" He cocked his head toward the door, listening to the sound of Stoner's angry roars and Redwing's howls of protest as Stoner dragged him away from the hallway near the trapdoor to the attic. There was a scuffle, then a thud as something heavy hit the floor.

"Redwing's getting better," he said thoughtfully. "When he first joined us here, Stoner could've stopped him in less than five seconds. He's been learning."

"He's had good teachers," Rick said wearily, slumping back into the chair in relief.

"Yes, indeed he has." Charonsky paused for a few seconds, waiting until Stoner came down the hallway dragging Redwing's unconscious body by the heels. Stoner left him outside the door and came back into the room.

"You shouldn't tease him that way, comrade," he said, taking a deep breath. "I thought for a minute I wasn't going to be able to stop him."

"You need your practice, too," Charonsky said, with a meaningful glance at Rick. Stoner colored and dropped his eyes. "And besides, Stoner, I was not teasing him. If Langtry hadn't come to his senses, I would have let it go on until Redwing was finished with her."

Charonsky turned and stared at Rick for a moment, frowning. "You need a shave, and something for that swelling on your lip . . ." He looked at his watch. "Stoner, get this man into the shower and get a clean set of clothes for him. Let him shave and do whatever you can for that lip—maybe some makeup, if need be."

"Makeup?"

"Yes, makeup," Charonsky said. "In a little over an hour we're going to make a video tape. Oh, let Miss

Barnette clean up, too, and get her something to wear. If there're no women's clothes here that fit her, she can wear men's clothes."

"You're the boss," Stoner said amiably. "I'll send Mitchik up for the dame. C'mon, pal," he said, nudging Rick's leg with his foot. "You're gonna shower and get cleaned up. And it's about time, too, if you're asking me."

When Rick returned to the attic forty-five minutes later, Fran was leaning against one of the rafters, watching him with a thoughtful expression on her face. She had been grateful for the opportunity to shower and change her clothing, but she was wondering at the reason for this sudden largesse from their captors. She plunged her fists deep into the pockets of the faded, too-large blue jeans she'd been given, hiking up the man's white dress shirt in order to do so, staring thoughtfully at Rick all the while.

"What have you done, Rick?" she asked coolly. "Sold out?"

"What do you mean?"

"These clothes. The shower. These people didn't give them to us out of the goodness of their hearts! You did something to earn them for us, and I want to know what."

"I don't know what the hell you're talking about," he snapped. "I promised them I'd help make a video tape for them to send to DIA headquarters. To help us maybe get the hell out of here. Why?" he added, a truculent, defensive expression on his face. "Would you rather have your filthy clothes back?"

"They were clean in a way these can never be!" she retorted angrily. "What was the price, Rick, for your shower and a shave and some fresh clothes? I see you made out a little better than I did," she added, scornfully looking him up and down, taking in the neatly pressed gray slacks and the light blue knit sport shirt. "Your clothes fit."

She paused, hating herself for the way she was attacking him, but she was unable to stop herself. From almost the very first moment they'd met, he'd made her feel as if she was something less than a loyal, patriotic American, as if there were something intrinsically wrong with operating a business and earning a decent profit, implying that there was something selfless and noble about working for the government as he did. And now, after he had practically shamed her into helping the DIA with this case, he was now the first one to capitulate, to cooperate with their captors.

"Can you look at yourself in the mirror and call yourself a man, or do you see nothing but—nothing but a turncoat?" she taunted.

"Fran, shut up. You don't know what you're talking about," he said quietly.

She had to avert her gaze from the pain in his dark brown eyes, but his hurt didn't make his betrayal any easier to accept.

"Trust me, please. I wouldn't do anything to hurt my country—or you. I know it's asking a lot, but that's all I can tell you. Trust me."

"Oh, that's all you can tell me, is it? For my own good, I suppose. No doubt it's classified information." She suddenly stood up and walked over to stand face to face with him. "I know this much, Rick. This is the first decent treatment we've had out of these people—and isn't it significant that it comes immediately after your long session downstairs with our friend, Charonsky!"

"Please. You don't know what you're saying." His face was white with anger; little muscles jumped and bunched in his jaw as he struggled to maintain control. "Please stop, Fran."

She stared at him for a moment, fighting the urge to throw herself into his strong arms and weep, to release the fear and uncertainty she couldn't help feeling at this puzzling new turn of events. She wanted things to be the way they were back in the mountains, at the cabin, before they'd been recaptured by Stoner and Redwing. There was none of this ambiguousness, this doubt then. Something had happened while Rick was downstairs; she would have been willing to bet anything she possessed on that. If he was so totally innocent, why was he now acting so evasive, so secretive? He definitely had something to hide, something he was so ashamed of that he couldn't even discuss it with her. Something was gravely wrong; she knew it intuitively.

"Don't you think that just because you got a shower and a change of clothing for us that I'll go along with you and your Russian pals in any fishy deals. Any deals you made, just leave me out of them. I'm not ready to sell my country down the drain even if you are!"

Her lips curled with contempt as he winced from her words, as if in actual, physical pain. If that wasn't guilt on his face, she thought with a sinking heart, she was the Easter bunny.

"And you were the one who talked about doing things simply from patriotism." She shook her head slowly. "You're some patriot, Langtry."

"Just shut up, Fran," he said in a dull monotone. "Just shut your mouth, before you go too far."

"Too far?" She gave a scornful laugh that threatened to turn into a sob of anger and regret. "How can I go too far, with you? You—you traitor!"

"Stop, Fran!" He seized her by the wrist, squeezing hard, trying to force her back around to face him. She twisted loose with a violent lunging motion and swung a looping, roundhouse right fist that connected with the side of his head just behind his left eye. He staggered

201

back, releasing her, groaning with the pain of having been struck once again on his aching, swollen, throbbing head.

"I've had about all the abuse from men I'm going to take in one day!" Fran stood defiantly in front of him, daring him to fight back. She didn't soften or relent when he just held his throbbing head and turned away, groaning.

Rick Langtry had one hell of a lot to answer for, as far as she was concerned.

"Okay, lovebirds," came a derisive voice from the opening of the trapdoor. "Let's get downstairs. We've got a movie to make!"

CHAPTER ELEVEN

On Wednesday morning an overnight express mail parcel was delivered to the Federal Building in downtown San Francisco. Boldly lettered across the front of the eight-by-ten-inch parcel in red Magic Marker were the words: For Joseph Addison III.

Twenty minutes later Jack O'Brien, Pete Smith, John Simmons, and Jerry Whitworth were seated on plush armchairs in the VIP Conference Room, staring at a large-screen television set to which a video recorder had been connected. Addison sat at the head of the table, stopping and starting the tape to discuss various points of interest with the agents. He'd just frozen the action, and there was a lively discussion going on.

"Look through that doorway," Whitworth, who had flown over from the Reno office, said excitedly. "Where they let the camera drift away from the Barnette girl for a second—isn't that a calendar on the wall? Looks like the kitchen, from the cupboards and countertop that are visible."

Addison squinted at the frame, nodding in agreement. "I believe you're right, Jerry. Looks like one of those calendars given away by banks and garages every year . . ." He hit the zoom button, enlarging the frame significantly. "This year's calendar, all right. And the name of the bank is clear enough. But I can't make out

203

the address of the branch office underneath; can any-body else?"

There was a general negative rumble, so Addison pushed the play button, allowing the tape to resume. Rick Langtry's battered face filled the screen again as they moved in for a closeup. Jack O'Brien sucked in his breath at the swelling and bruises that remained visible beneath the caked layer of pancake makeup.

"This is Special Agent Richard Langtry," he said tonelessly. He displayed the front page of Sunday's edition of the San Francisco *Examiner,* and the camera zoomed in on the date. "As you can see, we're alive and well—as of this moment." The camera panned from Rick across to Fran Barnette in the chair next to him, then back to Rick.

"Alive, maybe, but he sure doesn't look too good, does he?" O'Brien said thoughtfully. "And look at the girl—she looks mad as hell. 'Course, I guess you can't blame her. She comes up for a long weekend at Tahoe and winds up in this friggin' mess."

"Ssh!" Addison hit the volume button and a low rumble emanated from the speakers. It continued for perhaps six or seven seconds, then faded. "Anybody have any ideas about that sound?"

"Car or truck going by outside the house?" Whitworth suggested.

"Hell, for all we know," John Simmons's deep bass voice growled, "it could've been generated by the mechanism of the video recorder itself."

"Possibly, but I don't think so," Jack said. "I've got a buddy on the San Francisco PD. He's their resident sound expert. If anybody can tell us what that sound was, he can."

"All right, O'Brien," Addison said. "You run over there after we break up here and see what you find out." He turned back to the screen, pushing the play button.

". . . We're cooperating in the making of this tape," Rick's toneless voice continued, "because we want to be released as soon as possible. This will not happen until the diskette that had been paid for is returned to a designated representative of the persons who are holding us captive. I've been instructed to inform you that you have seven days from now, Sunday night, to deliver. After that time, my life and that of Miss Barnette will be forfeited."

"Stop the tape!" Jack O'Brien said. Addison glanced at him with raised eyebrows, but did as requested.

"I don't know about the rest of you," Jack said, "but I take that threat seriously. These people are pros and they're perfectly capable of killing a couple of innocent people to make a point."

"Doesn't make sense, O'Brien," Addison argued. "Once they kill either one of them, they've thrown away their only bargaining chip." He paused, staring off into space, then shook his head decisively. "No, I think the thing for us to do is to play along with them—whoever the hell they are—for as long as possible. Negotiate, stall, keep them talking. Maybe even doctor up another diskette, if it comes to that . . .

"No, I just can't see them killing Rick or Miss Barnette, O'Brien." He shook his head again. "So far there's been only one death in this case—Cindy Linkwell, and she died from natural causes. I just don't see them starting to knock people off at this stage of the game. Hell, they're smart enough to know it wouldn't do them any good."

"Look, we don't know who the hell we're dealing with here," Jack retorted. "What makes sense to you and I might not even register with them. If they're terrorists—"

"That's never been proven," Addison interjected quickly.

"Not proven, maybe, but don't forget the Aramas connection, and the strong indications from brother agencies he had ties with the PLO." Jack stopped, an impatient look on his face, then went on. "At any rate, I disagree with a policy of stalling and negotiating and hoping for a change of heart from these people. I want us to be a hell of a lot more active, not just sit around and wait for things to happen!"

"Hear, hear," Jerry Whitworth murmured, clapping his hands in approval.

"What is this, a mutiny?" Addison looked at them for a moment, wearing an expression of annoyance mixed with amusement. "Look, men, I know Rick is a personal friend, as well as a professional colleague, and believe me, I—"

"I want your authorization for unlimited overtime and travel until this thing is cleared up one way or another," Jack said flatly. "And it'd be nice to have some more men to help us out. The surveillance on the *Vostok* has resulted in exactly nothing—no sign of Rick or of the two guys who picked them up at the cafe. And nobody seems to have seen the van—in spite of the good description we have." He paused, drawing a deep breath. "And now this—this tape. It's obvious they're miles from the damned ship we've been pinning all our hopes on, so we're back to square one. I need help and I need it badly."

"I'll volunteer," Whitworth said at once. "I might not be as young as I used to be and I know I've been behind a desk for too damned long, but I still know how to wear out the shoe leather tracking down leads when I have to. If you'll have me, I'm in."

Jack shot him a grateful grin, nodding.

"Count me in, too," Simmons said. "Authorized overtime or not—I'm not going to sit around on my fat butt while one of our boys is sweating out his life."

206

"I'm in, too," Smith said tersely.

Addison threw up his hands. "All right, O'Brien, looks like you've got your team. You run the show, of course. Daily reports to me by close of business—and I want to be phoned at night in case of significant developments. Clear?" Jack nodded, and Addison got to his feet, tossing the remote control unit for the VCR across the table to Jack.

"I'll leave you to it, then. It's nine forty-five now . . . I expect my first report by five o'clock this evening."

"You'll have it," Jack promised. As Addison walked toward the door of the conference room, Jack added softly, "And thanks, chief."

"What the hell," Addison said gruffly. "I kind of like the guy, too." The door closed and Jack turned to the members of his team with a purposeful expression on his round face.

"First off," he said, "let's have one more look at that tape, start to finish, no interruptions. There's something we're missing . . ."

About forty miles to the south and on the other side of the bay, Rick and Fran languished in the dusty attic, the tension between them almost palpable. It had been three days now, Fran remaining on her side of the attic, spending most of her time on the thin but relatively clean mattress that had been brought up the evening after they'd made the video tape; Rick remaining several feet away, on his mattress. There was a pile of blankets as well for use during the chilly nights, and a bucket for emergency use between regularly scheduled visits to the bathrooms. To Fran's gratitude, it hadn't been necessary to use the bucket.

She looked over at Rick. He was lying on his mattress

with his back to her, but she could tell from the rhythm of his breathing that he was awake.

"Rick?"

"Hm?" he replied without turning over.

"Do you think they'd actually do it? Kill us, I mean, if they don't get what they want?"

He sat up and rubbed his face for a moment, as if he'd been sleeping. He looked over at her and she realized that most of the swelling had gone down; the only remaining discoloration on his face was the black eye she'd given him. The split lip was healing nicely, and with the swelling down, he was able to speak and eat normally for the first time in several days.

"Yeah," he replied after a few seconds, "I'm damned sure they mean to kill us—if we're not rescued in time."

"Rescued? You don't think they'll be able to make a deal with the DIA?"

Smiling ruefully, he shook his head. "No way, Fran. The information they thought they were buying is a hell of a lot more valuable than a couple of lives. DIA would let a dozen people die before they'd turn that diskette over to communist agents."

"I see," she said in a small voice. She looked up at him, her hazel eyes enormous and solemn. "That doesn't leave us many options, does it?"

"Only three. The first of which is release." He laughed. "I just can't see them turning us loose—not after all they've gone through to hang onto us. There's something else they've got to be thinking about— Charonsky. He's known to every agent in the DIA as a member of the KGB, though he's listed with their embassy as a cultural attache." He paused, lifting an eyebrow. "Are they ready to acknowledge that Charonsky —KGB—is running this operation? Indications were that Linkwell thought she was dealing with a terrorist organization with mideast tie-ins." He came closer and whispered, "I'm afraid they won't release us, knowing what we know, Fran."

"You mean—?"

"Ssh!" He pointed toward the trapdoor below which was posted an armed guard at all times. "Don't let them find out we suspect."

"You said three options. What are the other two?"

"Escape or rescue." He laughed sardonically, indicating the entire attic with a gesture. "I've been over this place with a fine-toothed comb at least fifty times. We're not getting out of here, not without tools, unless we go through that trapdoor." He paused, shrugging. "And you know as well as I do, there's an armed guard there, twenty-four hours a day. Not kids like Boris either— these guys are pros."

"Are you sure there's no way?" she pleaded, and he was forced to look away from the hope and honesty radiating from her lovely hazel eyes. He shook his head negatively, though he was relatively certain that, had he been on his own, he would have been able to overpower the guard during a bathroom visit and go out through a second-story window. A relatively short drop to the ground, and he would be gone.

He pushed the thought from his mind. The instant he did such a thing, Fran would belong to Redwing. Charonsky had promised this would happen, and Rick believed him. The prospect of Redwing having his twisted pleasures at Fran's expense was a prospect he was not prepared to face, even if it meant losing his own life.

He blinked in astonishment at the realization that had been lurking on the edge of his consciousness for several days: he loved Fran Barnette. There was no other explanation for the thought process he'd just put himself through. He would protect Fran, even at the cost of his own life. By any definition he could imagine, this meant he loved her—and coupled with the feelings he was aware of, this meant he was *in love* with her. He was surprised and a little apprehensive, though all in all, it was an exceedingly pleasant feeling.

"That leaves only rescue then." She lowered her eyes and sighed. "And by Sunday night."

Damn it, why'd he have to find out so late, Rick wondered. It was ironic. Rick Langtry, one of the DIA's most notorious womanizers, finds himself head over heels in love, when he most likely had less than four days to live. It wasn't fair.

"Yeah, by Sunday night," he agreed, forcing his mind back to their conversation with an effort.

"Can they do it?" she asked softly.

"Oh, it's possible," he said.

"But not likely, right?"

"No, not very likely, Fran. I'm sorry."

"Oh, Rick, we're going to die!"

"Hey, don't think like that! Hope for the best. Jack O'Brien and the rest of the boys could come busting through that front door at any moment. Hell, they could be on the street outside right now, just waiting to come crashing in for us! Don't you give up on me, Fran." He sat down beside her and put his arm over her shoulders, comforting her. "Not after all we've been through together."

"Boy, that's for sure." She laughed softly. "We have been through a lot, haven't we?"

"We sure have. And I want you to know I think you've been one hell of a trooper, right through it all."

"Oh, y-you're just saying that," she said shakily, laughing through her tears.

"I am not," he declared. "I wouldn't say it if I didn't mean it." He paused a moment, then added, "I might be a lot of things, but I'm not a liar."

"I wish I could believe that," she said. She looked at

him with yearning. "Oh, how I wish I could believe that." She was remembering how quickly Rick had capitulated when Charonsky made his demand that they assist in the making of the videotape. Rick had almost cheerfully gone along with the Russian, she remembered, while she had resisted as best she knew how.

"Have I given you cause to doubt me, Fran?" he asked quietly.

"I—maybe. I don't know, but I think so." She looked at him for a moment, chewing on her bottom lip, then burst out, "Oh, Rick, why did you give in to their demands so easily? Are you afraid they would hurt you if you didn't?"

"Hey, all we did was make a tape for them," he said with a carelessness he was far from feeling. He felt her contempt, but if he countered that contempt with the truth, it would bring about the very result he'd been trying to avoid all along. "It was no big deal, Fran. It wasn't treason or something equally wicked. Don't be so hard on yourself—and me."

"Is that all, Rick?" She stared into his eyes for several seconds. "All those long trips you take to the bathroom —you're sure you're not cooperating with them behind my back?"

"Fran, please listen to me," he said seriously, looking into her eyes. "Please think whatever you want of me, but always remember this one thing: I would never do anything to harm my country. No matter how things might look to you, always remember that." He stared into her eyes until it was as if she could touch the honesty radiating like warm beams of sunshine.

"I—I'd like to believe you . . . I *do* believe you, Rick!" She was silent for a moment, then burst out, "Oh, Rick, I've been acting like such a heel these past few days! I've been acting like—like *you* were the enemy, instead of these animals."

Drying her eyes, she looked up at him, her thick lashes wet with tears. "I'm sorry. I guess I've had some wrong ideas about proper conduct under these circumstances. I should have known you wouldn't do anything really wrong. Can you forgive me?"

"Forget it." He beamed, ridiculously happy to be back in her good graces. "I'm just glad you're not mad at me anymore."

"Not at you, but I'm sure mad at myself."

"Don't be, Fran."

"Listen, Rick . . ."

"Yeah?" He looked at her when her voice trailed off, and was astonished to see her blushing. He smiled. "Well?"

"Oh, I just wanted to say something to you, that's all. I don't suppose it's really very important now." She looked up at him with an expression of such yearning that he understood that whatever she had to say mattered, if not to her, then to him.

"Go ahead," he said quietly. "Please."

"It's just that—if we're going to die in a few days— and it's starting to look like that might happen—well, I just wanted you to know . . . I mean, I'd hate anything to happen to you without telling you—" She paused again, and he placed his finger gently across her lips, stopping her from continuing.

"Hush," he whispered. A tremendous feeling of release had burst in his chest while she was speaking, and all the confused, jumbled emotions he'd been struggling with for the past several days suddenly coalesced into one meaningful, easily understood decision: he loved her. In spite of her stubborn, willful, opinionated ways, he was unable to squelch the feelings he had for her for another moment. Maybe he'd been right all those years, guarding himself from deep commitment to a woman, but now, with death only a matter of hours away, what

212

was the sense in fighting his feelings any longer? "I love you, Fran," he said hoarsely, as if the words had come up from some raw, unused portion of his throat. "I love you. This is the first time I've ever spoken those words to a woman, but it feels so right to say them now. I love you," he said, laughing, the shine of tears in his dark eyes. "I love you!"

Her eyes lit up with wonder and happiness. "That's what I wanted to tell you!" she said, taking his hand and squeezing it tightly. "I don't know why it was so hard for me to get it out, after—after what we . . ."

"What we've done together," he finished, smiling into her sparkling hazel eyes. "I know why you were embarrassed, honey. It's because I was such an idiot before. You said you loved me at the time, but I was too stubborn to admit—even to myself—that I was in love with you." He paused, a wondering expression crossing his face. "Hell, I didn't even know it myself—how could I have told you?"

"Oh, Rick, why am I so happy all of a sudden?" She gazed up at him, her full lips curved in a smile of joy.

"You keep looking at me like that and I'm going to kiss you," he warned, and she laughed, daring him, wanting him to. He lowered his mouth to cover hers, and as their lips met and their tongues touched and probed, tentatively, delicately at first, then eagerly as they found acceptance and welcome. Rick's heart soared with happiness and he realized at that moment that whether the rest of his life consisted of fifty years or fifty minutes, it was inextricably bound up with the woman he held in his arms.

"Ooh, Rick." She sighed as their lips parted at last. Her breath came quickly; her heart was pounding like a trip-hammer under the satiny skin of her breasts. "Why have we wasted all this time?"

His eyes searched her face eagerly. "Do you mean— do you want—?"

"Oh, yes, darling, yes!" she exclaimed joyously. "Let's get these damned clothes off!"

"But what if the guards decide to check on us?" he asked, hesitating with his fingers on the buttons of his shirt. "It'd be pretty embarrassing."

"They've never come up at this time of day before. Why should they start now?" She looked around the attic for a few seconds, biting her lower lip thoughtfully. "But if you're worried, why not pull your mattress over on top of the trapdoor? That way, if somebody does decide to come up, we'll at least hear them in time to cover ourselves."

"You're not only beautiful and sexy," he said, smiling, "but you're smart, too!" When he came back to her and began unbuttoning his trousers, he felt his throat thicken.

"You're not so bad yourself," she murmured, hooking her thumbs into the elastic of his shorts and pushing them down over his hips, until they fell away to the floor. She felt his manhood pressing against her smooth soft belly, warm and firm with growing desire.

"Shall we get comfortable?" he suggested.

"Umm," she said, lowering herself to the mattress, pulling him down beside her. "Let's do . . ."

His lips covered hers for another deep, searching kiss that seemed to last forever while his big, warm hand roved over her eager body, stroking, loving, feeling, probing all the warm secret places a woman loves to have the man she loves touch her. When he moved his mouth away from her lips, it was to nuzzle the soft delicate skin of her throat, traveling up its graceful length to nibble gently on her ear while sparkling showers of sensation made her body tremble with happiness and anticipation.

"Oh, baby, baby," he murmured thickly, "I love you so much. I wish I'd realized it sooner . . ." He moved down to her breasts, cupping them together with his hands and adoring them with lips and tongue, licking and caressing and sucking until she thought she'd burst from the sheer pleasure of it all.

"Rick, Rick," she whispered, reaching down and gripping him, finding him firm and ready for her. "Please . . . don't make me wait."

He raised up then and came over her. Her thighs parted as his face loomed above hers, the fiery core of her aching for him. She gripped him tightly and pulled him forward, and he moved eagerly into the sweet firm grasp of her, sighing with pleasure.

They moved slowly, softly, with great delicacy and consideration for one another, until they were unable to withstand the sweet, sharp pangs of pleasure any longer, and then their bodies began slamming together with heightening urgency, faster and faster, until she cried out his name and they exploded together in a mutual convulsion of the most intense pleasure either of them had ever known.

"Fran . . ." he said after they had laid locked in the ultimate embrace for several moments, until their heartbeats had returned to normal, "it's even better than it was before, back at the cabin. If this is what love does for a guy, then I'm sorry I've been missing out on it all these years."

"I'm not," she said, smiling mischievously. "I'm glad you never knew until now."

He shifted position slightly, and her legs tightened around him, imprisoning him in their warm, blissful grasp. "Don't move," she gasped. "Please."

"I was getting a charley horse," he said. Wrapping his arms tightly around her, he quickly rolled over on his back, remaining locked together with her. She looked down at him, smiling happily, her rosy-tipped breasts suspended enticingly just inches from his face. Unable to resist, he reached up and caught one with his lips, teasing it gently with his teeth for a few seconds before drawing it into his mouth and sucking eagerly. When he released it, he moved quickly for the other one.

"You have such beautiful breasts," he said with a happy sigh when he withdrew a moment later.

"I just love what you do to them," she said breathlessly, giving an experimental little push with her groin, her hands spread wide on his chest. "Oh, my," she breathed, her hands curling into fists full of dark, coarse chest hair.

"I could get to like this, I think . . ." Laughing, she bent down and covered his mouth with kisses, moving urgently against him all the while.

"Fran, hold it," he protested. "It's too soon for me . . ."

"Oh, no, it's not," she said happily, and after a couple of minutes of her eager kisses against his lips and throat and ears, he realized to his delight that she was absolutely correct.

The sunlight from the one lone window was shining in at a steep angle by the time they lay exhausted in each other's arms. They'd spent the entire afternoon locked together in lovemaking, and Fran reflected that in spite of their precarious situation, she'd never known more intense happiness.

"We'd better get dressed," he murmured. "Getting late."

"Um, right." She moved against him with a contented sigh. "Love me?"

"Love you? Lady, I'm absolutely nuts about you."

They glanced around in alarm at the sound of the trapdoor pushing against the mattress Rick had placed over it, and Fran scrambled quickly into her oversized men's shirt, covering herself. Charonsky's well-groomed head appeared in the opening after the trapdoor crashed open. He eyed the heaped up bedding designed to delay interruptions with an ironic smile, then turned to Rick and Fran.

"Ah, my friends, I see you have had a reconciliation. Wonderful!"

"What do you want?" Rick asked tonelessly, averting his eyes from Fran's puzzled glance at him.

"Finish dressing, then get down to my room." Charonsky looked pointedly at Fran, to ensure she was listening. She had turned her back and was finishing dressing as swiftly as possible, but it was obvious from her unnaturally stiff posture that she was absorbing every word of their conversation. "We need some more information, Langtry. You didn't think those new clothes and the good food were going to come so easily, did you? After all, we expect a return on our investment." He smiled as he started back down through the trapdoor. "Quickly, Langtry."

As the trapdoor closed with a *thunk,* Fran spun around and glared at Rick through a film of tears. "And to think, I believed you! Stupid, stupid me! Well, no more, you—you damned *traitor!*"

"Fran, listen!" But she had turned away, and with a sinking sensation, he realized that it was just as well. There was nothing he could say that would convince her of the truth—nothing that would not place her in immediate danger. He was faced with the bitter choice of losing the woman he loved no matter what he did, and there was not a thing he could do about it.

"Well, what have you got for me, O'Brien?" Addison was asking Rick's partner at that very moment. It was almost five o'clock and Jack had entered the office a few moments ago with a manila folder containing his written report. He sat down uninvited in the straight-backed chair Addison kept to discourage lengthy visits from his underlings, and opened the folder on his lap. Addison frowned at this lapse in protocol, but said nothing.

"Plenty, for one day's work," Jack said eagerly. "Number one, the sound none of us could identify. Sergeant Bryan Collins at SFPD identified it as a BART train, three or four cars long."

"Well, fine." Addison grunted. "But the damned BART line completely encircles the bay area. We already know—or think we know—that they're still in the bay area, so just what good does it do us to know that it's a BART? Not that I'm denigrating your work, O'Brien," he added quickly.

"Of course not," Jack said dryly. "I know you'd never do that, Mr. Addison. But it does help us. You'll soon understand how." He shifted the top paper to the back of the sheaf of papers in the folder.

"The real good news is that we're almost positive they're being held in Hayward. We got a tight blowup of the paper Rick was holding—the *Examiner.*" He passed a photographic print across the broad mahogany desk. Addison took it and frowned at it, squinting.

"Look, Mr. Addison," Jack said with exaggerated patience, getting to his feet and pointing at a spot on the photograph. "Right there, above the dateline. See? It says Hayward Edition."

Addison pursed his lips dubiously. "I see it, but that doesn't necessarily mean they're in Hayward, does it? Couldn't they have purchased the paper somewhere outside of Hayward—Castro Valley, say—and brought it to this place they're being held?"

"Yes, of course that's a possibility that must be considered. However, I called the circulation department of the *Examiner* and discovered that most of the small cities and towns grouped around the bay have their own editions of the paper. It gives them a forum for the reporting of community affairs, local politics, stuff like that." He paused, shaking his head. "So it's pretty unlikely the paper was bought out of town and brought in. Possible, but not likely."

"Whatever," Addison said reluctantly, shoving the photo back toward Jack with a broad-tipped, well-manicured finger. "We'll go on the assumption they're in Hayward. So what's next? Hayward might not be nearly as big as the city, but it's still too damned big for a house-to-house search to get done before next Sunday evening."

"That's true. But we might be able to narrow down the target area by a hell of a margin." Drawing several photocopies of maps from his folder, Jack spread them on Addison's desk. "I got these from the Rapid Transit people—BART. These maps show the routes and every stop on the entire system." As he spoke he pushed most of the maps aside, leaving only the maps of Hayward and Castro Valley.

"Now is when that mysterious sound really begins to help us out, chief." Addison glanced up sharply at Jack's use of the slangy title popularized by Langtry, but Jack's attention was all on the maps, his round, freckled countenance preoccupied and serious.

"Remember that sound?" he asked. "Seven point five seconds of rumble that we now know is the sound of a passing BART train." He held up a finger for emphasis as he went on, "More importantly, a BART train passing a given point at full speed."

Addison frowned, staring at the maps spread before him on the desk in confusion. "Make your point, O'Brien," he said. "I don't have all damned af—" Suddenly, his face cleared in comprehension, and he nodded slowly. "Ah, I see what you're driving at now!"

"Exactly," Jack said eagerly. "The train is running at full speed—not gathering speed, and not slowing down for a stop. That means it almost has to be between this station, here, Hayward station on 'A' street, and the next one up the line, here, at Bayfair. That's about a ten- or twelve-minute run—more than enough for the train to get up to full speed and hold it for several minutes. And that means, if we're anywhere near being right about all this—"

"—That our people are being held somewhere in this vicinity!" Addison's blunt forefinger stabbed the map on the BART line, about halfway between Bayfair station and Hayward station. He stared thoughtfully at the map for a few seconds, then his lower lip gradually protruded, expressing his dissatisfaction. "Hell. That still leaves one hell of a lot of territory to cover, O'Brien. Both sides of the track, several blocks from the rail line, for how many miles?"

"It's not as bad as it sounds," Jack countered. "In the first place you've got to be within one block—or less— of the BART tracks in order for the sound of the train to be loud enough to be picked up on videotape. We know this because we've made tests.

"And in the second place, we know we're looking for an older, two-story house, from what we saw on the tape. The stairs, the old-fashioned cabinet work, and so on. . . . We can eliminate everything of only one story immediately, and that takes in one hell of a lot of houses in this part of the country."

Addison pulled at his lower lip while he considered all this for several seconds, then he looked over at Jack and nodded in reluctant admiration. "O'Brien, I've got to admit it. You've done some first-rate detective work here."

"Thanks, sir." Jack smiled tightly. "But all the fancy detective work won't be worth a tinker's damn unless we find them before this time Sunday—less than ninety-six hours from right now." He began gathering up the papers and stuffing them carelessly into his manila folder. "I don't suppose there's any chance of picking up another half-dozen men, is there? They'd be a lot of help, canvassing the neighborhoods between Hayward and Bayfair."

"Sorry, Jack." Addison shook his head regretfully. "There's just no one available. This is not the only high-priority operation we have going now, you understand. As a matter-of-fact, I'm taking a lot of flak as it is, what with leaving Smith and Simmons and Whitworth assigned exclusively to you for the duration of this operation."

"All right, then." Jack sighed as he tucked the folder under his arm. "How about requesting some help from the state and local boys? The California Highway Patrol, the county sheriffs—hell, even the Hayward Police Department."

"What can they do for us we can't do better?" Addison asked with a trace of impatience.

"Well, they could help us find that damned van for one thing!" Addison's eyes flicked up at the insubordinate tone of voice, but Jack met the older man's glare unflinchingly. After a few seconds Addison nodded.

"All right," he conceded. "I'll put in the request for cooperation and assistance. Give me all the particulars on the van before you leave if you've got them with you."

"Sure." Jack opened the folder and began extracting scraps of paper. "By the way, we want the van located, but don't want the driver hassled. No arrests. Stop and identify, that's all. Once they've located the damned thing for us, we'll put a tail on it. Five'll get you ten it'll lead us straight to where Rick and the Barnette lady're being held."

"Well, it's a long shot," Addison said. "But maybe worth a try."

"At this stage of the game," Jack said, sliding everything pertinent to the van across the top of Addison's desk, "long shots are just about all we have left. For Rick's sake, and for Fran Barnette's sake, I hope one of them pays off, and soon."

CHAPTER TWELVE

"I just hope something happens—and soon." Fran Barnette's silent plea echoed Jack O'Brien's sentiments exactly. *"Anything—just so it gets me away from Rick Langtry!"*

She stared blindly at the sloping roof of the attic, eyes blurred with tears as she remembered the way he had leaped up to do the bidding of his new master. Charonsky waggled his fingers and Rick Langtry jumped through hoops.

Could this be the same man who had only moments before made such powerful, thrilling, deeply satisfying love to her? The same man who had leaped unarmed at Stoner on Pier 39, disabling him with one blow? It was shameful what some men would do in order to avoid a little discomfort, she thought, flushing with shame on his behalf.

Fran felt the hair stirring on the nape of her neck, and she spun around. Redwing was staring at her from the trapdoor opening, his mouth hanging stupidly open, an expression of such evil on his coarse, pockmarked face that she was unable to suppress a shudder of revulsion and fear.

"Uh, supper," Redwing said, blinking. He placed a white paper bag of fast-food sandwiches on the attic floor and slid it a few inches toward her, then slowly retreated from view, never taking his eyes from her face.

She moved over to retrieve the food, though she wasn't in the slightest hungry. As she did so, it occurred to her that her first reaction at the sight of Redwing ogling her so openly was to wish for Rick's presence. If he was there she'd be safe . . .

"You son of a bitch," Rick said coldly as he strode into the bedroom Charonsky had appropriated for his own use. He slammed the door in Stoner's face, catching the big man by surprise. Immediately, a small, nickel-plated automatic pistol appeared in the Russian's hand, aimed unwaveringly at Rick's stomach. He ignored the threat, slouching down into the arm chair without waiting for an invitation.

"What the hell was the reason for that crack? You know damned well I haven't been passing you bastards any information, classified or otherwise!"

Charonsky gestured with the pistol, chuckling, as Stoner burst into the room. He glanced at the Russian and raised his eyebrows inquisitively.

"Want me to stay, or what?"

"Comrade," Charonsky said, staring coldly at the big man. " 'Do you want me to stay, *comrade?*' "

"Do you want me to stay, comrade," Stoner repeated tonelessly, avoiding Rick's eyes. Charonsky waved him away.

"The help you get these days," he said as Stoner closed the door. He glanced at Rick as if for sympathy. As always, the Russian agent was impeccably dressed, his sartorial splendor belying his insistence on the egalitarian term, comrade, from his subordinates.

"Ah, well, this assignment will soon be over, and I can return to Mother Russia."

"Back to the worker's paradise, eh?" Rick grinned

sourly. "Bet you can hardly wait, can you? Better stock up on that fancy clothing, comrade. I doubt like hell you'll find the like at home, don't you?"

"I see." The Russian nodded slowly. "You attempt to put me in the position of defending my homeland by ridiculing things about which you know nothing. Fortunately, Langtry, I am not so simple as to fall for such an obvious ploy."

"Fine. Then why the hell am I here?"

"You Americans never cease to amaze me!" Charonsky laughed out loud. "You're so naive. You want everything spelled out for you in black and white. No shades of gray, no subtleties to confuse your childlike minds with adult reasoning . . .

"In the Soviet Union our national game is chess. You Americans play baseball. No wonder you are the way you are."

"Yeah, we're a bunch of dummies all right. Maybe that's why we've been to the moon and you people haven't."

"The moon?" Charonsky snorted. "You worry about the moon? You should be worrying about keeping yourself alive, Langtry! It is now Wednesday, and we've had no response from your Mr. Addison of the Defense Intelligence Agency. You must make him understand that you will die if the diskette is not returned to us—to me."

"What can I do?" Rick shrugged, spreading his hands. "I've already helped with the videotape. If that didn't do the trick, I don't know what will."

"You will speak to him on the telephone. You will remind him of your situation here."

"Sure, whatever you say. I'll happily speak to him on the phone for as long as you want me to."

"Tsk, tsk," Charonsky said, holding up an admonishing forefinger. "I am not so naive as to permit you to

225

speak long enough so that a successful trace can be made . . . then you do agree to speak to Mr. Joseph Addison?"

"Hell, what choice have I got? Sure, I'll talk to him." He glanced at his wristwatch. "But it'd better be pretty damn soon. He usually leaves the office before now."

"Not these days," Charonsky said confidently. "He seems to be working longer hours of late." Smiling, he gestured toward the bedroom door, waiting for Rick to precede him. "Come. The telephone is downstairs."

Rick tensed alertly as they moved toward the staircase leading to the ground floor. This was the first occasion on which he'd been taken downstairs since they'd made the original video tape, and he'd been in pretty rough shape that day, unable to be as observant as he should have been. This time he'd try to learn more about where they were being held.

"It's in the kitchen," Charonsky said as they reached the landing of the stairs. Rick hesitated, and the Russian pointed.

The telephone was a wall unit, hanging just inside the door, next to a large, older model refrigerator. Rick smiled cynically as he observed that the number had been removed from the unit in an obvious attempt to keep him in the dark as to the location of the house. Shades or blinds had been drawn over every window within view, and a light rectangle on the kitchen wall opposite the phone undoubtedly delineated where a calendar had once hung. Someone had taken pains to disguise the location, which made it all the harder for him to understand why some careless individual had left an envelope lying in the dust on top of the old refrigerator.

He craned his neck experimentally but was unable to see the face of the envelope. However, he decided, if he was unable to figure out a way to capitalize on such a major blunder, perhaps he didn't deserve to get out of this mess alive. Carefully marking the location of the envelope, he turned to face Charonsky.

"Here is what you must say." Charonsky handed him a sheet of paper on which someone had neatly printed a few lines. "Say nothing else, Langtry. Should I remind you what will happen to Miss Barnette if you attempt to deceive me?"

"No." Rick quickly scanned the printed lines, learning nothing new. "You want me to just read this, or should I kind of put it in my own words?"

"Put it in your own words, so it sounds natural." Charonsky cocked his head and narrowed his eyes. "But keep in mind that my English is very good. Good enough to know if you are trying to pull something."

"Okay." Rick turned so that his shoulder was between Charonsky and the old refrigerator. The Russian stood just outside the kitchen, leaning against the doorway on the dining room side, watching Rick. "Just give me a couple of minutes to memorize the sense of this, okay?"

"Of course," Charonsky said with a weary sigh. "If you need it for such a small amount of dialogue." He rolled his eyes and shook his head, muttering in Russian. Rick chose that moment to make his move. While he held the sheet of paper with his left hand, ostentatiously studying the few lines of information, his right hand sneaked quickly up and scooped the envelope from the top of the refrigerator. He crammed the envelope into his pocket without so much as a glance, unable to stifle a huge sigh of relief as he realized he'd gotten away with it.

"Well? Are you ready?" Charonsky demanded grumpily. "Any longer and maybe Addison will be gone for the day."

"Do you want me to call collect or—?"

"Just dial direct and quit playing games with me!"

Grinning, Rick dialed the familiar number while Charonsky hovered, looking over his shoulder.

"Defense Intelligence Agency, Mr. Addison's office," Beth Ann's voice chirped in his ear. "May I help you?"

"Hi, Beth Ann. It's Rick Langtry. Is the old man there?"

"Rick! He's—yes, just a second! I'll get him for you."

"Rick, boy, where are you?" Addison said when he came on the line. "Did you get away again? Is the Barnette—?"

"Mr. Addison, please be quiet," Rick interjected, when Charonsky shook his head emphatically. "I've just got a minute, so you'll have to listen. I've been instructed to inform you that the time limit has been cut back to Saturday instead of Sunday. The tape must be returned by Saturday or Miss Barnette and I will be killed.

"Now, when you have the tape ready to turn over, Saturday, you will personally take it to Fisherman's Wharf. You will board the first tour boat to leave the dock after twelve noon, and you will remain near the rail on the starboard side of the boat. Oh, make sure the diskette is wrapped in a waterproof package. When you are told to drop it over the side, do it immediately. Got it?"

"I think so," Addison said, "But—"

"No buts, chief," Rick said when Charonsky began shaking his head in emphatic negation. "You are to be alone and you are not to go near a telephone until you are back in your office. You will be under observation from the moment you leave your office, and if you violate these instructions in any way, Miss Barnette and I will be killed. They mean business."

Charonsky reached across Rick's shoulder and broke the connection then, cutting off Addison's protests in mid-sentence. Rick replaced the handset.

"That was fine," Charonsky said. "Do you think he will do as ordered?"

Rick shook his head. "Hell, your guess is as good as mine. I hope he does, for Miss Barnette's sake."

"Yes, the lovely Miss Barnette." Charonsky took Rick's elbow companionably as they started back up the stairs, and Rick almost fainted with the temptation to disarm him and make his escape. He could have taken Charonsky out with his elbow and been down the stairs and out through the front door before the two guards in the living room had time to react.

"You are quite fond of Miss Barnette, are you not?"

"I suppose so," Rick muttered, wondering uneasily what the Russian was leading up to.

"In love with her, in point of fact? Oh, please don't bother to deny it. I knew you were, the first time I saw the two of you together!" Charonsky nodded and smiled. "And when Stoner told me of the circumstances of your recapture, well . . ." He gestured gracefully with his manicured hands. "Unfortunate," he continued. "Of course it has given us an effective way of neutralizing you through all this." He chuckled, tapping the wall at the side of the staircase with his knuckles. "This old place would never have held you if you were on your own, eh, Langtry?"

"Probably not," Rick agreed.

"There you are, then." The Russian chuckled smugly.

"Tell me something, as long as we're discussing Miss Barnette," Rick said. "Would you really turn her over to that damned Redwing if I—if I pulled something?"

"Oh, indeed I would." Charonsky's eyes were as hard and cold as marbles. "Redwing needs special handling, Langtry. From time to time I see that his . . . special tastes are indulged. You'd be amazed at how faithful that makes him, simply amazed."

"Special tastes," Rick muttered. "I can imagine."

"No, I am quite sure you can not," Charonsky contradicted bleakly. "Nobody could, unless they'd seen—seen what he likes to do. Well, here we are, then," he said briskly, as they arrived at the ladder leading up into the attic. Stoner leaned back against the wall in a straight-backed chair, a paperback book open on his chest. He looked up and nodded curtly at Rick.

"I do hope our efforts bear fruit," Charonsky said as Rick started up the ladder. "In my own way I've become rather fond of you and Miss Barnette. It would be an unhappy occasion if I had to order your deaths."

"Yeah, well, I don't think Fran and I'd be too thrilled about it either," Rick said, then pushed up through the trapdoor into the attic.

"So here you are, back already." Fran watched coldly as he closed the trapdoor and stood up. "What'd you tell them this time, hero? Anything they asked for, no doubt."

"Damn it, Fran, shut up and listen—"

"I don't think so. I'm not interested in your alibis—or your lies." She flung an arm in the direction of his mattress. "There's your supper. I'm sure you must be hungry, after a busy evening of collaborating with the enemy. Collaborating always gives one such an appetite, don't you agree?"

"If you'd just shut up and listen for a minute—!"

"All right, let's hear what you have to say, Agent Langtry. I'll listen."

"Fine." Rick stared at her for a moment, his chest heaving as his breathing gradually returned to normal. He'd never known anyone who could make him angry so quickly. When he felt calm enough to proceed, he removed the crumpled envelope from his pocket with a flourish.

"What's that?" Fran's eyes were wide with hope.

"This . . . this is an old gas bill," Rick said as he scanned the envelope. "But it does confirm that we're in Hayward, the way we thought. And look at this, we now have the street address. 720 Archibald."

"Big deal," Fran said, her shoulders slumping in disappointment. "I thought you had something for a minute."

"It is something, damn it! Don't you feel better, just knowing where we are?"

"It doesn't mean that much to me," she said disspiritedly. "I don't know this area at all. I wouldn't know Hayward from—from Oakland! My home is in southern California." She snuffled. "And right now I wish I'd never left there."

"Fran, I'm sorry we got into this mess." He touched her on the arm, and she shook him violently off.

"Don't touch me, Rick."

"Touch you?" His eyes narrowed into slits as he stared at her, hurt and angered by the way she was treating him. "Seems to me we did a little more than just touching, and just a few hours ago. You're really something, Fran, the way you can turn it off and on at will. Just about the time I think I know where I stand with you, you go all cold and icy on me again! An hour ago you said you loved me. And now—"

"—And now I realize just how much of a weakling you really are!" she interrupted, her hazel eyes blazing. "You'd do anything to help these people, wouldn't you? Anything, as long as they didn't hurt you!"

"Fran, you don't understand."

"No, I sure as hell do not! It's very hard for me to understand how you can be so much of a man one minute and the next instant be kowtowing to these animals the way you do! It's enough to make me sick!"

"I wish I could explain," he muttered.

"Explain? I don't need an explanation! I need a man

231

here with me, Rick. I need somebody who could come up with an escape plan—somebody who could get us out of here! But no, you seem content to just sit on your duff and wait for the wonderful DIA to spring us!" Her lips twisted bitterly. "The DIA. I wish I'd never heard of that particular agency."

"Believe me, I wish the same thing. I'd give anything if you weren't involved in this damned mess." He walked over and put his hands on her shoulders, pulling her to him. She resisted, but his strength overcame her and she stumbled into his arms. She stood stiffly as he held her, resisting the almost overpowering urge to relax against him and let him hold her, protect her. Conflicting emotions troubled her as she felt his warm breath against the skin of her neck and felt his hard, muscular body pressing urgently against her. In some ways Rick Langtry was the very epitome of the kind of man she despised: arrogant, macho, filled with an overwhelming sense of his own importance.

On the other hand, he was kind and thoughtful . . . and it was good to be with him. He was the heroic type of man all her friends in high school and college had coveted and schemed for and hoped someday to marry. And the fact that her knees were turning to water as he held her, that all he had to do was look at her in that certain way and she felt weak and languorous and filled with desire . . . that had to be considered, too.

If only she could have remained in ignorance about certain aspects of his character, she would have been able to accept him unreservedly. She'd thought for a while that she could go on deceiving herself, even after the conversation with Charonsky the other day while Rick was taking his turn in the bathroom downstairs; she'd wanted him so badly that she'd been able to block that conversation out of her mind for a brief time. Then Charonsky had entered the attic while they were still lying there in the afterglow of their lovemaking and burst her bubble with just a few well-chosen words, reminding her that Rick had sold out. The short conversation with Charonsky flooded back into her mind as she stood there, and she pushed herself back away from Rick, out of his arms, remembering . . .

"You think your American agent is a pretty splendid fellow, don't you, Miss Barnette?" Charonsky had asked languidly, leaning against one of the uprights in the attic.

"He's okay," she had said cautiously.

"Quite skilled at making love, of course." Charonsky had smiled and gestured with his manicured hands. "A handsome bachelor, in San Francisco . . . how could he be otherwise, unless he was homosexual. And we know he is most definitely not, don't we?"

Fran had turned away from his insinuating glance, not replying.

"Just so you don't get any romantic ideas about Langtry and the famous DIA," Charonsky had said idly, "I want you to know that he sold out to us. He's cooperating with us to the fullest extent."

"Sold out? Rick? I don't believe you!"

"Don't be a fool, Miss Barnette! Do you think we provided you with new clothing and the excellent food you've been receiving simply out of the goodness of our hearts? Quid pro quo, Miss Barnette, quid quo pro. Something for something. You're a businesswoman; you know how it works."

She had looked at him, stunned, unable to disguise the devastating effect of his words. After a moment Charonsky had chuckled and moved toward the trapdoor. From down below they could hear the approach of Rick and Stoner, escorting him back from the bathroom.

"I suggest you don't permit him to know, Miss Barnette. He's under the impression that you trust him, at least to a degree. For our purposes, it's better that you don't reveal just how much you know." Charonsky's smile had grown wider as he started down the stairs. "Stay on good terms with him, Miss Barnette. If only for my sake. Hmm?"

Good terms, was it? Well, she supposed that what had happened this afternoon would have to be considered "good terms." She looked over at Rick now, pushing the memory of her conversation with Charonsky out of her mind.

"Trust me, baby," Rick said, and that was the worst thing he could have said, from Fran's point of view. All the pent-up anger and self-disgust at having made love with him that afternoon, all the suspicion and hopelessness flooded back in a rush, blinding her to anything else.

"Trust you! Is that the best you can come up with? Trust me?" Her eyes blazed as she stared at him, jerking away as he reached out for her.

"Maybe it's all I can tell you." His eyes were bleak as he looked at her. She sighed, and her body seemed to sag as the burst of anger abruptly left her, leaving her weak and merely disappointed.

"God, how I wish I could trust you, Rick."

"You can, Fran! You must!"

She shook her head slowly, an expression of resignation in her eyes. "I'm sorry but I can't. I have to believe the evidence of my own eyes, Rick. Why are they giving us new clothing to wear? Why do we eat steak and chicken, instead of cabbage soup, as they gave us on the *Vostok?* I'm not so stupid that I can't see the changes in our treatment, Rick. And I'm not so stupid that I can't figure out that you must have done something pretty drastic to earn it!" She paused, chuckling bitterly. "You know, when I saw you lay out poor old Stoner with one punch, I thought you were just one hell of a guy. I thought you were trying to protect *me.*" She gave a brittle laugh, and the expression of contempt and pity on her face was so painful he was forced to look away. "Imagine my surprise when I found out you were simply trying to save your own skin from torture."

"Fran, where the hell are you getting such ideas?"

"You're not the only one who goes downstairs alone, Rick," she said. "They talk to me, too."

"And you believe *them?*" he asked incredulously, cursing the day he'd fallen in love. Here was an aspect of love that the song writers and poets rarely wrote about, he reflected. When you are in love, you are utterly open and vulnerable. Her contempt was a hundred times more hurtful to him than her anger would have been, and he was powerless to defend himself from her charges. Damn Charonsky, he thought bitterly. God damn the man and his twisted, convoluted reasoning! Wasn't it enough that he, Rick, was cooperating minimally with them, in order to save Fran from Redwing? Did he also obtain some weird, twisted kind of kick from turning them against one another?

"I believe what I can see with my own eyes," she said evasively. "I just know that things have been better for us since you started . . . cooperating with them. Since we made the tape, we've had better food . . . and these mattresses, and—and the clothes."

"Sure, we helped make the tape, Fran! Hell, you were there. Tell me what I did that night that you wouldn't have done! Go ahead—tell me how I betrayed my country! Jesus, all I did was read a short prepared statement. You heard it!"

"You've cooperated since then," she said stubbornly. "How about tonight?"

"Tonight—! Oh, the phone call." He sighed wearily and threw up his hands. "Yes, I made a phone call for our Russian friends. I told Addison they wanted the damned diskette back and how to deliver it, and that if he didn't cough it up by Saturday, we'd be dead ducks. Yeah, I cooperated."

"Saturday?" Her eyes widened. "I—I thought we had until Sunday before . . ."

"Yeah, well, they've moved up the deadline twenty-four hours for some unknown reason." He paused, frowning. "Maybe Jack's putting the heat on and they're afraid they'll be caught if they wait around too long. Maybe—ah, hell, I don't know. Maybe it's just that they're getting impatient."

He walked over and sat down on the edge of his mattress, looking at the paper sack of food. Opening the bag, he looked at the french fries slowly congealing with distaste, then refolded the bag and pushed it away.

"Saturday. That means . . . we've got less than seventy-two hours from now." She came over and sat down on the other end of his mattress, leaning her chin on her knees. "Isn't there some way we could break out of here?"

"I wish there was, Fran."

"Damn it." She rocked back and forth on the edge of her mattress, an expression of frustration on her lovely face. "I almost wish I was a man. I'll just bet I could figure something out."

I almost wish you were, too, Rick thought glumly. *Because if it weren't for the threat of Redwing hanging over you all the time, we'd've been out of here by now— or at least one of us would have.* Sighing, he got to his feet, gazing longingly up at the small, filth-encrusted window in the gable at one end of the attic. The last waning rays of the sun struggled against the dust and dirt, barely penetrating into the attic.

Another day gone, he thought with a sense of foreboding.

Jack O'Brien glanced up at the gathering twilight as he got out of his car and walked toward the real estate office in one of Hayward's half-dozen shopping centers. This case wasn't doing much for his marriage, he thought glumly, noting that it would soon be dark; this would be the fifth day in a row he had worked until long past dark. He took out his ID and his badge as he stepped into the office.

"O'Brien, DIA," he said, flashing the badge as one of the real estate agents trotted over with an eager, helpful smile. "I called this afternoon, made an appointment with Mrs. Pearson."

"One moment, sir. I'll get her for you."

Jack strolled over and looked at the bulletin board which took up a large piece of one wall of the small office. Three by five cards with descriptions of houses, commercial buildings, lots, and other properties completely covered the cork surface. Some of the cards were brittle and yellowed with age. Jack scanned several of the cards, nodding with satisfaction. He'd come to the right place, all right.

"Mr. O'Brien? I'm Madelyn Pearson."

Jack turned and smiled at the stylishly dressed, middle-aged woman addressing him in a low, husky voice. She wore her peroxided hair in an old-fashioned bouffant style, and her face was a bit too heavily made up, but it was obvious that she had been stunningly attractive once, and not that many years ago. Jack felt himself grinning foolishly as she stepped closer.

"On the phone this afternoon, you said you were specifically interested in an older home . . . ?"

"Yes, in a way. But I wouldn't want to give you the false impression that I'm in the market for a house,

Mrs. Pearson," he said hastily. "You see, I'm trying to locate a house in connection with a current investigation. All I know about it is that it is located within one block of the BART tracks, and that it's somewhere between the Hayward 'A' street station and the next stop up the line, at Bayfair."

"Mr. O'Brien, I'm a realtor, not a magician. Do you realize how many houses you're talking about?" Madelyn Pearson raised her finely arched eyebrows in disbelief. "Literally thousands!"

"I know that, Mrs. Pearson, but please hear me out." Jack glanced around the crowded office. Three of four of the desks in the room were occupied by sales agents, two of whom were presently occupied with feverish sales pitches over their telephones. The third agent, a fat, round-faced young man, listened avidly to their conversation. Jack leaned forward and said quietly, "Isn't there a more private place where we can talk, Mrs. Pearson?"

"In my office," she said in her husky, attractive voice. Jack followed her the length of the office, toward a door in the rear of the room. Opening the door, she stood aside, gesturing for Jack to precede her into the room. He stepped in and looked around. Sparsely furnished, with only a large, scarred wooden desk, swivel chair, visitor's chair, and a filing cabinet, the office's chief attraction was that it was relatively private.

"Sit down, Mr. O'Brien, please. And call me Madelyn. The reason for the 'Mrs.' has been gone for some years now."

"Oh? I'm sorry to hear that, Madelyn."

"Don't be. He was a real son of a bitch. I was never this happy while he was alive."

"Um, I see." When Madelyn was comfortably ensconced behind her desk, Jack cleared his throat and explained: "I was referred to your office because you do

238

specialize in older homes. Maybe it's a long shot, Madelyn, but I'm looking for a two-story house, probably built around the turn of the century or so." Reaching into the inside pocket of his jacket, he extracted an envelope and handed it to her. "I apologize for the poor quality of the prints, Madelyn. These are Polaroids shot from a video tape earlier this afternoon. They're the only available shots of the interior of the house—at least they're all I've got. . . ." He fell silent, watching Madelyn Pearson as she studied the grainy photographs intently.

"It's pretty obvious why you're so sure you're looking for a two-story house." She replaced the prints in the envelope and returned it to Jack. "The guy in the picture is seated almost in front of the landing of the staircase. And from what I could see of the cupboard and counter past his shoulder, I'd be inclined to go along with your estimate of the house's age. Certainly not any newer than 1930 or so." She stared shrewdly at Jack for a long moment. "What the hell is going on, Mr. O'Brien? And I know you're not just looking for a house, so don't kid me."

"If I'm going to call you Madelyn, you'd better call me Jack." He hesitated briefly, then shook his head. "I can't tell you anything about the case, Madelyn. National security. But I can tell you this—if I don't find it, and fast, two innocent people will probably lose their lives."

"The guy in the picture?"

"He's one of them."

"I see. How can I help you, Jack?"

"I was hoping I could look through your listings of available rental properties. I'd bet money the place is rented. You don't use your own house in cases like this . . . not if you have any brains at all, anyway." He looked up with a hopeful expression. "If the listings are in any kind of systematic order, it'd be a big help."

Madelyn snorted with amusement as she tugged a large, heavy loose-leaf binder from a drawer of the filing cabinet and dropped it in front of Jack on the surface of her desk. The binder appeared to contain at least a hundred pages.

"Yeah, they're in order," she said with a grin. "Chronologically by the dates we accepted them as rentals. I'm sorry, Jack, but if you want to find your old house, you're going to have to go through the book, page by page, checking every listing individually."

"Great." Jack stared at the thick book and sighed. "I don't suppose there's any chance you'd let me take it back to my office? I'd return it in the morning, Scout's honor."

"No chance, pal." She laughed to relieve the sting of her rejection. "Tell you what, though—I'll go put on a fresh pot of coffee, and I'll keep the office open until you've had time to go through the entire book. I've got some paperwork to catch up on anyway." She smiled warmly as Jack reached for the binder. "It's not as bad as it looks. They're only three listings to the page."

"Thanks, Madelyn."

He hitched his chair up next to the realtor's desk and opened the binder to the first page. As he quickly scanned the first three listings—none of which were two-story houses—it occurred to him that he really should stop and call Barb to let her know that he was working late again. Then something caught his eye and he leaned over the book, jotting a note in his pocket notebook.

What the hell, he sighed, Barb had known what she was getting into when she had married him . . .

CHAPTER THIRTEEN

When Fran went downstairs Friday morning to use the bathroom facilities, she was pleased to see that her escort was Stoner instead of Redwing. She and Rick had not spoken to each other since Wednesday evening, except when absolutely necessary, and she now welcomed even the minimal human contact that Stoner provided. He, at least, did not display the unhealthy interest in her body that Redwing did. And Rick as well, she reminded herself with a trace of bitterness.

"Looks like you folks'll be out of here tomorrow," Stoner informed her as they reached the door of the bathroom. Fran paused with her hand on the doorknob as Stoner smiled. "Bet you'll be glad, huh?"

"Yes, of course. It seems as if we've been here forever."

"It has been quite a while. Five days." Stoner paused and cleared his throat, as if embarrassed by what he was about to say. "Y'know, Miss Barnette, speaking just for myself, I'm damned sorry you had to get mixed up in all this. It wasn't necessary, when you think about it."

"How do you mean?"

"Well, if you'd just turned that damned diskette over to me, back in Tahoe, instead of calling those DIA people in, all this could've been avoided." He looked at her with sympathy on his broad, craggy face. "Men like

241

Langtry and me, we're pros. We're always aware that things can happen to us. But you, you're really an innocent victim."

"Why don't you just turn me loose, then?" Fran asked.

"If it was up to me, I would," Stoner said. "But Charonsky's running things, and—" he broke off, blushing, as one of the doors down the hallway opened and one of the other guards emerged with a towel around his neck. "Well, enough said, I guess. You'd better go ahead and use the bathroom now."

The other guard, Mitchik, nodded to Stoner as he passed by them on his way to the staircase. The guards used the downstairs bathroom most of the time, Fran had observed; at least none of them had ever seemed to need the upstairs bathroom when she was around. Mitchik glanced at her as he walked past, and she felt a chill stir the downy hairs on the back of her neck. Mitchik had looked at her as if she were a dead woman already.

When she finished her shower, Stoner escorted her back to the attic with no further conversation between them. Stoner volunteered nothing further and failed to respond to her one attempt to draw him out. She was vaguely troubled as she climbed back up into the attic and immediately went to "her" area. She sat down on her mattress, drawing up her knees and resting her chin on them, staring thoughtfully at the weak gray light filtering through the grimy panes of the one tiny window. She was only minimally aware of Rick moving down out of the attic with Stoner to use the facilities; not speaking to him or acknowledging his presence had become a habit now.

That cold, impersonal look from Mitchik continued to trouble her, as well as the awkward, fumbling attempt at an apology from Stoner. For that was what the big man had been doing, she was in no doubt about that.

At least this time Charonsky had made no appearance, she thought with a feeling of gratitude. She detested the suave, oily Russian, with his insinuating smiles and snide remarks about Rick, the nasty little hints about Rick's "cooperation" and how it had so improved their situation.

Rick seemed to be gone for an unusually long time this morning, and when he finally did climb back up into the attic, she turned around and studied him closely. He looked up and their eyes met briefly, and she felt a little tingle shoot through her in spite of her resolve to disentangle herself from him. It seemed that she could intellectually make a decision to distance herself from him, but emotionally, it was not quite so easily accomplished. Each time their eyes met, or they happened to brush up against one another, a turmoil of feelings were stirred up deep within her.

"Good morning," he said in that low baritone voice that never failed to stir her.

"Good morning, Rick." She smiled tentatively. After all, she reflected, if they truly were to be released tomorrow—and Stoner had told her it was true—the least they could do would be to part on cordial terms. As Rick had pointed out, they had been through a lot together; and besides, it would cost her nothing to be courteous to him now.

"One more day," she said brightly, "and we're out of here!"

"That's right," he said disspiritedly. "One more day."

He turned away and went to his mattress, unable to face the hope shining brightly from those magnificent hazel eyes of hers for another second. He sat down with his back to her, staring blindly at the steep sloping roof that formed the walls of their prison, replaying his most recent conversation with Stoner in his mind.

"Listen, Langtry, I probably shouldn't be telling you this," Stoner had said in a low voice, just outside the bathroom, "But what the hell—you and I are pros. You're on the losing side this time," he said, shrugging, "but it could've just as easily been me."

"Okay, we're both pros," Rick said evenly. "But we just happen to be on opposite sides, so don't get too choked up over me, all right?"

"Look, I'm doing you a favor," Stoner said, glancing up in surprise. "If you don't want it, fine."

"Sorry, Stoner." It was true, he realized: Under different circumstances, he and Stoner might have been friends. "It's just been a little tough, lately."

"Sure, I understand." Stoner looked up and shook his head a little, an expression of regret in his eyes. "Thing is, Langtry, we got our orders this morning. You and the girl are to be taken out on the bay and put aboard the *Vostok,* no matter what goes down with the DIA and the diskette. You know enough about Charonsky to blow the whole bay area operation, so they can't let you go."

Rick nodded. It was as he had feared. "I suppose we'll get a bullet in the head out on the Pacific."

Stoner nodded. "You first," he admitted, ducking his head in embarrassment. "Redwing's supposed to get the girl for a few hours, before . . ."

Rick swore softly and bitterly. "I was afraid of this."

"Yeah, well, I don't much like it, but there it is. You and I are pros, Langtry, and I hope that when my time comes I can go out like you—quick and clean, a bullet in the back of the head and it's over. But I gotta admit I hate the thought of Redwing and that woman, I really do. She just doesn't deserve that."

"Help me, Stoner." Rick gripped the big man on the arm, urgency in his voice. "You can't let it end like that!"

"Yeah, I know. I've seen what Redwing does, and it makes me want to puke, thinking of—well . . ." He paused, rubbing his chin with a large, blunt thumb. Abruptly, he nodded. "All right, here's how it'll go down. We take you out on the bay in a cabin cruiser we'll pick up at the marina on Saturday morning, and meet the *Vostok* as she pulls out on high tide. Redwing's going to board the *Vostok* with you. Things have gotten a little too hot for him in this country."

"The two of us, on the *Vostok* with Redwing?" Rick's face twisted with emotion. "Stoner, I'd kill her myself to spare her that."

"Listen, Langtry, I respect you as a professional, and I'd like to think you respect me, too. On that level, anyway. Yeah, I know I'm a free lancer, selling my services to the highest bidder. To some people, that makes me a traitor, I suppose." He gave a shamefaced grin. "Me, I always thought of myself as a kind of soldier of fortune. But, damn it, there's things even I can't stomach, and what that crazy Redwing does to women is one of them. Langtry, I give you my word—I'll make sure you get it fast and clean, the both of you. If it gets me in hot water with Charonsky later, so be it. At least I'll be able to look myself in the eye a year from now."

"Thanks, Stoner." Rick swallowed the thick, hot knot of sorrow in his throat, trying not to think of the impending death of the woman he loved. "I appreciate it."

"Don't be stupid enough to try anything beforehand," Stoner warned. "You'll just get your girl messed up that much sooner, and there won't be a thing I can do to help in that case."

"Right. I'd hate for that to happen."

Now, as he turned and looked across the space separating him and Fran, he realized that he had spoken the truth. Stoner would be performing an act of mercy by granting Fran a quick, clean death. And it was fitting that he, Rick, would die immediately afterwards, so they would be together in death . . .

He jerked around at the sound of the trapdoor opening. Redwing stepped up into the attic, followed an instant later by Mitchik, who was holding a large, stainless steel automatic pistol which gleamed in the dim light of the attic. Redwing stared at Fran for a moment, then turned to Rick, his coarse features twisted in a grin. Warily, Rick got to his feet, uncomfortably aware that Mitchik kept the gun pointed at him all the while.

"Over here, Langtry," Redwing snapped. When Rick hesitated, Mitchik stepped aside, cocking the heavy automatic and aiming at Rick's knees. "Damn it, I said move!"

"All right, I'm coming." Rick walked slowly over to where Redwing waited, wondering what was going to happen. Surely they hadn't decided to kill him now, leaving the field free for Redwing to have Fran with no interference.

"Over here, Mr. DIA bigshot." Redwing gestured with a pair of shining steel handcuffs, pointing at one of the cross braces nailed to the slanting rafters of the attic. "Get over here and wrap your arms around this baby, Langtry."

"Handcuffs?" Rick hesitated, looking from Mitchik to Redwing and back again, his eyes narrowed with thought. "Why handcuffs, Redwing? And where's Stoner?"

"I'm just about through screwin' around with you, wise guy," Redwing roared. "Get your ass over here, right now, and wrap your arms around this brace! I want to see splinters in your cheeks, DIA man! And don't you worry about Stoner—I'm in charge now."

Across the attic Fran gasped at Redwing's last statement. "God help us," she whispered, watching with horror as the two armed men threatened Rick.

"Listen, you don't need the cuffs, Redwing," Rick pleaded. "You've got us cooped up here in this attic, armed guards right down below the trapdoor, there's no—"

"Hit 'em, Mitch!" Redwing yelled, his face mottled with rage.

Rick spun around to face the threat from the other man, but he was too late. Mitchik swung the heavy pistol in a short, vicious arc, striking Rick on the side of the head and knocking him to the floor. Fran stared, appalled, as Rick lay unmoving on the dusty attic floor. How much more could he take? How much could any man take?

Mitchik shoved his pistol into his belt and took hold of Rick's shoes, dragging him by the heels over to where Redwing waited. They pulled Rick's arms until they extended beyond the supporting brace, then snapped the steel cuffs tightly on his wrists. Rick moaned softly, slumping to the floor, his upper body sagging against the cruel bracelets.

"Okay, let's get outa here," Redwing muttered after a moment.

Mitchik went over and started down the ladder without so much as a glance back at Fran or Rick. Redwing hesitated at the trapdoor for a moment, staring at Fran with open lust.

"I'll see you later," he promised hoarsely. "And this time, there won't be anybody to bust us up, baby. Just you and me, 'til I'm damned good and ready to let you go."

"I'll kill myself first."

"No, you won't, lady." Redwing smiled and shook his head knowingly. "You're just not the type. Not you. If I thought for a minute there was any danger of that, I'd cuff you, too. String you up so tight you wouldn't be able to hurt a fly. But there ain't no chance, lady. You're the type who keeps lookin' for the cavalry to come chargin' in and save you, right up to the very last minute."

Numbly, Fran watched him disappear through the trapdoor, realizing that he was correct in his assessment of her character. It was true. Her imagination had always been an asset in her life until now, enabling her to be more successful and creative than some less imaginative competitors. Was it now to be her undoing?

She hurried over and knelt beside Rick, examining this latest injury as gently as possible. He groaned when she brushed the thick black hair back to see where the gun butt had struck. She sighed in relief: it had been a glancing blow, and the skin, though abraded, was not broken. Swelling was minimal. He would be okay in an hour or so.

"Fran . . . ?"

"Yes, Rick, I'm right here. Just relax and rest."

"Don' leave me, Fran." His speech was thick and hard to understand, as if his tongue had swollen in his mouth. He reached up and caught the hand that had been softly brushing his hair back, clinging to it desperately. "Don' ever leave me!"

"I'm right here, Rick. Just relax and rest. I won't go away, I won't leave you."

"Tha's good," he muttered, his eyes fluttering closed once again. "Tha's real good, 'cause I love you so mu . . ." His voice trailed away as he lapsed into unconsciousness.

Fran felt the hot sting of tears behind her lids as she sat there on the dusty attic floor with Rick's battered head resting in her lap. Life was so confusing. Just when she thought she really understood the situation they were in, something like this had to happen, shattering all her previously held convictions about what was true and untrue.

Because there was one thing for sure, she thought with a grim little smile. What Redwing and Mitchik had done to Rick, they had done on Charonsky's orders —and the treatment they'd given him was most assuredly not the treatment they would have given to a collaborator.

"Come in, Jack, come in. Let's hear what you've got for me today." Joseph Addison showed his large square teeth in a smile as Jack O'Brien walked into his office carrying his folders full of reports and supportive material.

"Sit down, Jack," Addison said with an expansive gesture. "Sit down."

"Thanks." Jack lowered himself into the visitor's chair and spent a moment arranging the papers in the bulging manila folder. He looked more uncomfortable with each passing moment, until he looked up and blurted, "Mr. Addison, Beth Ann tells me that Rick called here Wednesday. Why wasn't I and my task force informed?"

Addison lowered his eyes and looked away before replying. "It's true that Rick called," he admitted after a moment. Leaning forward, he placed his large, manicured hands flat on the polished mahogany surface of his desk, an earnest expression on his face. "It was my decision not to brief you on the call, Jack. For one thing, I didn't want to put undue pressure on you."

"Undue *pressure?*" Jack looked ready to burst into tears. "Mr. Addison, do you have any idea how much sleep I've had in the past week? Or how many times I've seen my wife?"

"I know you've been working very hard, O'Brien," Addison said. "Perhaps you should take some time off."

"I'll take some time off when Rick's back here safe and sound and not one damned minute before." Jack seemed to regain control of himself, leaning back in the chair and staring at his superior with open dislike. "Tell me about the phone conversation," he said bluntly. It was not a request, and Addison looked a little startled.

"Of course, of course," he said quickly. "Well, there wasn't much to it, really. He, uh, he simply relayed instructions from his captors on where and how to turn over the diskette on Saturday."

"Saturday?" Jack leaned forward alertly.

"Yes." Addison put a finger inside his collar and ran it around his neck, which was slowly turning a dull, brick red. "It, er, seems that they've moved up the deadline by twenty-four hours. Why, I don't know."

"I see. Now they say they've got to have the diskette by Saturday evening or they kill Rick and Fran Barnette. Is that it?"

"That's what he said," Addison said, nodding. "And that's what I mean when I said I didn't want to add to the pressure already on you, O'Brien. I—"

"Mr. Addison," Jack interrupted, as if the older man hadn't spoken, "*tomorrow* is Saturday."

"Yes. I know it is."

"Did you intend to tell me about the new deadline at all, or were you just going to wait until one of the bodies turned up?"

"Now see here, O'Brien," Addison sputtered, gripping the arms of his chair and halfway getting to his feet. "I'm getting a bit tired of being badgered! It so happens that I run this office, not you, and I'll make the decisions. Now I don't have to tell you that we stand just about the chance of a snowball in hell of getting the okay to turn that STEALTH data over to those kidnappers in order to save two lives!"

"So what're you saying? We just write them off?"

"Well, no, not in so many words. But damn it, Jack, we've got to live in the real world, son."

"Y'know, what bothers me is that we could've worked something out if you'd told me about the call. Now there's not much time for coming up with a fancy idea."

"Maybe it's not as bad as you think." Addison sank back down in his chair.

"Well, you're going to have to explain your reasoning on that one, chief," Jack said with a snort. "From where I sit, it's about as bad as it can get. And you tell me you've been sitting on the phone call for two damned days, when we could've been using the time to work something out—!"

"Look, let me give you all the details about the phone call, Jack," Addison said. "Maybe we can salvage something of the situation, if we put our heads together. The call came in just a few minutes before five o'clock . . ."

It was shortly after six o'clock in the evening when Jack joined the other members of his task force in the main part of the office. Simmons, Smith, and Whitworth were sipping coffee from styrofoam cups, slouching wearily in the government-issue swivel chairs spaced around the room. They looked up and nodded wearily when Jack appeared.

"Well, what a cheerful looking crew!" Jack rubbed his hands together briskly, hoping to convey an optimism he was far from feeling. "Okay, I'll take your individual reports, then we'll discuss the plan for tomorrow—which is Saturday, in case any of you yahoos have lost track of the time." Pausing, he looked around, waiting for a volunteer to start things off. When no one spoke, he pointed at Whitworth.

"Jerry, how're you coming with hunting down the van?"

Whitworth put his coffee cup down, a weary, discouraged expression crossing his face. "Jack, I don't think anybody had the slightest damned idea how many vans in this state fit the general description of the one we're looking for! I've spent all of yesterday and part of today over at the DMV in Sacramento looking through the records. Even with computer printouts, there're just thousands and thousands of possibles. Frankly, I think we're spinning our wheels with this approach. If this was a nice leisurely murder investigation, where time was of no importance, maybe it'd pay to track down all possible registered owners of vans, but we're looking at a deadline here, and I don't think we stand a chance of making it."

"I agree, Jerry. Forget about the van for now." He turned to Simmons. "How're you coming along with that list of two-story houses in Hayward?"

"Knocking it down pretty fast," Simmons said. "Just have a few left, and if Jerry's dropping the hunt for the van, maybe he can give us a hand running down the ones that're left."

"Maybe, but Jerry figures in my plan for tomorrow. Smitty, you've been giving John a hand running down the houses, haven't you?"

"Yeah, we've been working together, just in case we did come up with the right place." He chuckled dryly and made a shooting motion with his finger aimed like a pistol. "Be a hell of a note to dig the place up, then not be able to report back in because they just added you to the catch."

"Okay, you guys have done well. But right now, let's talk about tomorrow. I've got some news—some good,

252

some bad." For the next several minutes, he filled them in on Rick's phone call to Addison on Wednesday evening, and on Addison's decision to withhold the information from Jack and the task force. "We discussed it at some length," he said pointedly, when the others expressed outrage at their supervisor's action—or lack of action.

"Now, about tomorrow. Addison will go out on the tour boat as ordered, carrying a faked-up diskette wrapped in a waterproof package. He'll make his drop when he's told, just like the man said." Jack paused, holding up a finger for emphasis.

"Now, I figure they've got to have one man on the tour boat with Addison to give him the word on when to drop the diskette over the side. You also have to figure they'll have a boat out on the bay somewhere, set to intercept the tour boat in a location where it won't attract too much attention to itself—probably on the back side of Alcatraz, where the tour boats make a wide turn, or maybe where it turns around, under the Golden Gate. Either one of those places would make a good rendezvous point, where a small boat could make its approach . . .

"Okay, so we're looking at probably two men on the small intercept boat, and one man—or woman—aboard the tour boat with the old man. Smitty, I want you to be on the tour boat with Addison. Stick to him like a second skin, but for Chrissake's don't give it away that you're an agent—at least until after the contact goes down. Take a date along with you, dress up like a tourist. Beth Ann volunteered to help out. Ask her to go with you."

Smith nodded. "You want me to pick up on who makes contact with the old man, then tail 'em when the boat docks, right?"

"You've got it. Addison will give you a signal when

he's contacted to help identify the contact. From that moment on they belong to you, Smitty. Stick with 'em, don't let 'em out of sight."

"It's not gonna be easy." Smith frowned. "If I stick that close, they're gonna make me, Jack. It's impossible to maintain close surveillance without being spotted, if you're talking one man tailing an experienced agent. You know that."

"Sure, I know it. I want them to spot you. The whole idea is to provoke some action—create a panic." Jack paused for a moment, checking the styrofoam containers scattered across the desk tops in the room, looking for some warm coffee. He found a cup and took a sip, grimacing. "Simmons, you finish checking the houses in Hayward. The rest of us'll be in on Addison's bait and switch operation. The crap's going to hit the fan when they open that package and find another phony diskette anyway, so we're going for broke tomorrow."

"I just hope we don't get Rick killed, foisting off another fake on them," Whitworth muttered.

"You and me both, buddy," Jack said fervently. "But you and I both know that there just ain't no way the government's going to turn over what these clowns want—not for a dozen Rick Langtrys. We're hoping they'll realize they can't win, and let their hostages go."

"Quite a gamble," Whitworth commented.

"You're telling me."

"I've got a question," Simmons said in his deep, gruff bass voice. "That tour boat operation doesn't start up until after lunch, right? So how about a couple of you guys helping me finish up checking out the two-story houses tomorrow morning? That way I'd be available to help out in the afternoon, if I'm needed."

Jack hesitated a moment, then asked, "About how many houses are left to be checked out, John?"

"Hell, I can tell you exactly how many there are."

254

Simmons reached into his pocket and withdrew a small, tattered notebook and consulted it for a moment. "There're eighteen houses left on my list. Now, working by myself, driving from place to place and going through my spiel at each place, I can do probably four, maybe five houses in an hour. If Jerry and Smitty stick with me and help out, we could finish them off by 11:00 A.M. and shoot back up to Fisherman's Wharf in time to see the tour boats off."

"Good thinking, John. I'll come along as well, and we'll really knock it out in a hurry. Divide up the list among the four of us. Give me five houses, you keep five, and give Smitty and Jerry four apiece. Everybody carry two-way radios, just in case, since we'll be working alone. You make contact, give a good loud squawk and the rest of us'll come running."

Simmons rolled a sheet of paper into a typewriter and began tapping the keys. Five minutes later each man had his list of two-story houses to be checked out first thing tomorrow morning.

Jack sat down at his desk and wearily sipped the lukewarm coffee he'd found, studying his list of five addresses. The third address on his list was 720 Archibald.

At that moment, forty-odd miles to the southeast in Hayward, Fran Barnette stood watching as Rick used the sharp edge of one of his handcuffs to scratch a message into the soft pine of the cross brace to which he was cuffed. The words, deeply scratched into the wood, read: Langtry, Barnette, Sov. Ship *Vostok*, Sat A.M. Op Chief Charonsky, KGB.

"There," Rick said with grim satisfaction. He used his sleeve to rub some dust into the fresh scratches so they wouldn't be so noticeable. "If Jack or any of the guys get this far, they damned sure won't miss that."

"How do you feel, Rick?" She reached out and gently

touched the side of his head where he had been struck. He winced, then steadied under her gentle touch. "There's very little swelling. Let's have another look at your pupils."

"Dad always told me I had a hard head," Rick said as he turned and stared wide-eyed. "This last week has sure been proof of that."

Fran leaned forward and stared into his eyes, turning his head slightly to get better light on his face. His eyes were so dark and the light filtering through the dirty window was so weak that she had a difficult time making out his pupils, but when she finally located them they appeared to be of equal size.

"They look okay," she said softly. His warm breath on her throat and cheeks brought a flush to her face. "Your eyes . . ."

"My eyes can't see a damned thing but you, Fran," he said huskily. "Listen, it's very important that you believe me. We might not have much time left, so you can take this as a dying man's declaration, if it'll make you trust me any better——"

"Just hush," she interrupted, placing a finger across his lips and shaking her head. She knew what he wanted to say, and she was uncertain of what her reaction should be. There was still much that troubled her, many things she did not understand. "And don't give me that 'dying man' routine, Rick. You'll be just fine in a day or two."

"I love you, Fran," he whispered, drawing her near, his lips moving against the soft skin of her throat. He felt her trembling at his touch. "I think I must've loved you from the first moment I saw you, but I've never had the guts to admit it until a couple of days ago. I love you, lady, and I don't care if the whole damned world knows it!"

"If you love me so much . . . maybe you can tell me

the reasons for your peculiar behavior in this attic during the past several days." He flinched at her words and looked away, and she felt the disappointment rising anew at his reaction of what just had to be guilt. "Someday, when you feel like it," she said comfortingly.

"Yes, someday, I will," he replied, his eyes squeezed shut, afraid she would see the grief and fear for her if he opened them and let his thoughts show.

She moved up against him, laying her head against his broad back, her arms wrapped tightly around his chest from the back. She could feel his breathing under her cheek, and sighed with a combination of sadness and relief; sad that she would be soon parting from Rick, who with all his faults was still the most fascinating man she'd ever known, and relief that she would be out of this mess, away from this filthy attic and back to her life in southern California once again.

She sighed. In a way, she would be very sorry to leave him. In spite of everything that had happened, everything she knew about him, she continued to feel an emotional entanglement with him, a pull toward him unlike anything she'd ever felt for any other man.

"Fran, do you see that piece of paper over there against the wall, in the shadows?" he whispered after a few minutes.

"Umm-hmm," she replied.

"Would you get it for me, please?"

Reluctantly, she stood up and moved away, her skin tingling with warmth where they had been in physical contact. She picked up the crumpled envelope and brought it to him, after glancing disinterestedly at it. "What is it, Rick?"

"Oh, hell," he muttered, after smoothing it out and looking at it. "It's just that old gas bill I stole the other day when I made the phone call to Addison." He tossed it aside and it landed a few feet away, with the printed side up. Fran glanced at it, remembering how she had ridiculed Rick about it on Wednesday.

The address read 720 Archibald. Big deal, she thought. Too bad Jack O'Brien didn't have the address. Maybe then it would have done them some good.

"Look," Rick whispered. "The sun's going down."

She looked up at the window, which was streaked across with a brilliant pattern of reds and oranges. There must be clouds out over the ocean, she thought idly.

"Yes," she murmured. "One more night and we're out of here. This is our last night in this damned attic."

"Yeah," he said, but his tone was utterly joyless. "Our last night in the attic." *Or anywhere else,* he finished the thought silently.

CHAPTER FOURTEEN

When Fran opened her eyes on Saturday morning, the first thing she saw was Rick, looking down at her with a weary smile. She had pulled the mattresses over next to him and arranged the blankets so he would have a modicum of comfort in spite of his awkward, handcuffed position at the cross brace, where he was unable to comfortably sit or lie down.

"It's Saturday!" she exclaimed.

"Yeah." He smiled wearily. She saw the dark pouches under his eyes and felt a surge of compassion. "Saturday."

"Did you sleep at all?" she asked.

"Had to stand up most of the night." He gestured at the pile of mattresses and blankets she'd so carefully arranged the night before. "Fell asleep on the pile you arranged for me, but it collapsed and woke me."

"Oh, Rick!" she said impatiently, giving him a little shake. "You should've woken me. I would've fixed it for you."

He shook his head. "You were sleeping so peacefully I just couldn't. It would've been a crime."

"But you didn't get any rest! Don't you ever sacrifice your own rest for my sake, you hear me?" She smiled, doing a little dance step around the attic. "This is the first day of our freedom, mister, so let's have none of that morbid behavior!"

"Okay, it's a deal." He managed a smile, his heart breaking at the fate that awaited her in a matter of hours.

Fran spent the next few minutes dragging the rest of the bedding and mattresses together, forming a kind of chair for him to relax on. He groaned with pleasure as he sank down on the improvised seat, taking the weight off his feet and legs.

"Not exactly a Hepplewhite chair, but you can't beat it for comfort, right?" She sat down in front of him, cross-legged, and smiled at him, wondering why he remained so glum, determined to cheer him up. They would be parting soon; she didn't want her memory of him to be of this sad-faced, exhausted young man before her now. Remembering the way he had been in the cabin in the mountains, after they'd escaped from Stoner and Redwing, she felt a flush of warmth flooding her cheeks. That was how she would remember him, she decided: the happiness and fun, before the deceit and dishonesty spoiled everything.

"Know what the first thing I'm going to do when I get out of here?" she asked gaily. "Walk. Just walk around where I can smell the grass and flowers and look up at the sky again. Stand by the ocean somewhere and listen to the surf. How about you?"

He hesitated before replying, filled with admiration for her. Whether she actually believed they were going to be released today, or was merely keeping up the pretense in order to keep their spirits up, there was a sort of blithe gallantry about her, a cheerful insouciance that he couldn't help responding to. What a woman. If he was to meet his maker today, he decided, he certainly couldn't do it in better company.

"I don't know," he said, playing along with her. "I

260

think maybe—" He broke off at the sound of the trap-door crashing open. Redwing's rough, pockmarked face appeared in the opening and swiveled automatically to leer at Fran for a few seconds. He placed a paper bag on the floor.

"Breakfast. Eat quick, 'cause we're moving out of here this morning."

"Soon?" Fran asked.

"Soon." Redwing looked at his watch. "It's just after eight. I want us out of this hole by nine. So eat your breakfast and make your visits to the toilet."

"Redwing," Rick called. "How about these cuffs?"

"Yeah, I guess you're gonna need to be moving around." Redwing climbed the rest of the way into the attic and walked over to Rick. Taking a small silver-colored key from his pocket, he unlocked the cuff from Rick's right hand. When Rick stepped back away from the post, stretching his arms and groaning with pleasure and relief, Redwing reached up and gripped his wrist and whipped it down behind his back. When Rick began to struggle, Redwing shoved the muzzle of his revolver up against the back of Rick's neck.

"Get the other one back here," he snapped. Reluctantly, Rick lowered his left arm and stood stolidly while Redwing snapped the cuffs closed behind his back.

"How the hell am I supposed to eat?" he said.

"Just have to get your girl friend to feed you, Langtry." Redwing snorted with amusement at the furious expression on Rick's face. "I ain't takin' no chances with you, man. Charonsky said to watch you like a hawk, and that's exactly what I'm doin'." He stepped back a pace. "You need to go to the can, Langtry?"

"You going to hold it for me?" Rick asked furiously.

Redwing colored slightly. "I'll unlock 'em long enough for you to use the bathroom."

"All right, then. I do have to go."

Fran watched them leave the attic, Rick backing down the ladder with extreme caution while Redwing kept him covered with his revolver from above. An uneasy sensation threatened to spoil the optimistic mood she had worked so hard to create; they were certainly not treating Rick like a prisoner who was about to be released. They had handcuffed him, and kept a gun on him at all times. It occurred to her that they were treating him more like a prisoner on death row than anything else . . .

Jack O'Brien gulped at the fiery liquid in the styrofoam cup and looked at his watch for the dozenth time in the past five minutes. Though he was early for the eight o'clock meeting with the remainder of the task force, he couldn't escape the uneasy sensation that time was quickly running out.

Taking a huge bite of a jelly doughnut, he glanced out the plate glass window of the doughnut shop just off the freeway in Hayward, where the members of the task force were to assemble before parting to complete their search. He grunted with satisfaction at the sight of John Simmons pulling into a parking slot and getting out of his car. A couple of minutes later, the big agent was joining him in the small booth, carrying a cup of coffee and a sack of doughnuts.

"Morning," he rumbled in his gravelly bass voice. "Want a doughnut?"

"Morning, John." He glanced at the bulging sack. "No, thanks. I had something already."

"Good. I want 'em all myself anyway."

Jack chuckled and took a sip of his coffee. Within the next five minutes the other two members of the force arrived and joined them in the booth. As they sipped their coffee, Jack gave them their last minute instructions.

"Everybody got their walkie-talkies?" They all either nodded or held up the small handsets, and Jack went on, "Good. Now, these things have enough range so that we shouldn't be out of touch with each other at any time. Anybody comes up with what he thinks is the place—buzz us and give the code word—gymnast, and the nearest cross-street. Don't attempt anything on your own! Wait until we're all there and can go in together. We don't want anybody getting hurt at this stage." He looked at them. "Any questions?"

"Yeah," Smitty said laconically. "Can we blow these slime bag kidnappers away when we catch them?"

"You know the rules, Smitty," Jack said. "No shooting unless necessary to save lives—especially your own." He glanced at his watch. "All right, it's exactly eight fifteen. If nobody comes up with the house, we'll assemble back here before heading back to the city. Check in with me when you're through with your lists."

"Right, Jack."

"Okay. Good hunting."

Jack waited until the rest of the team had gone in their separate directions, then paid the check and left the doughnut shop. He drove toward the first address on his list, after consulting his Thomas Brothers map of Hayward. Fortunately, the first two houses were located within half a dozen blocks of one another, so he was on his way to the third address by nine o'clock.

He glanced down at the list on the seat next to him, then reached for his Thomas Brothers map, muttering, "720 Archibald, 720 Archibald. Where are you . . . ?"

"Okay, let's get a move on, damn it." Redwing gestured impatiently with his automatic as he herded Fran and Rick toward the van parked in the garage at 720

Archibald. A door in the kitchen led directly into the attached garage, so it wasn't necessary to go out of the house to enter the garage. The familiar van was the only vehicle inside the garage, which had the atmosphere of long vacancy; no garden tools hung on the walls, no cluttered workbench. Just four walls, cobwebs, and the wide hanging door.

"Morning, folks." Rick jerked around in surprise at the sound of Stoner's voice. The big man had been seated in the passenger seat of the van, and he tipped his hat at them as they climbed in through the side door.

"Stoner. We thought you were gone."

"Nope, I'm not gone. I couldn't miss out on the end of the show, could I?" He winked almost imperceptibly at Rick as Redwing climbed into the driver's seat and started the engine.

"Damn it, I told that dude to meet us at the marina at nine," Redwing swore as he put the van into reverse. "Here it is damned near ten after nine already, and we're just leavin'. I knew we shoulda skipped breakfast, damn it!"

"What do you care?" Stoner asked lazily. "Hell, we're paying for the damned thing, ain't we? What do they care if we show up at nine or nine fifteen, or even nine thirty? Hell, it's all the same to them. They don't care when we get to the boat."

"Boat?" Fran's voice rose sharply. "Boat? I thought—"

"Yeah, we know what you thought," Redwing said, leering at her in the rearview mirror. "But you folks are takin' a little boat ride this morning. Remember the *Vostok?* Well, you'n me have a nice, private stateroom waitin' for us, lady. Think of it—a nice, slow cruise to the Soviet Union, and just the two of us to enjoy it!"

Fran sucked in her breath in dismay, reaching down and gripping one of Rick's handcuffed hands. He squeezed her hand tightly, trying to convey reassurance with his eyes, but all he saw in her face was hopelessness and despair. A tear appeared on her thick lashes, and he leaned forward and kissed it away.

"Now you understand," he whispered huskily. "I played along with Charonsky as far as I did to keep him from giving you to Redwing." He paused, and added bitterly, "And it was all for nothing."

"Oh, Rick, I'm sorry." She sobbed quietly against his shoulder. "I've been so wrong about you!"

"Just hang on, baby," he said. "It won't be much longer, I promise you. I won't let it happen. Redwing's not going to get his filthy hands on you. That's a promise."

"Oh, Rick, how will you stop him!" She shook her head. "I'd rather die!"

"Hang on, baby." He looked up at the sky as the van rolled backwards out of the garage. From his position on the floor of the van, he couldn't see much, but he hadn't had a good look at the sky in several days and he greedily drank it in now. It was one of those rare, crystalline days when the skies were washed clear and the temperature balmy; a day of such rare beauty that life was suddenly poignantly sweet. Fran lay against his chest, trembling with dread, her optimistic, insouciant mood thoroughly crushed by Redwing's words.

"You guys get the place cleaned up?" Stoner asked idly, as Redwing drove through the streets, heading toward the marina.

"Mitchik's supposed to be finishin' up," Redwing said. "Not a hell of a lot to do, really . . ."

"Gotta clean up the attic," Stoner pointed out. "Get rid of that bedding and so on."

Rick caressed Fran's hair, thinking furiously. *Damn you,* he cursed himself, *think of something!*

* * *

Jack pulled up into the driveway at 720 Archibald at almost exactly a quarter past nine and looked at the house with quickening interest. A two-story Edwardian house with ornate gingerbread trim, the place had the abandoned aura of a house long vacant, though he knew full well from his session with Madelyn Pearson, the realtor, that the place was under a year's lease.

He unbuttoned his jacket as he walked up to the front door, reaching around and loosening his snub-nosed .38 in its hip holster as the door chimes died away. After several seconds he punched the doorbell again. He had heard movement on the other side of the wall, and he was determined to get an answer. He savagely punched the doorbell several more times, and was finally rewarded by the sound of feet crashing down a flight of stairs.

"All right, all right, damn it. I'm coming!"

An instant later the door was jerked open. Jack stared at the young, dark-complexioned man standing before him and instinctively knew he had found the house where Rick and Fran were being held prisoner. The young man looked at the hand-held radio in Jack's left hand, then back up into his eyes.

"Cops!" he exclaimed, his eyes widening in panic.

He thrust out his hands full force, taking Jack by surprise. Jack went sprawling off the porch and onto the lawn, the wind knocked out of him. The dark-complexioned young man pelted up the street and around the corner, disappearing just as Jack raised up on his elbow and drew his revolver.

"Damn it," Jack muttered as he got to his feet. He picked up the radio and thumbed the transmit button. "All right, guys, I've got the place," he said. "Come to 720 Archibald."

He stared at the radio with disgust when there was no

reply. He shook it several times, then thumped it with the heel of his hand. Damn. The fall off the porch must have damaged it. He was on his own.

Cautiously, he approached the front door, which was gaping wide open. The house felt empty, but he followed standard procedures, keeping his weapon drawn, entering each room with extreme caution. When he entered the large, old-fashioned parlor, he recognized it immediately as the room in which the video tape had been filmed. The door which led from the parlor, just beyond the landing of the staircase, led into the kitchen. There, on the wall, was a rectangle of lighter paint where the calendar which had appeared on the video-tape had hung.

He hurried through the downstairs rooms with the growing certainty that he was too late; that Rick and Fran had been removed to whatever fate had been decreed for them by their captors. By the time he finished searching the ground floor and was on the second story, he was dashing from empty room to empty room, throwing the doors open and charging inside without a thought for proper procedure. The second story was empty, and he was almost ready to despair of finding a quick clue as to what had happened when he spotted the ladder which led up into the attic. His heartbeat quickened as he reached up and pulled it down. It moved smoothly, on oiled hinges, as if it had been used recently, and frequently.

"I knew it!"

When he emerged in the attic and saw the piled up mattresses and blankets and the unused waste bucket, he knew that this was where Rick and Fran had spent the last several days. He walked around the wide space, searching for anything that might tell him what had happened to his partner. He spotted the old gas bill envelope and nodded grimly. Rick would have found that. Rick would have discovered where they were being held, if at all possible. Jack examined the gas bill envelope, but there was nothing on it beyond the address of the house and the name of the lease holder. He shoved it into his pocket. Chances were just about ninety-eight percent that the lease holder had given a phony name, but it had to be checked out.

Why were all the blankets piled up around the cross brace at one side of the attic, Jack wondered. He walked over and moved the blankets around, looking at the floor and the base of the rafter, finding nothing. As he raised up slowly, examining the rafter and the cross brace, he spotted the words scratched into the brace and yelped with joy.

Rick had figured out a way to help him. Jack pelted down the stairs, out through the front door, and skidded to a halt on the front lawn. Two elderly women gawked at him in avid curiosity.

"If you're looking for the men who live here, they're gone, mister," one of the elderly ladies quavered. "If you're a burglar, I promise I won't tell anyone I saw you."

"I'm an intelligence agent, ma'am," Jack said, flashing his identification. "You saw them leave? How long ago?"

"Oh, it wasn't but a few minutes ago, I guess. They left in that old van of theirs just a few minutes after nine o'clock."

"Van? What color van?"

"Oh, it's blue, I guess. Blue or some kind of green, I have a hard time telling them apart sometimes."

"Never mind about that," Jack said quickly. "You say they just left?"

"Mister, it couldn't've been more than five minutes before you come pulling in to the driveway." The old lady peered narrowly at him. "Say, what'd you do to

268

that boy to scare him off that way? He run out of here like the hounds of hell was after him."

The other old woman snorted. "Hmph. It was the other way around, Florence. That youngun' just shoved him right off the porch and run right over him."

"Thanks, ladies," Jack said, hurrying to his car. "I don't suppose either of you have any idea where the closest marina is?"

They shook their heads almost in unison, and Jack twisted the key in the ignition. With a wave he roared out of the driveway and headed down the street, filled with new optimism.

"All right, in the boat." Stoner gestured with his revolver, standing with his back turned to the marina, facing Fran and Rick. Redwing was fifty feet away, talking animatedly to the man from whom he'd rented the small cruiser.

"You going to shoot us now, Stoner?" Rick asked. "What if I just refuse to board? What if we decide to run?"

"It won't work, Langtry. We'd just shoot you and go on. We're leaving the country anyway, so it wouldn't make much difference in the long run."

Stoner noticed that Rick was looking down the boardwalk where Redwing was shaking hands with the fat, bald, middle-aged owner of the boat. "Shoot him, too, if you were thinking about trying to attract his attention. I wouldn't advise it." He gestured with the revolver again. "Go on. Get aboard."

Rick stepped lithely aboard the small cruiser, spreading his feet quickly when the small boat rocked a bit under his weight. With his hands cuffed behind his back, it was awkward trying to move around on the deck. When Fran came aboard he was able to do nothing to steady her. She took his arm and clung to him while Stoner came aboard.

Rick looked around. He knew nothing about boats, but this one looked expensive to him. It was perhaps twenty-five or thirty feet in length, with a streamlined profile. A rakish curved bow with chrome handrails all around and a dazzling white canvas canopy above the cockpit area, where the controls were located, gave the boat a classy appearance, at least to the uninitiated. The cockpit was directly above the small area of deck where the three of them were standing; directly below the cockpit was a narrow door which apparently led into the cabin. It was toward this door that Stoner prodded them now.

"Go on, get inside. Move it, now."

Rick opened the door and stood aside, permitting Fran to enter first. He followed her into the cabin, stooping slightly as he passed through the doorway, and looked around, impressed. The luxurious interior reinforced his opinion that he was aboard an expensive piece of marine machinery. Thick carpeting covered the floor, and the fixtures in the cleverly arranged room appeared to be expensive and well-made.

"Nice, eh?" Stoner asked, standing in the open doorway.

"Listen, Stoner," Rick asked, ignoring the comment, "how about taking these damned cuffs off?"

"Not a chance, Langtry," Stoner said flatly.

"You . . . you haven't forgotten your promise?"

"I haven't forgotten." Stoner stepped back through the doorway. "You folks just relax now. We'll try to make this as pleasant as we can." He closed the door, and they heard the sound of a key in the lock.

"Locked in," Fran said hollowly. She sat down on the sofalike bench that ran along one side of the cabin. "What promise?" she asked.

"What? Oh, nothing, really." He started to reply further, but they felt the boat rock slightly as Redwing stepped aboard. An instant later there was the whirring of the starter, followed by the muffled, powerful-sounding murmur of the engines.

Rick staggered slightly as the boat began moving away from the marina and heading out into the bay. When he had his balance back, he took several deep breaths, then vaulted straight into the air, simultaneously whipping his handcuffed wrists under his feet and forward. When he landed lightly on the carpeted floor, his hands were in the front.

"There, damn it," he said. "That feels a hell of a lot better."

"Wow. I guess I'd almost forgotten you were an Olympics gymnast."

"This is the first time it's ever been of any practical benefit," he said grimly. "But I sure as hell don't feel quite as helpless this way." He sat down next to her on the bench seat and looked deeply into her eyes.

"I want you to know something, Fran, before this is all over with, one way or another. These last few days, back in the attic—is it clear in your mind now that I wasn't betraying you or my country?"

"Hush, darling," she said, shaking her head, feeling the sting of tears behind her lids. "I just wish we had more time to spend together. I'm sorry that so much of our time has been spent at each other's throats. I'd like the chance to do it differently."

"It wasn't your fault, baby," he said soothingly, taking her hand and rubbing it gently. "It was just exactly what Charonsky wanted. It wasn't enough for him that I played along as far as I ethically could. He got some kind of weird, perverted kick out of keeping you and I at odds with one another." He shook his head ruefully. "And when you add to that my lifelong aversion to

271

commitment . . . well, it'd be a miracle if things had been any smoother between us."

"I—I guess so," she agreed, sniffing. "Oh, Rick, I feel so terrible, the things I was thinking about you! I couldn't wait to get away, because one of the things I wanted to do was to get far, far away from you."

"Well, we beat the odds, didn't we?" he asked, holding her hand to his lips and kissing it. "At least once."

"Yes," she said, smiling at the memory of their love-making. "We beat the odds that time."

"I just feel like an idiot, that's all."

"Don't feel that way, not at all. The KGB are experts at manipulating people, Fran. And Charonsky's one of the leading experts in the KGB, or he wouldn't be stationed out here where he is, on the edge of Silicon Valley. What kind of a chance did you, an innocent bystander, a businesswoman from southern California, have against the likes of Anatoly Charonsky?"

"None, I suppose, but . . ." She fell silent, then looked up at him, wide-eyed and fearful. "Rick? What's going to happen to us now? Are they going to get away with putting us on that ship and taking us to Russia? Can things like that happen? I mean, don't they have to look at passports and like that before you can leave the country? And what about you? Redwing said that he and I—" She grimaced with distaste and looked away for a moment before going on. "Rick, what have they got planned for you?"

His eyes turned flinty. "They've got a cold, watery grave planned for me, Fran. But I'm going to do my level best to try and keep that from happening."

"But if something happens to you, Redwing—"

"Stoner won't let that happen to you, Fran." He stared at her for several seconds, until she understood the grim message in his eyes. She nodded slowly. "He gave me his word."

* * *

Jack slammed on the brakes of his government Plymouth and skidded to a halt in front of the marina office, leaping out of the car before it stopped moving. He jerked open the door of the office and yelled at the fortyish, hennaed woman behind the counter, "Do you people rent boats?"

"Well, yes, sometimes, but—"

"Have you rented one in the past half hour or so? To a party of four, maybe five? One woman and three, maybe four men? Good-looking woman and a slim, dark-haired man?"

The woman shook her head. "I've been trying to tell you, we haven't rented any boats in days, but I think Joe Chapman just rented his Chris-Craft out to a group that fits that description."

"Joe Chapman? Where can I reach him?"

"Well, he's gone. He met them down here and turned over the keys and stuff and got paid, but I'm sure he's on his way back home by now. You can probably reach him at home in an hour or so. We have his number, if that'll help."

"Damn!" Jack slammed his fist down on the counter. The woman jumped back a little, startled. "How long ago did they leave?"

"Not more than five or ten minutes ago. You just missed them."

Jack hesitated for a few seconds then took out his identification folder and flashed his badge and government ID card. "I need a fast boat, and I need it right now. I'll take care of the paperwork later. If anything happens to the boat, Uncle Sam will reimburse the owner."

"Well, the marina owns a little runabout . . . it's fast enough to pull skiers, so I suppose it's fast enough for your purposes." Turning, she took a key from a cork board behind the counter. "Come with me, Mr.—?"

"O'Brien. Jack O'Brien."

"All right, Jack, let's get you squared away." Out from behind the counter, she appeared much more relaxed. She flashed a wide smile at Jack as she led him toward a small, fast-looking runabout tied up near the office. Jack stared at the boat and felt a tinge of apprehension. With its plexiglass hull, leather seats, and large, authoritative-looking outboard motor, the runabout was more boat than he'd operated in the past.

"You're gonna try and catch up to Joe's Chris-Craft, right?"

"Right." Jack shot her an amused glance. "Think this baby'll do it?"

"Oh, it's plenty fast enough, all right." She pointed toward the bay, which sparkled under the clear azure skies. "It's just that on days like this there's one hell of a lot of pleasure boat traffic out there. You might have a little trouble finding the right boat, that's all."

Jack looked in the direction of her pointing finger and his spirits plummeted. The dazzlingly clear, unusually balmy day had apparently brought out dozens of amateur boating enthusiasts. The dark cerulean blue waters of the bay were speckled with pleasure boats of all colors.

"I'll find them," Jack said grimly. "I'll find them, because I know where they're headed."

Rick backed up against the bulkhead near the door, flattening himself as much as possible so he wouldn't be seen at once by a person opening the door.

Fran sat on the bench seat staring wide-eyed at the door, wondering who was going to enter the cabin, Stoner or Redwing. Less than a moment ago, they had heard a brief, violent struggle and a single pistol shot from above, followed by the splash of a heavy object falling into the water.

"A body?" Fran had whispered to Rick, and he had nodded.

"Probably. But which one?"

Now they waited for the answer to their question. They felt the motion of the boat as a heavy body came down from the cockpit. Fran stared at the door, but could see nothing but a blur of clothing; no distinguishable features which would have told her if it was Stoner or Redwing.

The door flew open. Redwing stepped inside and crouched with his pistol held in both hands, swiveling quickly to cover the entire room. His eyes were wide and alert, and in less than half a second he realized that Rick must be behind him. He started to spin around but he was too late. Rick kicked out and sent the gun flying. It hit the deck and skidded up against the bulkhead opposite where Fran was seated.

Redwing dived toward the gun, and Rick fell on him, trying to get his cuffed hands over Redwing's head and around his neck, but Redwing guessed his intention and tucked his head low, against his chest, bull-like, and kept squirming toward the gun. Desperately, Rick tried to get a grip, but Redwing was fast and powerful and wasn't handicapped by a pair of handcuffs.

Fran watched, unable to move, her heart pounding inside her chest like a trip-hammer. *Do something!* she shouted inwardly, but remained paralyzed as she watched the two men struggling desperately. *Rick is fighting for our lives!* she thought, but in spite of her eagerness to help him, she remained unable to move.

As Redwing's fingers reached the walnut grip of the heavy automatic pistol, she was galvanized into action. Jumping up, she crossed the cabin in two steps. She brought her heel down on the back of Redwing's hand

275

with all the strength of her right leg, then twisted her foot, grinding it back and forth.

With a bellow of rage and pain Redwing released the pistol, rolling over and kicking Rick back and away, cradling his injured hand to his chest and glaring murderously at Fran. Quickly, she scooped up the pistol and pointed it unsteadily at Redwing while the two men glowered at each other, their chests heaving.

"Shoot him, damn it!" Rick sobbed.

"I—I can't!" she cried, squeezing the trigger. She pulled and yanked, but the trigger wouldn't move. Redwing's eyes glittered with renewed hope, and he began sidling toward the open door that led out onto the deck.

"The safety," Rick yelled. "Take the safety off!"

"The—oh, here!" She thrust the gun toward Rick. Redwing's foot shot out, kicking the gun from her hand. Rick dove toward the gun, which was skidding toward the rear of the cabin under the table. Redwing dove through the open hatch out onto the deck and vanished from view.

"Stoner's gun!" Rick yelled. Fran stood in the center of the cabin, unable to move. "He's after Stoner's gun, damn it! Get down!"

He scooped up the automatic, thumbed off the safety, and followed Redwing out onto the deck. Fran stood motionless for a moment, then turned determinedly toward the opening which led to the deck. That was her man out there defending their lives; she would not put her head in the sand and wait while he put his life on the line for her. *Whatever happens to Rick Langtry,* she resolved fiercely, *I am going to be a part of it! Now, and for the rest of my life!*

Pausing in the opening, she saw Rick, leaning back against the transom, aiming the automatic at something above and beyond her. She spun around and saw Redwing, turning with Stoner's revolver in his uninjured hand. There was a tremendously loud crack and Rick fell backwards. He reeled along the transom, then collapsed on the deck.

Fran's eyes slowly rolled up in her head and she began falling to the deck. As she spun slowly into the inviting velvety darkness, she was vaguely aware of another shot, followed by a splash, then an excited voice yelling Rick's name, but it was fading too rapidly for her to identify the speaker. She swirled down into the darkness of unconsciousness, almost grateful for the oblivion.

Jack O'Brien watched the big man topple from the small cabin cruiser into the waters of the bay with a sense of satisfaction. Holstering his .38, he sat down and guided the rented speedboat slowly over to the cabin cruiser, standing and tying a short white rope to the chrome railing around the transom.

"Rick!"

He saw the supine figure of his partner in the slowly spreading pool of blood, as still as death. Just beyond, in the opening leading into the cabin, Fran Barnette lay on her back, motionless.

"God, I'm too late." Jack groaned, and then his heart soared at the sound of a sigh and a slight movement of the boat.

One of them, at least, was still alive.

CHAPTER FIFTEEN

The metallic blue Mazda RX-7 sped down the winding highway, flying across the picturesque, gossamer bridges that arced high above the narrow inlets along the Pacific Coast Highway, encountering one spectacularly beautiful vista after another as it rounded each curve with graceful precision. The lovely blonde at the controls of the car reached up and brushed a tear from her cheek.

"Hey, what're the tears about?" her companion asked.

"It's just that all this is so very beautiful," Fran responded. "And I came so close to never having the opportunity to share it with you." She glanced over and smiled at him through her happy tears. "You know, Rick, I thought you were a goner, back there on the boat."

"I probably would've been," he said, gesturing at his right arm, which was encased from the wrist to the elbow in a plaster-of-paris cast. The bullet from Redwing's gun had smashed through muscle and tissue, causing a simple fracture of the ulna as it ricocheted off the bone during its violent passage through the arm. "If he'd been a better shot, and if Jack hadn't come along when he did, it would've been all over. I never even got off a shot, and old Redwing was just taking his sweet time, aiming carefully for the coup de grace, when Jack's bullet took him right through the throat. One hell of a shot," he added admiringly, "especially when you consider it was made from a moving boat. Lucky, damned lucky."

"Luck had very little to do with it," Fran said firmly.

"Yeah, I know, honey." He patted her on the knee with his left hand, chuckling indulgently.

"Don't you dare patronize me, Rick Langtry!" She shot him an exasperated look. "I know what I know, and it wasn't simply luck that caused things to happen the way they did."

"Okay, okay. I can respect what you believe."

He turned away then, looking through the window on his side of the car in awed disbelief at the brilliant blues and greens of the ocean smashing against the beach a hundred feet below the roadway. On a narrow, rocky beach, several dozen seals were sunning themselves and frolicking in the surf. He thought about his last remark—that he could respect Fran's beliefs. With a mild sense of surprise, he realized he'd been telling the truth. He could respect Fran's beliefs, and even more importantly, he was secure in the knowledge that she would at least tolerate his beliefs where they differed from hers.

It was what happened when you agreed to love someone and commit to them, and to spend the rest of your lives together, he reflected with a sense of contentment. Sure, he knew that there were differences between himself and Fran—and so did she—but their love for one another was strong enough to overcome the differences and to concentrate their attention on the many areas of agreement instead.

"What're you smiling about?" Fran demanded, interrupting his chain of thought.

He shook his head. "Oh, just thinking about you and

me . . . how funny it is that we're winding up together."

"What's funny about it?" She took a hand from the steering wheel and squeezed his knee. A little thrill coursed through his leg at the contact.

"We started out at odds with each other over almost everything," he said thoughtfully, catching her hand and stopping its movement with a chuckle. "You, the hard-driving, successful businesswoman, aggressive, demanding—"

"And you," she interrupted with a flash of mischief in her hazel eyes, "Mr. Macho—the original he-man, swaggering around with your chest thrown out all the time. The very antithesis of everything I ever said I wanted in a man."

"Well, us he-men come in handy every now and then, don't we?" he asked, grinning.

"Oh, yes," she admitted softly. "You certainly do. And if you can stand my occasional bitchiness, I can put up with your little attacks of macho."

"The good thing about all this is that we're deeply in love with each other," he said, squeezing her hand gently. "When we finally got around to admitting that to ourselves, everything else started falling into place."

"Yes." She smiled. "How's the arm holding up? Need another pain pill?"

"No, it's okay." He flexed his fingers experimentally. The pain was still there, but didn't seem as acute as it had earlier. "No pill," he decided.

He leaned back and let his mind wander for a moment. It had been one hell of a day. After a three-day stay, he'd finally been discharged from the hospital early that morning. The attending physician had warned him against becoming overly dependent on the pain pills; so far, he'd only taken two.

He smiled as he remembered the madhouse in the

hospital room. Everyone had shown up for the occasion: Addison, Jack and Barbara O'Brien, John Simmons, Smitty, and even Beth Ann. Fran Barnette, of course, and her friends from Tahoe, the Hillers, had been there to greet him. Jerry Whitworth had come by the previous day to wish him well and to inform him that he'd put in for retirement. Rick glanced fondly at Fran, admiring the capable way her slim hands rested on the steering wheel of the car, recalling the scene several hours earlier . . .

"Rick, my boy," Addison had said jocularly, "I want to wish you all the best in your new job. I called Matthews, your new boss at the L.A. office, and he's really looking forward to having you on his crew."

"Yeah, I'll bet." Rick winked at Fran and Jack O'Brien, who were listening closely to the exchange. "You probably told Matthews I was a real hot dog and a troublemaker, and to watch me like a hawk, right, chief?"

"No, no, of course not," Addison sputtered, flushing. When he saw that his denials were being ignored, he grinned and spread his hands. "Well, there might have been a little something like that said," he admitted, "but after the coup we just pulled off, I couldn't really bad-mouth you too much, now, could I?"

"Coup?" Fran asked.

"Sure." Addison's chest seemed to swell as he took a step closer to Rick, beaming. "We rolled up an entire network, thanks to our boys, Langtry and O'Brien. Charonsky's been declared persona non grata and run out of the country. Aramas had been picked up and charged with espionage and extortion and whatever else the FBI can think of." He paused, frowning. "Too bad about the guy Jack surprised at the house in Hayward. We haven't got a clue to his whereabouts."

"Sounds like the one they called Mitchik, from Jack's

281

description," Rick said. "Very minor character, or seemed to be. If we had to lose one, it's good it was him."

"I suppose . . ." Addison brightened, rubbing his hands together. "Damned fine job, anyway, Rick. We've suspected Charonsky for a long time, of course, but suspecting it and proving it are two separate things. Thanks to you and Jack, we were able to nail the bastard."

"Thanks, chief." Rick held out his left hand, and Addison pumped it enthusiastically. "Listen, while it hasn't always been what you could call a pleasure working for you, I have to admit it's always been damned interesting."

"Yes, it has been, hasn't it?" Addison chuckled. "Good luck, son. And if I can ever help, you call me."

After Addison disappeared through the door, Beth Ann hurried over and took Rick's hand. "Don't you worry about your paperwork," she said warmly. "I'll take care of everything for you as soon as I get back to the office. He signs everything I put in front of him, so there won't be any trouble with your expense sheets or travel reimbursements, not this time. Just leave it to me."

"Ah, thanks, Beth Ann." He gave her a bear hug with his left arm. "It's been a real pleasure working with you these past few years. And I mean that, lady, I really do."

Beth Ann took out a lacy handkerchief and dabbed at her eyes.

"Oh, I just hate good-byes!" She started to turn away, then quickly returned. "Now don't you forget, Rick. You've got thirty days of convalescent leave before reporting to your new office. I want you to relax and enjoy yourself."

Rick looked over at Fran, who smiled into his eyes.

"Oh, I think I'll manage to keep him amused, Beth Ann," Fran said.

John Simmons and Smitty each came up and shook hands, and Rick thanked them for the extra time and effort they'd put into helping Jack track him down.

"Hey, don't worry about it," John Simmons rumbled in protest. "I like to think you guys'd do the same for me—or for any of us in the same predicament."

"I like to think so, too," Rick agreed. "Still, I want to thank you guys. It was a helluva job."

"Ah, I'm just glad everything turned out all right," Simmons said, coloring with pleasure at the praise. He glanced over at Fran and grinned. "It *did,* didn't it?"

"Yeah, it did. Go on, get out of here, you old reprobate," Rick said with a fond laugh. He grinned and waved at Smitty as the two men left the room together.

At last they were alone, except for Jack and Barbara, and Fran's friends, the Hillers. Jack glanced over at Rick during a lull in the conversation and raised his eyebrows questioningly.

"Well, ready to do it?" He cocked his head. "Sure you don't want to change your mind?"

"No way." Rick smiled at Fran. "If this lovely lady hasn't changed her mind about me, I'm ready."

"You're mine, fella," Fran said with a laugh. "I picked up the license this morning, and Jack's got a preacher waiting less than five minutes from here in a lovely little chapel that overlooks the Golden Gate Bridge. Shelly's got the flowers, and Todd will drive us over there. There's no escaping it now, Rick."

"I wouldn't want to," he said quietly.

They were married in a simple ceremony, with Jack and Barbara and Shelly and Todd as their witnesses. The minister, a distinguished-looking older man, conducted an old-fashioned service with plenty of thee's and thou's and beautiful language from the King James version of the Bible. Rick and Fran had tremendous lumps in their throats when the old preacher at last declared them husband and wife, and their first kiss as a married couple was touched with reverence and the solemn appreciation of the step they had taken.

Now, Fran tore her eyes away from the magnificent scenery outside the car long enough to glance at her new husband and ask, "What's all the wool-gathering about, Mr. Langtry?"

"Just thinking, Mrs. Langtry." He lifted his chin, indicating the highway ahead. "Y'know, there's a damned nice motel up ahead in Pismo Beach. What do you say we stop there? Have dinner, some wine, maybe get a room for the night? Aren't you getting tired of driving by now?"

"Who, me?" She smiled brightly, her hazel eyes twinkling with mischief. "I've only been driving a little over four hours. Are you quite sure there isn't something else on your mind, oh, husband of mine?"

"Of course not," he said, pursing his lips thoughtfully, wearing a reserved, judicious expression. "I was just thinking of you, wife of mine. Since I'm unable to share the driving with you, I was concerned that you might be getting all tuckered out, that's all. But if you're okay . . . ?"

"Oh, I could go on for hours," she assured him, biting back a smile.

"Well, that's settled, then. We might as well keep plugging away, try to make your place in Anaheim by tonight." He glanced casually over at her lovely profile and was shaken anew at the intensity of his feelings for her. He wouldn't have thought it possible for a man to love a woman so deeply. "It's just as well," he said casually. "I probably wouldn't be able to do anything about consumating our marriage anyway, with this damned cast on my arm."

Half a mile ahead the cluster of buildings around the large motel loomed into view—a steak house, service stations, a few touristy-looking bars, and other business establishments. Fran looked over at her husband and winked as she activated the turn signal and began slowing for the turn-off.

"I'll bet you'll be just amazed when you find out what all is possible, even with your arm in a cast."

"Hmm. Amazed *and* delighted?" he asked thoughtfully.

"Mmm-hmm," she almost purred as she pulled off the highway into the parking lot in front of the motel. "You just sit here and rest," she said throatily. "Gather your strength while I go register."

"The lady's a tiger," Rick said. She grinned and gave a little twitch of her rump as she hurried toward the office.

An hour later Fran raised up on her elbow and smiled fondly down into the lean, tanned face of her husband. His dark brown eyes were filled with love for her, and his left hand continuously caressed her, almost as if it were unable to stop.

"I love you, Rick Langtry," she whispered. "I want to be with you always."

"Always isn't long enough," he said huskily, pulling her down for another deep, satisfying kiss.

As their lips met and their bodies surged eagerly together once again, Fran realized that everything that had happened in her life up to now had been worth it; the pain and heartaches of earlier, unsuccessful relationships had all been leading her to this, the beginning of the rest of her life with the husband she was so desperately in love with. And, from the ardor with which he was responding to her now, a husband who was also desperately in love with her.

Life was beautiful.

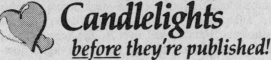